The Life & Times Of A Full Figured Fashionista II.

I'm No Angel.

Written by Dominique Ali.

Dedication

This book is for anyone who has lost their way for a little bit, but always find a path that will lead them back to who they are.

Chloe

I can't believe Hennison pulled that stunt at The All White Attire Ball! I swear I could feel every dagger Clair threw at me with her eyes. That was her night, and his brief announcement dulled the evening. I knew how hard she worked on perfecting it, mainly because I was the frequent flunky that did most of the legwork she requested. I also knew that after our mini holiday break I had to make it up to her, God only knows how the hell I will do that. She's Clair freaking Winters; nothing I could do short of rewinding time would atone me.

Getting out of there without someone making goo-goo eyes at me was a task. As I passed by partygoers, I heard the oohs and ah's, the 'Oh, that was so sweet' comments, with scattering sounds of various women sucking their teeth; I could only imagine they paired it with the rolling of their eyes as I was too embarrassed to look in their directions to confirm. Finding Dee once I made it pass the crowd that had accumulated at the base of the stage; we lingered for a few minutes as to not cause a scene by leaving so abruptly. Increasingly becoming uncomfortable, I then felt the sensation of being watched fall over me, and it felt similar to when I went out for the first time after the breakup with Malik. Heading towards the stairs, I gathered our coats, and we left undetected.

Arriving home, I received a text from Hennison asking where I had gone. Quickly answering him, I put my phone away and stripped away the embarrassment I felt with each article of clothing I removed. Standing in the bathroom, while gazing at my reflection in the mirror, I tried to gage the night's events, and how to move going forward. Tired of Indulgence, and drama between myself, Hennison, and Jayshawn; I grabbed my nightshirt and went to bed. Whatever scheming I had to do would wait until morning.

With the holidays coming up within the next few days, I wondered where I would spend it. My invitation is still open to celebrate with Dee and her family, but I don't know if I have the heart to do it. After almost no sleep, I lay on the couch with my eyes closed in a vain attempt of hoping I would drift off.

Seeing the dawn peek out from the windows, I decided that I played possum long enough, and the aroma of eggs wafting through the apartment beckoned me to the kitchen. As I stood to follow the scent, there's a hard knock at the door. Answering with the same ferocity the banger displayed, I came face to face with a large arrangement of flowers; and when I say large, I mean HUGE!

There were at least six delivery men holding two bouquets of roses in glass vases trailing down the stairs. The one that knocked with the authority of the NYPD held up a wrinkled paper and asked for Chloe Major. Stuttering at first, I told him I'm Chloe. With a quick yell, he said, *"Bring 'em in, boys!"*

One by one each guy brought in their flowers and put them anywhere they found a space. Dee heard the scuffling of work boots as they stampeded into her tiny apartment, as she came out of the kitchen, spatula in hand. The last guy walked straight to me and handed me a white box tied with a red ribbon. Closing the door behind him, I sat on my makeshift bed/couch and opened it; Dee standing over me watching while simultaneously smelling the flowers urging me to hurry. Lifting the lid, I found a note sitting atop the tissue paper that hid whatever was underneath. Unfolding it, it read…

Ms. Major,

You rushed off so quickly that I didn't have time to say my goodbyes, or furnish upon you the other gifts I had for you. Please accept my invitation to dinner tomorrow night; Mr. Bassett will be at your apartment a quarter to nine if you agree to share a meal with me. I hope you consider my invitation. Hennison Black

Unfolding the delicate tissue paper inside the box, I found a mulberry Christian Eldinar cap sleeve evening dress with a boat neck neckline and plunging sheer back that had an ornate flower pattern. This dress hasn't appeared on the runway! Eldinar will make its debut it in the spring; I can't believe Hennison got it before it's introduced to the rest of the full-figured universe. Pulling the dress from the box, I held it against my body and looked at Dee for confirmation that Hennison had impressed me again. With a crooked grin on her face, she turned on her heels and sashayed her way back to the kitchen; the spatula leading the way.

Following quickly behind, I shouted, "Do you think I should go to dinner with him?"

Not looking in my direction as she placed eggs on a plate and handing it to me she answered, "Yes girl, go! He's obviously really into you, what's the worst that could happen? I mean, he could bore you to death with a dry sense of humor; but at least you would get a five star meal out of it." She said candidly.

Taking my plate to the bistro table by the window, I considered taking him up on his offer.

Jayshawn

I knew I would eventually run into her, especially at an event hosted by her company; but I had to save face and escort Tarin to the event. All I could do is hope that Chloe wouldn't make a scene like she did in the club. I'm pleasantly surprised to see her as we entered the event space, the only thing that could make the event better is as if I had planned it, and the woman I escorted is her. She looked so beautiful that I nearly forgot Tarin had a vice grip on my arm so tight my fingers tingled from lack of blood flow. Immediately she went on model mode, I swear I could imagine someone holding a fan to make her hair blow as we floated about the room greeting all the who's who of the plus fashion and publishing industry.

As we made our way from one group to the next, I ever so casually stole glances at Chloe. She seemed to enjoy herself as she and Dominique giggled. I must have let my stare linger a little too long, because I heard someone clearing their throat so loudly that it snapped me out of my trance. Everyone's focus was on me, as if they were expecting some sort of answer to a question that I cared less than a fuck about. Apologizing, I quickly regained my composure and continued to converse as if I didn't have a nagging urge to look over my left shoulder.

Playing my part as the dutiful boyfriend, I indulged Tarin's every desire to keep the evening running as smooth as possible. I engaged in meaningless conversations with models and photographers, retrieved drinks, and uttered a strategically placed complement to those who fished for one (which was practically everyone).

After serving my sentence, I figured it was time for me to indulge a bit. As I started walking toward Chloe, Tarin rushed at my side; picking up Sloan and her date as we walked, it looked as if we were all going to greet her. The language between us was strained, but I could tell she had been holding back emotions trying to remain professional. Just as I attempted to make her comfortable with me being there with Tarin, the devil showed his privileged, pompous face. Had we been in the street and not at an event that would damage my credibility along with his, I would have knocked him the fuck out!

He always waited until we were in social settings to take a stab at embarrassing me. I promise myself that one of these days I would be the one to knock him off his high horse and expose his dirty ass for what he really is! I wanted to break every bone is his hand as he touched Chloe. Oh, and that spectacle he put on apologizing to her took all the restraint I had not to run up on that stage, punch him, and press Chloe into my body firmly as I swept her from the room. I couldn't believe she was even falling for that store-bought charm he's throwing her way; in my eyes, he is the white version of Malik. She seemed like she was eating it up, it must have come in a can; ready for immediate consumption whenever the sleaze in him crept up.

I allowed myself a daily indulgence of thinking about Chloe, which always happened when I had a free moment in the office as it was next to impossible to form a thought at home because of Tarin. The distant ringing of my office phone snapped me out of my most precious of daydreams, and I'm instantly in work mode. Since letting go of Makayla all the office duties fell to me and trying to hold down the home front, making myself available to clients, and being on site for events and preparation I'm wearing myself out! I've got to find a new assistant ASAP! I know one thing for damn sure, my next assistant will be a man; I can't trust that if I hired another woman that she wouldn't betray me like Makayla did for a background singing gig, and community dick in her twat; but then again she has community pussy so I guess it's a match made in Hell.

After a day filled with appointments, vendors, press releases, and dumb ass caterers, I couldn't wait to get home and relax; thank God I had a potential applicants coming the next day for an interview!

Opening the door to my apartment, the scent of expensive perfume invaded my nostrils, and the sight of shopping bags littered my once pristine living room.

As soon as I stepped over the threshold Tarin is in my face giving me the 'where have you been?' look. Giving her the same crazy look back, she walked away muttering. Following her into the bedroom, I dreaded having long, drawn out conversations with her about nothing. No really, it always surrounded NOTHING! Whenever she's mad, she makes absolutely no sense. Either it was because Jerry the doorman didn't open the door fast enough, or the salad she ordered had six croutons instead of the three she requested. She had maintained her curvy figure by under eating, and overexercising, fearing that she would get back on the heavier side of being full figured like she had been when she was younger. Yes, she had been a full-figured model for Sloan when she started with Legendary Models, but now she had been demoted to an assistant because of her wild partying. Sloan gave her that title as to keep a watchful eye on her. After our breakup she had gotten into trouble with drugs, and between Sloan and I (me keeping my distance!) we tried to calm her down. But now I'm letting the past be the past, and to avoid an argument I'd suck it up and be the concerned boyfriend.

Walking into the bathroom where she is holding a pair of curlers hostage, I asked, "What's wrong now, sweetheart? Is it your hair? It's really looks great."

"No, it's not my hair!" she shot back at me. "It's you! You forgot that we have somewhere to go tonight, didn't you? Tonight is important to me, there will be people at Opulence Lounge tonight that can get my career back on track. I will not be a nobody assistant for the rest of my life. I had a moment of senselessness and Sloan won't let me forget it. You forgave me. Why can't she do the same? I mean, I appreciate what she's done for me, but it's time to move on. I'm leaving way too much money on the table by not doing what I came to New York to do."

"So, who exactly will be at Opulence, besides who we already know? Everyone knows that you work with Sloan and she's the best in the game. Working with anyone else would be a step down and you know it!" I tried to convince her.

"Maybe or maybe not." She uttered snidely as she continued to burn her hair into submission.

Walking back into the bedroom, I sat on the edge of the bed closest to the bathroom door contemplating if I should keep on my clothes or change. As the thought passed through my mind, my eyes drifted to the other side of the bed, where I made love to Chloe. The image is so vivid that it's as if I'm watching myself being with her; it was so real that I reached out to move her hair from her eyes and stroke her face. As my hand got close to where the sweat glistened on her forehead, the Tarin's screeching from the bathroom interrupted my fantasy.

"What's wrong?" I yelled as I ran to the door.

"This fucking curl won't lay the way I want it to!" She expressed resembling a five-year-old who didn't get her way. At that moment, I asked myself… WHAT THE FUCK DID I GET MYSELF INTO?

Dominique

Colder and colder the days are becoming with no one for me to cuddle up with at night to keep me warm. Cuffing season used to be my favorite time of year, you know; when people have to find a winter boo to make the cold sting of winter bearable. Someone to eat Chinese with, attend holiday spectaculars, and bring to my parents' house for the holidays to show them I'm growing as a person and can maintain a healthy and stable relationship (until the spring of the year, that is! When I shed the winter clothes, I shed the winter boo too.). Since my beak-up with Chase, the season has lost its luster.

For Chloe things are heating up with Mr. Black, for his sake I hope he's not trying to make a winter boo of my bestie. As long as he behaves himself I'll keep my thoughts to myself, but if he gets out of line with her, IT'S A WRAP; Like a doobie (a wrap hair style) with big ass pins! Anyway, I have to give him props for sending her the flowers and a gift. I would be grateful if Chase sent me a hate text right now; at least I would know that he was thinking of me. I miss him so much that he crosses my mind on the daily; I've even started waiting for him outside of his apartment to see if he brings anyone home with him.

Chloe doesn't know this, but sometimes when I tell her I'm working late because of the workload and the firms cutbacks; I really get a cup of burning hot coffee and sit in the park outside his building to get a glimpse of him. How crazy is that? I want to call him and invite him to my parents' house for Christmas; I know my mom is expecting us to show up together; but I don't have the heart to tell her I fucked our relationship up for an ex that until recently had sort of been stalking me.

Ramir for a long time couldn't let me go neither. Coming into work would be like entering a flower shop, endless gifts would be sent by messenger, some were sent to my apartment, and of course he's sends his snitching ass driver to give me love notes or take me somewhere; which I refused every time he offered, I wonder if Ra knew about the driver and Kasha's little arrangement; most likely he doesn't. Anyway, I know that the moment I gave in Kasha would be informed and would hurt my dad's business, or attempted to anyway. I couldn't risk that, especially when I know that I don't love Ramir. He was just an infatuation… unfinished business that I'm done with now. Kasha can keep her cheating ass husband; I have no need for him! The only thing on my agenda is getting my man back!

Not looking forward to spending another chilly night on a park bench, I called it a night early. I couldn't keep this up too much longer, I will have to face him; either on his terms or mine. As I walked through the park I had come to know well, I watched as people strolled, walked their dogs, and some even jogged in thirty degree weather; I guess the heat they built up with keep them warm enough. I don't know what it is about the holidays that always bring out the romantic in me, but it also fueled the loneliness I felt without Chase.

Getting home after midnight, I poured myself a glass of wine and passed out. Groggily waking up, I realized that I had overslept and staggered my way to the bathroom for a quick hoe bath or PTA wash (pussy, tits, and ass) and flew out of the door. Arriving at the office with not a second to spare, my gaze catches Elgin Reese, one of the people stationed in our office from the other company as part of the merger.

Damn Elgin is fine! He has to be at least 6'1, reddish brown eyes, creamy light brown skin tone, with juicy lips that bore the most beautiful smile I've ever seen. The epitome of a Metrosexual, he always dresses to impress in the most expensive, tailored suites money can buy; and he let no one see him without a fresh low cut Caesar with waves that would make you seasick as he floated about the office. He completely captivated most of the women in the office and believe me, he had swag out of this world! A few times I walked in on him smooth talking a female with all the sexiness a man has when speaking

Spanish. You guessed it, he's a mixed breed, and a fine one! If that's what mixing the races does, SIGN ME UP!

What am I thinking? Wasn't I just stalking Chase just last night, talk about deflecting. In all honesty, Elgin was just a nice piece of ass to look at; not long-term material. I've dated my share of men like Elgin, and it left me with nothing but a migraine. Attempting to walk past him as quickly as I could, I dropped my head (so he wouldn't see the blush in my cheeks) and sped walked past him briskly. Catching me by my elbow, I turned to find him staring intently in my eyes. I felt the heat in my body raise twenty degrees, I'm sure I was blushing so hard I looked feverish at this point. My heart pounded so hard, for a few moments that it is all I could hear. With everything moving in slow motion, I finally realized he was talking to me when I saw those beautiful lips of his moving.

"I'm sorry, what did you say, Mr. Reese?" I asked him.

"Mr. Reese?" Elgin questioned. "Is my dad here? Please Dominique, call me Elgin. Is it all right that I call you by your first name? I wouldn't want to make you uncomfortable. Your comfort means everything to me." He went on to say.

"No, no, Dominique is fine… Elgin. What can I do to you? I'm sorry for you?" I stuttered.

Not missing a beat, he retorts with a devilish smile, "Were in the office so you wouldn't be able to do anything to me right now; well not with all these cameras watching us, unless you're into putting on a show. But what you can do for me is set up a ten o'clock with Hershel; I'd like to go over a few things before he leaves the office for the holidays. Can you do that for me, doll?" He inquired.

"Yes, Elgin, I will schedule the meeting right away. Is that all?" I questioned as evenly as I could.

"For now," Elgin replied as he let go of my elbow and turned to leave.

I scrambled to my desk to the meeting in the agenda and alert Hershel. I can't believe I let him get to me. I've been in tougher situations and swam with the most ruthless of sharks, and I let a cute face and a dynamite smile knock me off my game; I must be slipping.

Chloe

I gave a lot of thought to going out with Hennison. For hours I paced the apartment and debated if I should get in the shower. When I finally arrive at the decision to shower, the next task was to convince myself that I would only try on the dress to see if it fit; not to get ready for the date. After I saw how magnificently in hugged every curve, the most natural thing next for me to do was to see what type of hairstyle I would wear with a dress like this for future reference. With the beautiful sheer pattern on the back, I would have to wear my hair up to highlight it. After about an hour of dressing, complete with hair and makeup, there's no denying it; I'm meeting Hennison tonight, and I was nervous.

It's easy to be clever when there are many people around to distract from the obvious intentions we have, but this time it would be just the two of us. I would have no one to act as a buffer while I get my bearings after he says something bluntly sexual or beat around the bush about beating up the bush; if you know what I mean. It's been so long since I've been on a date with a man, and I don't know if I could resist Hennison if he made suggestive moves. I don't want him to treat me like a hoe, so I've got to make him wait before I allow him to savor my body and make him sleep in the wet spot; well, that's assuming we sleep at all.

The last guy I was with I fell for, and he abandoned me to be with his ex; so from here on out, I'm operating on instinct and not feelings. I have to make smarter choices. Maybe Dee has it right. Use these dudes for whatever they could do for me and then move on. Before I could let another scorned lover thought race through my head, the buzzer rang and I knew it's my ride. With one last look in Dee's floor-length mirror, I grabbed my clutch bag and didn't look back for fear that if I did, I would get a glimpse of disappointment from the old Chloe.

Arriving at La Belle Figura Restaurant, we practically ran through the glass doors to escape the brutal winter winds. The maître d' escorted us to the rear of the restaurant to the private dining areas. The intimate atmosphere really set a tone for the night, and I became instantly comfortable with my dining companion. Conversation was slow at first, we made small talk and it quickly became an all-out laughing war. As we sat sipping on wine and other various distilled spirits; in our own private section we are free of other patrons and didn't have to be coy about our banter. We discussed the upcoming Fashion Weeks for straight sizes in New York and plus size in London. He didn't give away too many details about the direction the magazine would take when on location for both, but he said that he would love for us to visit his favorite locations while we were there on business; what happened after hours were between him and I.

Playing into the mood he set the stage for, I began to have an inner dialog about what would happen at the end of the evening, but honestly I didn't want to think too far ahead; I want to be in the moment and enjoy every minute of being the object of his infatuations, if only for a few fleeting hours. During a moment of silence, I unconsciously played with my wineglass, sliding it in slow circles with the stem between two of my fingers. I don't know where my mind drifted off to before he grabbed my hand, but after he did; I wanted his hand to be resting comfortably on my thighs.

While holding my hand and rubbing his thumb across my fingers, he asked, "Where were you just then?"

"Nowhere, I was just thinking about London. It would be my first Fashion Week with the company, and I'm mentally preparing myself for the work." I lied.

"Oh, because for a moment there I thought I was boring you. I would have to think of something else to do to hold your attention." He smirked.

"Something like what?" I probed.

"Oh, don't worry about that Ms. Major, whatever I do; I'll never lose your attention again." He expressed with a seriousness that I believed whatever he would do would have me catching my breath.

After dinning on exquisitely food specially prepared for us, I wanted to dine on what Hennison offered afterward; but I had to stick to the plan. That shit would be rough if we keep having evenings like this. In the car ride home he asked if I wanted to go to his place, with want in my eyes and lust in his I said no even though my kitty was purring *'YES DUMMY, YES!'* Ignoring the yelling from under my dress, I crossed my legs and held my thighs as tightly as I could without drawing too much attention to myself. That didn't help, I had to pull the dress to the side to do it; and as I did, his eyes went directly to my legs; which made my body shiver.

Pulling up in front of my building, Hennison got out first to keep Mr. Bassett from opening my door. Walking to the building, he thanked me for spending Christmas Eve with him, and I thanked him for the invite. Asking if I had any plans for Christmas Day, he invited me to spend it with him. Briefly telling that I would be with my friend and her family, I told him I would consider his offer. Grasping my lower back, I felt the pressure of his hand through my coat as he gently pulled my body close to his. Tilting his head to the side, he whispered "Goodnight Ms. Major" and gave me a deep, body humming, kiss. Still clutching my lower back and holding the back of my head as he played in my hair, I forgot that it's freezing outside; it felt more like the middle of August with all the heat that passed between us.

When he let me go I temporarily lost my footing, luckily he was quick thinking and jerked me to his side. Opening the door to the building, he said that he would look forward to hearing from me.

Before I heard the door click closed, I knew I would call him the next day; at least to say Merry Christmas if not come fuck me now. As I walked up the stairs, I formed a plan to make a smooth getaway from Dee's parent's house tomorrow.

Cassidy

I'm so glad this day is winding down; Cairo had me running from pillar to post trying to get our apartment ready for Christmas. I filled every hiding spot I could find in my house trying to hide his gifts; I just wish his Godmother wouldn't spoil him so much. I think she over compensates because his father isn't around. Let's face it, if he hadn't have died, he still wouldn't have bothered with Cairo. I know he loved him in his own way, but because of the circumstances of his birth, he couldn't outwardly show it. But that's the past, and what's done is done and I can't dwell on things I wouldn't change. My son is the best thing that anyone could give to me, and I will be the best mommy I can be for him.

Walking softly towards the radio, picking up some of his old toys on the way, I put my phone on the dock and searched for some holiday music to play; I loved to listen to it this time of year. Coming across one of my favorites, I danced to my favorite chair near the Christmas tree and sang along with the lyrics. Trying not to be too loud as to wake up Cairo, I grooved to the music. As I got into it, I got a text on my phone from Clair to open my door. SHIT! I said out loud. I didn't think she would pull this dropping by shit tonight of all nights, she's supposed to be in Atlanta.

Rising from my comfortable seat, I dragged my feet to the door and held it open for her to sashay through. Walking in with authority, she dropped her coat and bag in my hand and asked where Cairo had been. Telling her he was asleep, a wave of disappointment crossed her face. I felt so bad I almost offered to wake him up for her so she could say hello. But before I could let the words leave my mouth, he came running full force from the back of the apartment and leaping into Clair's arms. I guess my sleeping angel wasn't really sleeping but playing possum.

"Auntie Clair!" he yelled as he hugged her neck. "Mommy said you would be in Atlantic."

Clair slightly chuckled, "No sweetie, Atlanta. But I couldn't leave without seeing you. I brought you something." She stated as she pulled a small box from her pocket.

Putting the five-year-old down, she handed him a box; as I watched from behind her to see what was inside. His small hands reached inside and pulled out a tiny rose gold bracelet that had his name engraved on it. Instructing him to turn it over the other side read *Love Clair*; taking the bracelet from the child, she opened the clasp to place it on his wrist.

"Clair, it's beautiful. But that's too much for him; he will lose it." I tried to reason with her.

"There's more where that one came from if he does. I don't mind buying him the world if he wants it. What are Godmothers for?" She insisted as she spoke, but never took her eyes off of him.

I appreciated everything Clair does, but sometimes she really goes overboard. I want him to have the best, but there's a thin line between having the best of things and just plain spoiling him. He's an only child and this treatment can go real left, real quick. Nevertheless, I didn't object to the gift; he seemed to love it. Anyway, it's Christmas. What kind of fool would I look like if I took his gift away? Clair knew how to get her way, why should this be any different.

They chit chatted for a while and when I saw him yawn, I swooped in to usher him to bed. Putting him in the bed and pulling in his cartoon character blankets around him, he wanted to hear his favorite story about his dad. So I snuggled with him in the full size bed and told him the story he knew by heart about his father.

"Well," I began. "Your dad was a hyper focused man. His dream was to own his own business, and he worked very hard to achieve it. He was a talented photographer/Editor/Writer, and my company at the time sent me and a few other models to Cairo, Egypt for a photo shoot they called *Dessert Flowers*. We had known each other previously, so we knew each other well. We fell in love and that's how mommy got you." I tried to conclude quickly.

"But mommy, what happened after that?" he questioned.

With a deep bated breath, I tried to come up with a story a child would believe. "We loved each other very much, but life pulled us apart. When I had you, he was so happy he came to see you every day. Until his business kept him too busy to see us. We broke up and shortly after he passed away."

"How did he die mommy?" Cairo asked.

"I'll tell you when you get older." I uttered as I tried to complete the story.

"Ok." He backed down. "But I have one more question."

"What is it, baby?" I acknowledged as the image of a newborn Cairo dance in my head.

"Did I get my brown color from my dad?" He questioned softly.

"Yes baby, he was the most handsome man I had ever seen. Now go to bed or Santa won't come." I told him as I switched off the light and closed his bedroom door.

Letting out a deep breath as if I had been holding it until I could leave his presence, I came face to face with a distraught Clair; she leaned against the hallway wall with tears streaming down her face. Trying to hold back sobs, she walked into the living room and sat down. I touched her on the shoulder, and as I did, she stood up swiftly and grabbed her coat.

Putting it on as she walked to the door; she faced it as she said that one day I would have to tell him the truth. As I went to say something comforting to her, she changed the direction by telling me she hoped I would be ready for Fashion Week New York, because when we get to Plus Size Fashion Week Designers in London will be itching to outdo the straight size designers, those designers will ache to have Indulgence cover their shows. Not knowing how to reply, I simply said yes. That being enough of a response for her she ran out of the apartment leaving nothing but her perfume in her wake.

She's right. One day he would have to know the truth about his father. I'm just not ready to tell him, and by Clair's reaction she isn't either.

Dominique

Getting in late from work, I decided not to stalk Chase, It's too cold, and I'm too tired. The last time I was this deep in my feelings it was over Ramir; I just hope that an extensive amount of time doesn't go by before I can make things right. I expected to see my girl's face when I walked in, but she wasn't there. I guess she took Mr. Black up on his dinner offer. At least someone would get the "D" tonight.

Left to my own devices, I thumbed through my closet for the perfect "I lost my man outfit" to wear to my parents' house tomorrow. As I stood in the closet, I could almost see my mother's disappointed face as her dreams of grandchildren were becoming less and less attainable. With the fear of succumbing to the same disappointment, I half expected to be on that path to giving her what her heart longed for. I didn't intend to have a sexual relationship with Ramir again, nor was it my damn intention to get caught and lose the only man that I believe really cared about me pass what I could do with my body. But it happened, and all I can do is to be the cleanup woman and try to put my life together. That was the moment I realized that I was alone. I didn't have Chase to comfort my mind, and I didn't have a bed warmer (a random guy) to comfort my body. This is when I realized I had to grow up.

Throwing leftovers in the microwave, I settled into my bed to watch atrocious romantic holiday movies where two people who don't belong together somehow end up in love; you know the same BS over and over; the only difference are the character names and locations. Stuffing an overly nuked egg roll in my mouth, I wondered how I would get through tomorrow.

With rapidly fluttering eyes, I tried to find my phone to shut the alarm off as its repeated blaring felt like a nail being drilled into my head. Good thing I set the alarm before I went to bed, I didn't even know I was asleep until it went off the next day. Realizing what day it is, I ran into the living room to find a sleeping Chloe with the goofiest look I've ever seen on her face. Tip toeing to the accent table near the door, I picked up a small box under our tiny Christmas tree.

Leaping unexpectedly on her, she let out a loud gasp in surprise. Yelling my name as she swept her hair out of her face, she sat up on her elbows when she realized why I had done it.

"Merry Christmas boo!" she mumbled.

"Merry Christmas back at cha honey!" I replied.

"Look, I know today will be long so I wanted to get an early start; here's your gift, sweetie." I whispered as I handed her the small box. "By the way, you must have had a good time last night? When I came home, you were still out with old boy. How did it go?"

Slowly tearing the red and gold wrapping paper, the same goofy looked she had on her face when she slept crept back across her face. From her reaction, I could tell it went well; I wonder if she gave it up?

"Well, I'm waiting, Bitch! Where did he take you?" I urged.

Opening the present she babbled, "He took me to that new place that used to be next to that sandwich place we hated because you got sick from the cold cuts; it's called La Belle Figura now. Looking at the gift she changed subjects, "Oh,

Dee, this is beautiful! I can't believe you bought me a Quincy Monique scarf! I thought we agreed on a cap this year?"

"We did, but I saw it and I knew I had to get it for you. Do you like it?" I asked.

"Hell yeah! But the gift I got you isn't expensive; unlike you, I stuck to the spending cap; apartments are not cheap. Anyway, I hope you like it." Chloe uttered.

"Give me my gift, girl! I'm sure I'll love it!" I blurted excitedly.

Opening the envelope, I found a card that said:

To Dee:

I love you so much, you've been more than a best friend to me this year, so that title does you no justice; especially when the title of sister suites you best. I will love you forever! Merry Christmas, you sexy thang you! Love, Chloe

My heart melted at what she wrote, I always thought of her as more than my friend; it felt good to see she felt the same way. Under the card was a Coffee Gift Card. We both had the same idea; my gift would keep her warm as she trotted through the streets of London in a few days, while her gift would keep me warm as I spent crisp nights working up the courage to go inside of Chase's building to talk to him.

Getting dressed quickly, we called for a cab to my parents' house. I had pre-warned her it would probably be a very boring day. My dad would most likely be on some conference call, my mom would entertain the mass of people they would have invited to fill the growing space between them, and I would pray that something remotely interesting would happen so I could at least get a good laugh. I know today is especially rough for her because of all the shit that went down with China, which is the reason she didn't go home. I heard her talking to her mom as her voice cracked from fighting back tears.

Reaching our destination, we held each other as the wind whipped us back and forth as we climbed the stairs. Relentlessly ringing the doorbell, Godfrey opened the door. Greeting me as a father would, he picked me up and twirled me around the foyer. To me, he was more than an employee, he's a surrogate dad.

"Baby girl, I'm so happy to see you! It seems like forever since you last came to visit." He exclaimed.

"Yeah, I know, nobody told me that working put a damper on a girl's social life." I explained.

Briefly re-introducing Chloe and Godfrey, he explained that the party was in full swing and that my parents are entertaining the guests. Following the sounds of music and drunken laughter we entered the Great Room, and to my surprise the same stuffy people I use to loth seemed like the stick in their asses had become dislodged.

Finding the source of the good time, I saw a crowd gathered around Elgin. I can't believe my dad invited him to our house for the holiday. That pompous asshole could charm the slither from a snake! Seeing us approaching, he quickly turned his attention to me.

"Good afternoon, Ms. Lawrence, Merry Christmas. You look ravishing, as always." He stated ever so bolder than normal. "And who is this beautiful woman with you?"

"Merry Christmas to you too Mr. Reese, This is my best friend Chloe, Chloe this is Elgin Reese; he works in my department." I uttered as nonchalantly as I could.

"It's nice to me you. How long have you been working for Mr. Lawrence?" she asked.

"I don't work for Marcellus, we work together. My company and his sort of acquired each other and we've been making beautiful bottom lines since." He informs her smugly before answering her question. "I've been working in the same department as Dominique for the last few months, and I have to say she's very good as what she does."

As he let that phrase slip from his beautiful lips, one of my dad's colleagues whispered in his ear. He excused himself; but before he did, he shook Chloe's hand and kissed mine, allowing his kiss to linger for a few seconds longer than a gentleman should allow. Elgin was seriously making a play for me; it wasn't just something my mind conjured up.

Leaving the moment as quickly as it started, he left me with a heaviness that exited as soon as he did. Folding my arm in hers, Chloe whispered, "Intense isn't he?" nodding my head I changed the subject. Trying intently to find my parents and not run into Elgin again, I grabbed the closest Champaign glass and chugged it like it was a shot of Vodka.

After an hour or so of greetings and pleasantries among the guests and empty well wishes were given, we all sat down for a wonderfully catered dinner. As everyone congratulated each other on fiscal accomplishments, I could tell my bestie is as bored as I am. Leaving the table for a moment, she came back with an urgency I've only seen when she has to run off to work for some idiotic errand her boss sends her on. IT'S CHRISTMAS DAY FOR GOD'S SAKE! CAN THEY GIVE HER ONE DAY OFF! Passing out apologies to everyone, she gave my parents a hug as she excused herself.

Avoiding my glaring as I walked her out, I told her what I thought about that job of hers as she shook her head at my raving. Closing the door behind her, I realized that I had been using this party, and her leaving to prolong doing what I really want; and that was to call Chase. I started to send a text, but thought; if I called him, maybe he would answer.

Dialing his number, several scenarios flooded my mind all at once. I imagined him answering the phone and telling me he missed me, next was him cursing me out, and the last day dream he wasn't even in. I imagined a woman picking up the phone, giggling as she spoke 'Hello' into the phone. Yearning to hear his sweet masculine voice, he takes the phone and breaths the same words as the nameless woman. Not hearing an answer, he hangs up, leaving nothing but the emptiness of the dial tone. None of that happened. No one answered the phone, only the voicemail.

Quickly trying to speak, I blurted out, "Hi Chase, its Dominique. I'm calling to wish you a Merry Christmas, and I…" I hesitated, trying to figure out if I should be so bold as to say what I wanted, or hang up with the little shred of dignity I still possessed. Fuck it! I thought, just go for it. Letting out a deep sigh, I breathed, "I miss you, I'm so sorry about how things ended. If you would just talk to me, meet me for coffee or something and let me explain… I'm not ready for us to be over, let's work it out. Please call me."

Ending the call, I let the wall catch me as I fell back onto it. Wishing that Chase would see my missed call and would call back that I didn't see Elgin looking at me with an expression I had never seen worn by him before. At that moment I didn't know if it was anger or embarrassment, but I couldn't hold back any longer. I'm full to the brim, trying to hide the inner turmoil that was wrecking my soul. That's when the tears started flowing. I broke in that moment; I sobbed so hard that I was sure the entire dinner party would fill the corridor to see what had been going on.

Hearing the laugher of drunken party-goers, he whisked me into the guest bathroom. Once in there, he let me cry. I buried my face in my hands and caught every tear that fell with urgency from my eyes as I leaned into his chest. Realizing that I had totally embarrassed myself in front of the most gorgeous man in the office, I attempted to compose myself.

As I smeared the makeup on my face, trying to get it together, he touched both my shoulders. Easing his hands down to my arms, I followed his lead, lowering my limbs. Taking a piece of tissue, he cleaned my face. Wiping my tears as my chest heaved like a small child after a tantrum. Grabbing piece after piece, I slowly began to resemble the woman he met months ago.

I started to speak to explain what he saw, but in one swift motion of putting his finger to my lips he quieted me, while moving my hair from my face. This is the calmest and most gentle I've ever seen him. He's usually so aggressive and domineering; but not now. Taking comfort in not having to speak the madness of my life into existence, I allowed his caressing to go on. Really, I was too weak to fight it and put on the facade of being strong when all I wanted to do in that moment is crumble. Pulling me into a comfortable hug, I let myself melt into his arms. He cradled me like a precious baby; I have to admit it had been a long time since a man had held me, besides the feeling of being protected and cared for is all a woman wants to feel from a man, anyway.

Then it happened. Before I knew what was happening... we kissed. Here we are in my parent's guest bathroom on Christmas day kissing like as we did so, we breathed life into each other; which is ludicrous because we are so not compatible on any level. I forgot how good it felt to feel someone's lips pressed against mine; I fell into the embrace as if to have given the illusion that it had been Chase I kissed so passionately. I don't know how much time passed by when voices of the party-goers starting to get louder.

There was a wiggling of the doorknob that broke our trance, followed by knocking. Answering the persistent knocker, Elgin yelled that the restroom is occupied. Listening as quietly as I could for that person to leave, I reached for the door. As I did, Elgin touched my hand, and our eyes locked for a moment. Trying desperately to express with my eyes that I couldn't do what we were doing, he moved his hand. When he did, I peeked out the door before I walked vigorously my old bedroom to collect myself.

I practically galloped up the stairs, pausing only for a moment to see Elgin staring in my direction. For a second it looked as if he would call out to me, then he turned on his heels and walked back to the party.

Chloe

The isolated pockets of high profile business people who continuously congratulated themselves are becoming a little too heavy for me. Leaving Dee on Christmas was a horrible thing to do to her, but honestly it was like being at a high school party with her and Elgin pretending not to be attracted to each other. Seriously, I'm sick of the cat-and-mouse game between those two. I've been playing the same game with Hennison for months now. Jayshawn is no longer in the picture, he's made his choice and it isn't me, so now he and I have to live with what comes after. What that means for him is hopefully Tarin won't fuck him over again, and what it means for me is I'm now open to the possibility of exploring relationships with different men without attachments. He has no idea what he lost in me, and it's not my job to tell him; though it's my job to make sure my needs are met and for the moment that includes Hennison.

Flagging down the only cab that that crossed my path in four blocks, I gave the driver the address Hennison gave me. Arriving at an enormous cinderblock building with humongous wooden doors, I knew immediately that Hennison had a few tricks of his own planned. What he didn't know is that I had a few of my own he should watch out for.

Standing outside ringing the bell felt like an eternity as the blistering winter wind blew across my body. He answered the door in a black thermal and sweatpants; this is the most casual I've ever seen him. In the office he wears the most expensive tailored suits designers make especially to fit every facet of his incredibly sculpted body; but then I remembered we weren't in the office or a work-related event. We are alone in his enormous house with nothing but opportunity between us.

Taking my coat, revealing my Tony Pérez Hip-Hugging Jeans and Mateo Baptiste sweater, he led me to the living room. It was truly breathtakingly decorated; the only problem is that there was no one else here with him besides me and the bottle of Whiskey on the glass coffee table. Noticing the label, I realized it's the brand he's developing called Timeless Black. Seeing the loneliness of the space, I wondered where his family had been, and why hadn't they been spending the holiday together. I then put that quickly out of my mind, remembering my family situation. I miss my family, especially today.

Watching me intently, he asked, "Do you want to try it?" nodding in agreement, he laughed as I downed a small shot and damn near coughed up a lung.

"Sorry sweetheart, I should have warned you it has a bit of a kick." He smiles through a brilliant pair of lips.

Regaining my composure I assured, "No, no I'm good. I didn't expect it to burn that much good thing I have some food in my stomach." I breathed through heavy panting.

"Really, you've eaten already? I had hoped you would share a meal with me." He responded. "Well, I guess we'll have to settle for a few more drinks instead." And that we did.

Before long the bottle is empty, and he had gotten up from our place on the area rug and walked to the bar for another bottle. I know that if I didn't make a move now that I would miss my opportunity. With a guy like Hennison, this type of thing is usually his territory, but tonight it would be mine. Before he saw me, I took off my sweater to show the cami hiding underneath. Noticing the loss of my sweater, he stubbed his toe on the sofa, nearly dropping the bottle.

"Oh, my god! Are you ok?" I questioned between bursts of laughter.

Stuttering uncontrollably he uttered "yeah, yeah, and yes. It's just that I wasn't expecting…"

"Me to take off my sweater?" I finished for him. "I was boiling from the liquor and I thought it would be better to remove it or pass out in a puddle of sweat." I concluded because that wasn't exactly the sweating I had planned on doing.

"I can put it back on." I offered as I reach for it.

"No! Its fine, it just that… it was unexpected." He remarks tautly.

Pouring us yet another round of drinks, we talked a bit about the Fashion Weeks. This is about the time he decided to put the mack down on me. As we talked, he began by massaging my leg. When I began answering one of his persistent questions; he let his hand ease down to remove my Article 8 knee boots. Finally he was picking up on the subtle hints I had been dropping all night, massaging my feet first, then the rest of my leg. The more he closed the gap between us, the more the anticipation built up. Reaching up to my face I thought this is it, I get to taste those sweet lips again. WRONG! The strap from my cami had fallen to my shoulders. As he slowly placed it back, I tilted my head toward his ascending hand and it briefly grazed my face.

That was all it took! After all the months of flirting, surprise lunches, intimate dinners, and an abundance of gifts and compliments as quick as it takes for the pair of shoes you've been stalking for months to be released online and sold out, I was on my back and he nestled comfortably between my thighs; and his luscious lips that are made for the sweetest of daydreams were making their way up the right side collar bone.

I felt like he wanted to be engulfed by my body. Taking off his thermal, he traced the outline of my body starting at my breast his hand glided down my side stopping at my hips. In a swift motion, he raised my leg to reach higher up his torso. At some point the cami came off with the bra following closely behind. So there I was, in the very expensive house, among the most beautiful things money could buy, seriously about to get the most wicked rug burn ever. His kisses sent electric shocks to every nerve in my body, so much so I began to mentally reason with myself that the rug burn would be worth it.

Pausing between breaths, I had suggested that we do this in a more comfortable place. Reluctantly raising off me and helping me to my feet; breasts bouncing as they had lost the very luxurious Trina DeMartino harness (bra) I got from her last photo shoot with Indulgence for the Sexy Curvatures Edition. He locked hands with mine and led me back out into the foyer and up a twin staircase. The landing at the top of the stairs is just as massive and the ground floor. This house was beyond large and from what I could see he is the only one that lived in it. I don't know if in that moment my desire to comfort him grew more, or the possibility that this interlude is more than I originally thought it would be.

Entering his bedroom, I didn't have enough time to get a good look at the layout, because after opening the door he lay on the bed and pulled me on top. With my knees at his sides, I straddled him as we roamed each other's body. His icy hands on my fevered body slid up my back to my shoulders, and the mix just turned me on more. I clung to his head as we kissed. His hands seeking a home gripped my ass through the jeans and squeezed. Putting his arms around my waist as if to pick me up, he flipped me on my back and with his right hand placed between my breasts; he made an invisible line down my tummy, past my navel to the button on the jeans. Once undone he turned me on my stomach, mapped out kisses down my back and in one instant motion pulled the jean exposing my ass adorned in boy shorts underneath.

Gripping me firmly, he literally kissed my ass; both cheeks! When I arched my back, he took that opportunity to reach between my legs until his fingers reach a very damp destination. I couldn't tell up from down with all the feelings he's creating. Before we could go any further, he reached in the nightstand for a condom; I secretly hoped he had enough because I feel like repeat sessions happening for the rest of the day.

Entering me from the back, the breath that I had been holding for what felt like a lifetime I could finally let go of. We caught each other's rhythm quickly and instantly synched. I hadn't expected him to be so passionate with me; I had made up in my mind that sex with him would be rough and dirty; fooled me! As he stroked, his hands roamed my body. Gently squeezing, softly touching, caressing with lingering traces as if he was memorizing what made me moan deep and throaty or soft and sweet; maybe he was trying to decide which sound he liked the best.

Finding confidence, I pulled away from him, catching him off guard; his eyes looked as if to say "what are you doing!" What he hadn't realized yet is that this is my party and he's the invited guest, so it had now become my turn to call the shots. Turning around, and sitting on my knees, I pulled him into an intense, passionate embrace reserved only for a partner you've been with for a while, not for a casual fling. So why did I do it? Simple, because I wanted to know what it felt like to have a man WIDE OPEN for what I could do to him. Then realize what it would feel like if I took it away; to do that, I had to pull out every trick in the book. Like I said before, I'm not playing the part of the victim anymore. If my semi relationship with Jayshawn and train wreck Malik had taught me anything it's that handsome, successful, powerful men like unattainable BITCHES so from this point I will only be available when I want and not when I'm beckoned by one of them.

Breaking the embrace, I instructed him to lie on his back. Doing so, I got an eye full of not so little Hennison. As I tried not to stare, I noticed that it hadn't looked the way I expected it to. I've never been with a man outside my race, so I have to be honest because I didn't know any different. Like most women, I assumed the stereotypes had some truth to it. Instead of a "little pink Willie" he is surprisingly well endowed, and like the rest of his body he was a delicate bronze color; maybe he tanned naked, I thought as I straddled him.

Gliding down slowly on him, I had to adjust my body as to not hurt myself. Starting a slow wind, I heard the breath get caught in his chest then release. Picking up the pace, I let the slickness of my body engulf him; even through the condom, I knew he felt the wetness of me as the winces of exquisite pleasure washed across his face. As I saw the muscles in his arms and chest tighten and release, I speed up my pace and then slowed down to push him to the brink of explosion. There's power in a woman, men can't even imagine possessing; and I have to admit I loved the control I had.

Just as I got a good tempo, he flipped the switch on me! He put me on my back and began to long stroke me slow. Lifting my leg to meet his lips, he kissed and licked my calves like a man devouring his last meal. I have no idea how the rest of the night will play out, but I have to admit I love the direction is going!

Malik

Man, this shit here is crazy! The showcase really put me on the map! I've been getting calls for bookings left and right, and even a few of them have been for Cyn. She doesn't have the best stage performance, but that's nothing a few background dancers can't handle. So, you know what that means, right? Ya boy got to scout some new talent! I booked TNT for a gig at the Enigma club, hopefully his performance will bring in prize groupies willing to take a slim to none paying gig as a dancer. Who knows, I just might find my next big money maker. My only problem is China, she's been all over my ass about signing female artists; I thought I ended that conversation with her, but I guess I didn't come across firm enough for her to get the message. That's cool, I got plans for that ass, believe that!

As for my former competition JayShawn, that dude is finished! I heard he got back with that trifling ass girl of his Tarin; maybe I'll make her join my roster just to get under his skin. Word has it she's trying to stage a comeback or whatever that means for a former fat girl model; I don't really know, though I might put her legs in the air for good measure. At the moment I have more pressing matters to attend to, like getting this bitch out the door and on the next bus to Jersey. China asked if I would go home with her, but I'm thinking *"you must out of your mind?"* After the Chloe situation, I'm not about to be stuck with their family in close quarters; I don't even know if China told them anything, which would make things more awkward if we just showed up together. I'm not about that life! I'll just stay here and find me a shorty to cuff while she's away.

Finally getting her in a cab, I'm free to make moves that will put me in positions to make power play's and really launch my brand; maybe take it international! After making all the arrangements for

TNT, I have the rest of the day to chill. Because it's the holidays, the city slowed down to a crawl, and the only women that are out are the lonely, desperate, I don't need a man because I have my career chicks. Who the hell were they fooling? That money ain't going to knock the bottom out of your ass at night. Well, only if you get one of those Cree Cherry vibrators that the females are going crazy over. I heard my man at the gym telling a trainer it sold out as soon as it dropped; his girl even got one. I was trying not to listen, but then he said something that nearly got my dick hard. He said his girl dropped $350 on it! For a plastic/metal dick? Man, I can manufacture my own meat and distribute it for that kind of money. Between that and the music, I could be unstoppable; corner every market. I can just see it *"Malik's Magnificent Meat", twirling in a pussy near you!* Ok, the name needs some work; but the concept is there.

Walking in to Façade Bar and Grill, the place was a lot livelier than I thought it would be; the city had more singles than I thought who are alone on Christmas. Grabbing the only stool left at the bar, I shouted out my order quickly to the waitress as she passed by; it was so busy I nearly had to reach over the bar and grab her arm to get her attention. They are lucky the ribs here are some of the best I've ever had.

Adjusting my clothes, I sat back down and noticed this beautiful girl on the stool next to me. Glancing at her quickly, I saw she was giving me the "eye". Knowing what it meant, I flashed my pussy melting smile at her, and she blushed immediately. It was easy talking to her. The conversation flowed effortlessly into another without so much as an awkward pause. As we shared an early dinner together, I notice how her lips moved as she spoke; I heard the words she was speaking instead of imagining her juicy lips wrapped firmly on the "D". I must have gotten lost in thought when I faintly heard her call my name over and over. Snapping out of my daze, we continued to talk. I learned that she is from Detroit and she came to the city to design clothes, but currently works as an assistant. Telling her what she needed to know about me, we left together and decided to have a nightcap at her place. I can't believe a woman this beautiful and smart was alone on Christmas Day; why didn't a dude try to pull her? *"I hope she wasn't really a man under all that makeup."* I thought as we entered a passing cab.

Her place was nice enough. It was a one bedroom in Soho; which on a assistants income is more than a little hard to swing, but those types of details I'd have to find out later. It's definitely well decorated, so I know she's been here for a while and taken care of; maybe she has a rich daddy like Dominique who's paying her bills while she "finds" herself. If I play my cards right, she could be my next connect that could open up a few more doors to potential investors. But I'm jumping ahead of myself; let's see what baby is working with first. Taking a seat on her couch, I wait as she goes to the kitchen and comes back with a bottle of Cognac.

She speaks in a hushed voice, and leans close to my ear as she says, "This is very, very exclusive bottle of Cognac. It won't debut until fashion week, it just so happens that I have a few friends that pulled a few strings and voila here it is."

With a questioning look, I uttered, "oh you have skills like that, baby?"

"I have many skills Malik; maybe I'll share a few of them with you. But first, let's start with this." She concluded as she placed a glass into my hands.

When the sweet smelling amber liquid touches my tongue, my palette immediately awakens. It was like no other drink I had before; its soft flavor had a slight kick to it, but pleasant as it maneuvered to the back of my throat. Pulling the glass away from my lips, I looked over to see that she had been savoring that first sip just as I had. Watching her with her head slightly tilted back with her hair cascading away from her face, I saw how beautiful this girl is. Taking the glass from her hands as she finished the shot, I reached over and grasped her by the torso with one hand and used the other to caress her neck, bringing her closer to my lips.

Every inch of her pulled me in; her soft skin, the sweetness of her hair, the heat of her breath drenched with the sweet taste of the smooth liquid the once lingered there. I became lost in her; the next thing I knew she was on top of me, practically attacking my mouth with hers. Wearing nothing but her black bra and leggings, I drank in the moment and savored it. As my lips stroked her neck, several moans escaped her throat. Just as the heat was about to turn up another degree, she broke away from me with her arms outstretched in front of her as if to stop herself as she stopped me.

Composing herself quickly, she apologized profusely as she forced me from the couch and steered me towards the door. She slammed the door so quickly that I hadn't had the chance to ask her for her number. This has never happened to me before. Normally I'm the one rushing to get out the door and the woman is begging me to stay. Walking down the hall to the elevator, I knew what my next more will be. This broad did not understand who she is dealing with. No female ever left me with blue balls. I looked for a challenge and one had just fallen into my lap, literally. She had set the stage, and now it was my turn to write the next scene. She would see me again, and I would feel her again.

Cassidy

I'm so happy this holiday is over, now we can get back to business as usual. I need to get Cairo back to our normal routine and keep Clair's mind focused on New York and London's Fashion week; maybe if I did that I could block out the fact that I haven't heard from Kelly in a few days. I'm starting to like her, but she's flaking out on me. I hope she's not using me for my position at Indulgence, but if she had been, I wouldn't be surprised; this has happened before. Ever since my ex Shane jumped ship and left Black Publishing to write a gossip column for The Skyline Times, every lesbian within sniffing distance applied for her old job at Renegade Magazine, another one of Hennison's pet projects.

Instead of making myself upset, I decide to get some work done by going into the office a little earlier than normal. I can't lose my edge, if it gets out that I'm getting soft every wannabe blogger or assistant will pine for my job looking for a come up; not that Clair would ever let that happen, it's just that I don't need the aggravation.

Sitting at my desk starring at a blank screen, I tried desperately to put my relationship situation out of my mind. I mean, is it so wrong to want to spend my time with someone who wants to also spend their time with me? These days it seems like work will be my only mistress. Glancing at my calendar, I realized the New Year is around the corner; so there is practically no time to waste! Fashion Week is like the Super Bowl to the fashion industry, and if you're preparing now, you're already behind. Indulgence plans the next Fashion Week just as the current one is closing, as does most industry professionals; but I need to get all the schedules together for the next meeting or whenever Clair drops last minute bombs on us.

Concentrating so hard on the task at hand, I barely noticed that the office is filling up with rested employees; I hoped they enjoyed the time they had to themselves, because that's over now. Those rested faces will soon be replaced by overworked, underpaid, exhausted fashion zombies who'll be ready to pounce at a moment's notice if Clair deemed it so. Momentarily distracted, I saw Kelly sashay to her desk; she looked beautiful! For a second I rose from my desk to greet her, and then I hesitated and sat back down. I can't create a scene at work just because my sort of girlfriend had returned none of my calls. Hearing the phone in the distance, I answered it quickly, knowing it was Clair.

Our first meeting back went as expected. Clair thanked everyone for a successful All White Attired Ball; she was very pleased with all the investment money it brought into the magazine. Honestly, the petty show Hennison put on was the icing on the cake. He gave the paparazzi something to write about with the bonus of them now focusing on all the re-branding that has been going on throughout the company. Surprisingly, she didn't even mention that portion of the evening; I half expected her to address it, especially since as the evening wore on her eyes could slice Hennison and Chloe both into tiny pieces while she stared at them. Then with the predictability of a flea she ripped into the departments she thought had been slacking off.

After the carnage called a staff meeting ended, I followed her in her office with my tablet in hand; she rambled on as I attempted to keep my mind focused on what she was saying. Slowly coming out of my stupor, I heard her repeat with sternness "Where are we with Montreal?"

"Cassidy, where are you today? Break time is over, we need to get back on track!" She bellowed. "Isabella, that succubus; is trying to outdo us on everything! Every time I turn my back, she's in Hennison's ear about expanding her magazine. If he decided that Rouge is performing better than Indulgence, he'll cut our budgeting and decrease our circulation; that could lead to our eventual demise! I won't entertain that idea for a second, we have to out think that rod of a woman and our concepts have to be nothing short of spectacular. Are you with me, Cassidy?"

"Yes, yes, I am." I repeated. "I just had a few things on my mind. I'm with you one hundred percent," I assured.

"What's wrong, Cass? Is it Cairo?" she asked with worry in her voice.

"No, no, nothing like that. But now that you've mentioned it, he has been asking more frequently about his dad. He's getting more inquisitive about him by the day. One day sooner than later he'll need to know about him; that worries me." I confessed.

With shock in her eyes, she paused in what looks like a state of fear. Watching her body slump down, she turned to her desk and plopped down in the chair as if the weight of a thousand bricks were on her shoulders. Stumbling over her words, she acknowledged what I said and assured me we would both sit with him when he's old enough and tell him the truth about his dad. This is a very sore subject for me and a tender one for Clair; we both had been through so much and tried our best to shield Cairo that we both forgot to deal with the pain of it ourselves. Clair is more than my employer, but my best friend; an annoying, demanding, narcissist, but the Yin to my Yang all the same.

Leaving her office, I went back to my desk outside and took several deep breaths. I had been so off my game I forgot about Montréal, and the bomb I had dropped on Clair made her forget she even asked about it. Gathering up all the information I could, I frantically attempted to put together a Mock Up for the Montréal Music & Arts Festival.

As a medium for news, Indulgence had to showcase the festival in the magazine; especially since the who's who of music, film, fashion, and so forth would be in attendance. Many amazing indie designers have been discovered at this showcase that has gone on to become juggernauts of their profession that rule the game. If there was any place to present your talent to a myriad of people at once, this is it.

Even if you didn't get contracted by a major company or philanthropist, you could still have a chance of success from the social media coverage that is guaranteed to be in attendance.

As a representative for the magazine Clair had to be in attendance, as her right hand as did I. I hated to leave Cairo for so long, one event after another made it impossible for me to be with him for important things like parent-teacher conferences, school plays, story time, etc. In accompaniment with a grueling travel schedule this time of year it becomes impossible for me to schedule my feminine wax's; I'm practically growing a forest on my vagina.

Checking and re-checking the bookings over and over, I had finally decided it was perfect and to hand out to the staff. I would notify those who would travel with Clair and I a week in advance to make whatever arrangements they needed. To the average person this would be difficult, but when one has the privilege to work for Black Enterprise a week's notice was long enough for you to decide if your career or whatever else was more important to you. Is it harsh? Yes. But are the connections you can make worth it? HELL YES! Being in this business can put someone with drive, knowledge, and charisma to the next level with the right people in your corner. But piss the wrong people off, you can find yourself black listed; no pun intended.

Straightening myself, I put on my best resting bitch face and slow strutted down the short corridor. I have to admit I have one of the best model walks in the game to this day. These newbies are good, but some lack the passion, balance, knowledge, and awareness of their bodies in order to perfectly execute a signature walk that leaves woman jealous and men salivating; though for me it was sometimes the opposite.

Maintaining my fierceness as much as I could, I went to each department to the key people needed to be aware of the magazine's plans. When I got to Chloe, she had a mischievous grin on her face as she gazed into space; smiling at an invisible person. Momentarily interrupting the flashback she was having, she scrambled to grab the folder. Envious of the look in her eyes; a look I haven't had for a while. She asked, 'You ok?' stunned that I had let my game face go, I quickly answered and turned to enter Kelly's cubical.

She looked beautiful. I raked my eyes over her body; I had definitely missed her. She wore her hair in a shortcut, her makeup was light highlighting her features, and the dress she wore hugged every curve I longed to put my fingers on; but were at work and I can't be unprofessional. Looking up at me with the eyes of a goddess, she reaches her hand to take the folder. I saw her lips move, but I couldn't hear the sound it made.

Snapping out of my daze I heard her say "Cass, I'm sorry I didn't reach out to you but the holidays are hard for me can I come to your place tonight; we can discuss us."

"Sure." I said plainly as I turned on my Mateo Baptiste heels to leave. She shouted, "I'll come by at 10 ok?" dashing I rushed out of her presence.

The rest of the day was a blur. I looked forward to seeing Kelly. Truth be told, I really liked her, but I got the feeling she was hiding something from me; I just hoped it wasn't a secret that we couldn't get pass.

She arrived at my apartment on time; I had put Cairo to bed forty-five minutes earlier; so by now he had to be sleeping. Hopefully, whatever she wanted to discuss wouldn't be so heated to wake him. Walking in, she smelled amazing; her perfume reeked of sexual innuendo. Sitting on my couch, she explained why she had not contacted me. I was so enthralled by her sheer presence that it didn't matter what she said; I was just happy she had come. Stopping her in the middle of her speech, I handed her some wine she sipped slowly without taking a single breath.

I reached out to take her hand, and she immediately stopped talking; enough words had passed between us. Feeling that my moment was fleeting, I pulled her close and felt the softness of her lips. Her reaction at first was shock, I could tell by how she'd been slow to kiss me back. After a second or two, she let herself enjoy what was happening.

Massaging her lips with mine, she took the initiative to reach for me and pull me closer to her. She smelled so good, and her skin so soft; I temporarily wondered why I switched back and forth to men. Honestly, both sexes were crazy, and I can't say I preferred one more than the other; but in this moment Kelly's touch is what I wanted. I don't know if tonight we'll end up in bed together; I have no expectations of her, but if we did, I would show her that I can do more with my face than give the perfect resting bitch, but create orgasms that will rival the best effort a man can give. Being a woman myself, I know exactly the right places to make her entranced.

Jayshawn

I've never met such self-indulgent person in my life! Tarin was in the club acting brand new, like she hadn't taken a long sabbatical from modeling. She treated me as if I was the trophy on her arm to keep the women interested in whatever babble came from her mouth. Sure she got a few people interested in her comeback, she even got the attention of Philip Fuller, Creator of Mass Creation; but that means nothing if he doesn't ask her to walk in his runway show for London Fashion Week, which is basically the be all end all in the full figure fashion world. Though she's a massive pain in the ass, I have to admit that seeing her happy made me happy; a feeling I thought had been impossible.

She must have really been feeling a sense of accomplishment; when we finally called it a night and went home, she was all over me. In the same elevator where I fantasized about Makayla, and brought Chloe to my apartment for the first time, Tarin practically swallowed my face. I don't remember her being so aggressive; when we were together before she would play coy. Maybe that was an act, and this is the real Tarin I'm seeing.

Barely making it in the door, she had nearly undressed and had been attempting to undress me. Admittedly, this turned me on. The last time a woman had taken control like this, it was Chloe; damn, I miss her. Letting her skirt drop to the floor, she jumped in my arms and wrapped her legs around my waist. Not one to miss an opportunity, I undid my belt and pants in a motion so fast only the sound of the belt crashing to the floor gave away that I had been naked from the torso down.

Pinning her body between myself and the wall, I ripped the buttons on her silk blouse. As I pulled it apart, I heard a few of them hit the floor in what sounded like applause, as I put my lips to her chest and lick slowly on her breasts. Sucking air through clinched teeth, I could tell my deliberate kisses were having the desired effect. Leaning her head back to rest it on the wall, she thrust her hips forward to aid in a deeper penetration while she threw one arm above her head and brought her beautifully manicured fingers to the cupid's bow of her lips.

Bucking wildly against her, I could feel my body tighten and loosen; knowing what was about to happen, I bucked even faster as to get the release my body craved. Upon my release, the energy drained from my body. Dragging myself from her body as to not hurt her, she staggered a bit to find their footing. Backing away from her, I retreated to the bedroom, pulling my boxers up as I walked.

Stretched out across the bed, I caught a glimpse of her with the most devilish look on her face. With only her bra and black silk blouse still on, she strutted to me. Dropping to her knees, gently parted my legs. Watching her intently as to see what she does next, she kissed the inside of my thigh as I had done to her breast only moments before. Reaching up, she reached inside my drawers through the slit in the front and awaked the once sleeping monster who greeted her eagerly.

Wrapping her glossy lips on my penis, she began caressing her tongue gently on head, and then worked her way to the shaft. Getting into the movement, she released me only for a second to swiftly pull my boxers all the way off. Sucking me as if my dick contained the antidote to fix whatever pain she had been feeling inside; she became more aggressive. Regaining some of my energy back, I moved from her mouth to fuck her missionary; or so I thought. Stopping me before I could start, she got on top of me and rode in reverse. Tarin had definitely become a different lover than what she had been before; as she rode me I wondered if he had taught her some of these not so new tricks she had been performing on me. But now is not the time to discuss old lovers.

After finishing the second round, Tarin got off her now sore knees and went to the bathroom to fluff her hair and ran the shower. As I lay on the bed listening to the sound of the running water, I wondered if Tarin and I have what it takes to make our relationship work this time. Quickly falling asleep, I had only been briefly disturbed when I felt the weight of Tarin's body when she slid into bed; she smelled of Pomegranate body wash.

Waking up early and moving as quickly as I could without disturbing Tarin, I raced out of the apartment and to my one and only sanctuary these days; my office. Though pleasantly quiet since Makayla's departure, I need an assistant. Approaching my office door, I could barely see the door frame over the sea of people who were standing outside; let the interviewing begin.

The first girl that came in looked like she could be a potential candidate until she described how she entered the events business; she described all the best events she had attended, some of them being mine. When I asked her what she thought could improve any of those events, her answer was the men she attended them with. As she spoke, I could feel my stomach twitch and suddenly in a burst of energy I stood up and escorted her to the door with the usual "I'll be in touch" as I signaled for the next candidate to enter.

This has got to be the longest afternoon I've had since I opened my business. Sitting at my desk, I reached for the bottom drawer to pull out my favorite drink and poured a glass. Taking a swig, I heard a gentle knock at the door that was accompanied by a voice that asked "So, it's been that hard of a day huh?" looking up I expected to see another woman standing in my door looking to either make me hire her or attempt to get me to pay her rent for the month; both were wrong.

Seeing an impeccably dressed man in a brightly colored tailored suit, I pondered if he was here to book me as his event planner or if he was simply lost. He stood in the doorway with a puzzled look on his face as to say if it was ok for him to enter my office: gesturing for him to take a seat; he flounced to the seat.

"So, what can I do for you bruh?" I quizzed.

"I like a man that gets straight to the point." He remarked. "I'm here to interview for the assistant position; I hope I'm not too late. The posting said it was an open interview until 4:30 p.m."

"You… Sure. Ugh, do you have your resume? What are your credentials?" I asked.

"Well, I've been a personal assistant for five years with indie designer Nova Henry. I've designed her productions, helped to select venues, made traveled arrangements, managed all her bookings, constructed promotional materials, even choreographed some stage shows. I've gained a wealth of experience with Nova." He concluded.

"That all sounds great, I'm sorry man; what's your name?" I questioned.

"My name is Fallon. Fallon Toussaint." He replied.

"Fallon, that all sounds amazing to be honest. If all that you said is true, I could really use someone like you working with me. But why did you leave the assistant position with Nova Henry; Also, what could you bring with your employment that would help me improve my business?" I probed.

"I left Nova's employ, because it was time for me to move on and create a unique experience that would make me more well-rounded." He offered." As far as business, I've built a lot of great business connections in and around the music, fashion, finance, and entrepreneurial arena. I could help you build your clientele to reach the innermost desired areas of corporate culture; that would include foreign and domestic opening Jayshawn Thomas Signature Events to a diverse realm of clients ready and willing to spend top dollar to have their events specially tailored to their lifestyles where the only limit is there imagination. I've watched you, and you have the potential to be great and with my help you could be infinite."

"Well Mr. Toussaint, from what I see here on your resume and what I get from our conversation I can see that you are an amazing assistant. Nova Henry is a well-respected business woman and will be a force to be reckoned with if she finds out that her prize employee is interviewing for me. And to be frank, I don't care!" I said as a slow smile crept across my face. "Out of all the candidates I've interviewed today, you're the one I believe can really help. I know some work you've done; I've worked with Nova in the past. She will beat my door down for you, but I think you'll be worth it. Don't disappoint me, bruh; when can you start?"

With surprise on his face and dripping from his voice, he uttered, "Immediately. I can be here first thing in the morning to familiarize myself with the office and past and a current events, if that's ok with you."

"Be here at 9am." I proclaimed with certainty as I held my hand out to him. Shaking it with gratitude, he then left.

The days passed by in a blur of meetings, photo shoots, fashion layouts, and an endless stream of designers sending pieces of their collections to Indulgence to be featured in the Fashion Explosion Issue. This had good and bad consequences, of course; great because of the buzz it gave for London Fashion Week, and the goodies the staff will get when the Issue's finished, it is also vexing due to all the craziness it brought with it.

Cassidy is in work mode, keeping all of us lower assistants in line and under the critical view of her meticulous eyes. There would be absolutely no slacking off; especially since Clair has been ever present. Something is brewing in the office, or as the old folks would say, "something ain't right in the Kool Aid." There has been some more than a usual tension between Clair and Isabella, also between Cass and Kelly. Even the air in the office is different. Where it was pulsating and thriving, it's now eerie with a sense of uneasiness. I remember hearing career women in the bars where I used to work constantly complaining of when their careers are soaring that their personal lives are in the crashing. At the time I didn't put too much stock into what they had said, because Malik was a Prince to me and things couldn't have been better. Fast forward, I now understand exactly what they spoke of. It's difficult for a woman to have a career, be independent, and then switch to mommy, wife, or girlfriend mode at the stroke of a clock tick.

On the other hand, I couldn't be happier! Things are always busy at work, especially because we were all going to be hopping a flight soon to London. But besides that, Hennison and I have been spending so much time together we don't even bother hiding it anymore. We are the talk of the office; he stops by Indulgence unannounced and openly flirts with me as I attempt to keep a straight face. The first time he stopped by, Clair and Cassidy came stomping through the cubicles so hard I just knew the lifts on their heels would pop right off. He cleaned it up, he couldn't appear to be having a relationship with an employee, but honestly that cover had been blown the night of the Ball.

I know for certain he's had other office romances, especially in the Rouge office. I was on the elevator last week and I overheard one of the Rouge girls say to the other, "that's her." The other girl responded with bated breath, "I can't believe he turned us down for that. Isabella has to be upset." She uttered through clinched teeth. Smiling like a Cheshire cat, I couldn't help being mildly entertained by their dismay. But I wondered what they meant by Isabella being upset. In that moment, I wondered if he had sex with her. Would I be surprised if he hadn't; but I would've liked to have full disclosure if he had a relationship with her, be it sexual or otherwise.

Meanwhile, back at the ranch, Dee is slowly becoming a recluse; I talk to her, but sometimes she looks at me as if she's not there in the room. She's becoming a quiet storm and I'm waiting for the signs for when she is ready to become destructive. I know she suspects the growing relationship with Hennison. Concern washes swiftly over her face whenever I refer to him even in the smallest capacity so I keep '*the I'm screwing the publishing God*' talk to a minimum. Instead, I steer the conversation toward a more pleasant conversation; SHOPPING!

I bring tons of freebies home, most of them for me. Though Dee has the best curves I've ever seen on a woman, she's still too petite to wear the clothes Indulgence features. Instead, I bring her tons of shoes and accessories, and today's excursion is to find outfits to match. While online, she found a Pop Up shop in Brooklyn, so we made it a girl's day out. As we browsed through the printed tees, I casually asked her if she and Elgin had anymore flings in the bathroom at work or otherwise. Looking at me with the '*girl please*' look, I stifled a smile as I kept looking at tees that were way too Spring-ish for the chilly days we're still having. I love my friend and I want her to be happy, and these days she's anything but content.

"What's so wrong with entertaining Elgin's advances? He likes you and I know you find him attractive…" I began to say as she interrupted.

"You don't know that. What makes you think, I would give him a second of my time? He's not all that!" she spat at me.

Smacking her on the ass hard enough to make a sharp popping sound, I retorted "Because I've seen how you looked at him at your parents' house. Whenever he wasn't in your line of sight, I watched your eyes dart across the room until they found him; that's how I know, honey!"

"Girl, I was just looking for Martha's Beignets; you know she makes the best. And he just so happened to be hording the tray every time a server left the kitchen. I swear that man will become a diabetic." She concluded.

"Diabetic," I questioned. "Dee the only sweet treat that man wants in his mouth is you!" I said through bursts of laughter that echoed through the sparsely decorated room the event host is using. Giving me the *'girl bye'* look, I continued to provoke a response from her.

"Dee, he's handsome and goal oriented; don't count him out because you're still in your feelings over Chase. Has he even reached out to you after all this time? I understand that you hurt him, but that's no excuse for him to treat you like some dime store hoe. If anything, you're a five dollar hoe, at least." Smacking me lightly on the arm, she joined me in laughing. That is the first time I've seen her let her guard down long enough to give a genuine laugh. "But seriously," I continued. "This is not you. You used to be so vibrant, and not so long ago you were the one trying to help me through a tough breakup. Look, all I'm saying is there's nothing wrong with spending time with this

man; if anything at least he can help you take your mind off of Chase."
I concluded.

Finishing the day with lunch at TASTE IT Deli and Bakery, then Mani Pedi's at TIPS Nail Salon, we returned home with a full bellies and beautifully aching feet. As Dee carted her bags to her room, and I took a slow glance of the small living room that had now become a slash bedroom for me, I realized that I have no place to put my growing wardrobe. What started out as a necessity became a home and has now turned into an inconvenience. When I first moved in with my bestie, I had nothing and nowhere to go. Out of her giving me a place to lick my wounds and gather strength to move on, I grew, and I didn't even realize it. We talked before about me moving out and looking at how her home is starting to look like a dorm room we'll have to revisit that conversation. I don't want to leave her while she's going through this stupor, but we can't continue to live on top of each other like this. As she unpacked, I packed for London; I decided to talk to her about it when I came back.

Later that night at Hennison's place after sex so good my limbs winced with a mixture of pleasure and pain, my body became lethargic and it was lights out. If I hadn't had heard hushed whispers, I wouldn't even have roused from the comatose state I had been in. Reaching for a warm body only to grab a handful of air, I got out the bed and follow the direction of the whisper. In the hall near a large window I saw him sitting in the dark, phone in one hand, cognac in the other as the moonlight washed over his body. As I watched him, three things crossed my mind; 1. Damn this is a scene that would be the pivotal moment that changed the characters (if this were a book), 2. He looked sexy as hell in this moment, and 3. Who the hell was he talking to!

Seeing me standing halfway between him and the bedroom, he put the phone down on the small table next to him and walked towards me. He hugged me tightly, using my body to comfort him. This is not the confident Hennison I had seen countless times during various degrees of circumstances. He's always kept his cool, but tonight I saw for the slightest instant a look on his face that made me worry for him. I'm not in love with him, but I care about him.

"What's wrong?" I asked.

"Nothing sweetheart, just some business that couldn't wait until morning; come on, let's go back to bed." He concluded as we went back to his room.

As we lay together in bed, he rested his head on my chest and without thinking I stroked his head; playing in his hair. This is the most intimate we've ever been. All the times we've been together we were flirting or just recently having sex. Whoever was on the other end of that phone had made Hennison ominous, which made me feel unsettled. Damn Just when I had become used to our relationship being one way, he changed it up on me and added a new depth. If that phone call truly had something to do with Black Enterprise, I wonder if that would affect the day-to-day operations of Indulgence. That could be why Clair and Isabella have been at odds more than normal. Really, I'm speculating. I can't ask Hennison about anything having to do with the business; I know that if I asked, he would either avoid answering me or pull his dick out as a distraction. Our relationship has for the most part been about having fun and not being too serious, if I opened Pandora's Box I don't believe I could ever close it again; whatever it is we're doing, I don't want to lose it.

On the way into work I passed by all my co-workers who seemed to be on autopilot, all their movements were normal; but their eyes were dead. There's a kind of poison circulating through the magazine, I wonder if it will hurt its future. Luggage in hand, as soon as we finish the work day everyone who had to be on hand would have to get on the evening flight to London; most would fly commercial, the rest of us would board Black Enterprise private plane.

Having to team up once again with Kelly, together we had to design and execute the last photo shoot before leaving with designer Artemis Johns. As per usual Kelly is dead weight, I know I'm fucking the headman in charge but I'm still holding my own in the work department; but Kelly... who the hell was she fucking besides Cassidy that she could get away with only doing the most mediocre of tasks. The most work I've seen her do is accessorizing the garments with items from The Closet. I've been the person running back and forth to The Warehouse so that the scenes were properly set, assisting Artemis himself with whatever tragedy occurred in his world, interviewing and positioning the models Sloan sent from Legendary Models Inc. one of them being a familiar face. It seems Tarin has sweet-talked herself right into this gig. Either Sloan was getting soft or Tarin still had some pull in the business; either way, dealing with her was not how I wanted to end the day. I had no choice but to cast her because it was at Sloan's request that she be involved. Usually it would be a hectic but fun day, but she made it difficult for the photographers to get a decent shot. Did I mention that the photographers scheduled were in my charge as well? Every time she complained about an angle or the lighting, it set us back a half hour. It's not anyone's fault she didn't keep it right and tight while she was playing secretary; the re-touching of her photos will be catastrophic. Well, maybe not that bad, but she annoys the shit out of me; I'd rather have girl talk with Kelly.

Alone at my desk, I took off my shoes and wiggled my toes on the cold floor for relief. Leaning back in the chair, I vaguely heard heel clicks. Sitting up, I saw Clair standing in the opening of my cubical. She had never spoken to me directly, only through Cassidy; to what do I owe her presence, I thought.

"Ms. Major, I trust you're ready for the flight tonight. The plane won't wait for your, then again it may." She scoffs at me.

Not feeling enough energy to put up with her sudden burst of sarcasm, I gave her some of my own. "No, I don't expect the plane to wait for me. But yes, I'm packed and ready." I retorted as I pointed to my luggage in the far corner.

Glancing in the direction of my finger, she continues, "Good. I've watched you grow in the past few months here; I've got to admit regarding all the new hires you seem to be the most capable. I've hardly had to have Cassidy correct any of your work, and the clients seem to value your help and input; for that, I congratulate you. But I can't ignore what has been going on between Hennison and yourself. I'm not telling you who to mess around with, God knows we've all done our share in this business. With that being said, understand the difference between the pleasure of this business and results of doing that type of business; they've got consequences." She cautions.

Before I could utter a word, she strutted away slinging her perfectly crafted Nicolai Mikhail fur scarf. As she approached the elevator, like clockwork, the bell chimed and a gorgeous man stepped off with barely a glance in her direction. Speaking to each other coarsely, Clair simply offered "Hennison" Which he just as quickly returned "Clair" as he continued to his destination.

Smiling a brilliant smile, he asks "Hi beautiful are you ready?"

Stepping back into my shoes, I nodded my head to agree as he grabbed my bags and we started towards the elevator. Exiting the building, Mr. Bassett greeted us. Opening the door and taking my bags from Hennison, we made our way to the private runway. In the car, Hennison removed my shoes and rubbed all the achy parts of my feet. Grateful for his thoughtfulness, I motioned for him to come closer to me. As he did, we locked each in a kiss that would make porn stars blush. With the partition raised, we greatly use the forty-five-minute ride. I must say for a curvy girl on the heavier side of the curve I have excellent flexibility. Raising my skirt, I sat on his lap and rode him as we rode towards the airport.

Finishing just as we pulled up to the gate, we had just enough time to put ourselves back together. Stepping out of the limo, Mr. Bassett gave us a knowing smile. Telling us to enjoy our trip and have a safe flight, we thanked him as we climbed the steps to the aircraft.

Having a boyfriend who had a private plane had its perks! Oh, shit, did I say boyfriend? We haven't put a title on anything yet, and I don't want to be the one to make the first move; God, I just hope I didn't mistakenly say that out loud while in the heat of the moment. Entering the plane, I expected to see the usual suspects, but I saw a few new faces that I have never seen before.

Seated in a Queen like position was Clair, next to her Cassidy. Behind them sat Sloan Hill, former model and founder of Legendary Models Inc. Ingrid Indulgence's most notable stylist and good friend of mine, and behind them sat two faces I've never seen before. Interlocking his fingers with mine, Hennison introduced Gavin McLaren and his assistant, Phoenix Alexander. After this trip, I would never forget these names.

Fallon came into the office attacking computer files and contact listings like a mother inspecting your bedroom for dirty socks and dishes under your bed. Watching him work was a breath of fresh air, I had never seen an assistant actually work; in my mind all they did was book hair appointments and file their nails. Meticulously going through past event records and vendors, he found a few discrepancies.

The first being some outdated contracts, I had at least four vendors whom had been overcharging me for their services despite the revenue I helped them generate once the word spread that I had used their services. Next, he found that some of my safety procedures weren't being followed by contractors I hired to build/set the staging for events. Makayla should have been on hand to make sure they followed every procedure like it came from the Bible. As my assistant, Makayla shouldn't have let even the smallest detail fall through the cracks; I'm glad that scrub Malik is stuck with her ass now! The last thing Fallon found was that Makayla hadn't deleted none of her emails. She had hundreds of emails from her to Malik and vice versa about my business. Not just who was booking me, but everything down to where we were meeting when not in the office, the rates I charged, and mock up plans for their event; she had let the wolf in! Now I know how he had been able to cut me off at the knees these past few months, where I thought I had been slipping or becoming predictable; NEVER THAT! My work has always and will continue to be impeccable.

By the end of the day Fallon managed to straighten the mess Makayla made, set up a new system that would be easy for both of us to follow in case the other is out of the office, finalize a few last-minute wedding details for a very prestigious and wealthy couple, and on a whim call club PARADOX to reserve one of their VIP areas for

Tarin and myself. Of all the decisions I've made in this business hiring Fallon has to be the best, I just wish he could manage my personal life as well as the business; in that area, I'm losing my grip.

I waited in the lobby of my building for what seems like an eternity for Tarin to get her ass ready. I had dozed off when she sauntered off of the elevator to the chair where I'd been waiting that had become a temporary bed. Arriving at PARADOX and an hour and a half after my reservation, I didn't expect for my section to still be available and it wasn't. Pulling Tarin away from the club owner as she wildly ranted about never gracing his place with her presence again, I apologized profusely as I steered her towards the bar. Ordering the strongest drink I could think of, I attempted to calm her as the diva reared her well contoured face.

Taking her hand, I whispered, "Sweetheart calm down; it's not that serious; we were late getting here. Take this drink and relax."

Rolling her eyes, she retorted, "How can you be so nonchalant about this? Doesn't this guy know who we are? I could put in one call and he would never have another customer in here again; I'm still a big deal in this town!"

"Yeah, big deal" I uttered flatly as I mocked her.

"What is that supposed to mean, Jay?" she spat at me. "Do you think I don't have any pull anymore? You have no idea who you're dealing with, I have so many things in the works right now that if you knew what they were, you would kiss my very well maintained ass right now. Hell, I can even get your business back on track and maybe Malik wouldn't be running circles around you; how about that?"

Stunned at the words that poured out of her mouth, she continued. "I will be in the London show walking for Philip Fuller; if I play my cards right, I could be the new face for his Project Curves Collection. Matter of fact, I'll be leaving tonight on a non-stop to London, I would've told you sooner, but it simply slipped my mind. Oh yeah, and that girl you were slumming with (she paused to dramatically tap her chin), what's her name Chloe, right? She'll be there too with that sexy Hennison Black. Maybe I'll make her help me get dressed for the show, so she could smell Hennison's scent dripping from my body." She ended with a wicked grin across her face that has been similar to the Cheshire cat.

She laughed wildly as she took the drink from my hand and lifted it to her lips. As she put the glass down, she didn't expect me to reach out and grab her face and squeeze her mouth. For a few seconds I forgot she was a woman, I forgot that we were in a public place; I forgot that I loved her; or did I? All I could see was red! Letting her face go as my hand smeared her lipstick, I slowly came back to myself and stood up slowly to find sanctuary in the men's room.

Walking ferociously to the bathroom, I kicked myself for losing my cool; I shouldn't have let her push me that far! She knows that Hennison, and she is a very sore subject with me and her incorporating Chloe in that mix brought out a fire in me I didn't know I still had for her. Pausing for a second to look at my reflection in the dirty night club mirror, I knew I had been lying in that moment; I knew that I still had feelings for Chloe. What the hell was I doing here? Not just in this club, but with Tarin. I don't know what I'm doing; I have love for Chloe, but I had been so fixated on having a second chance with Tarin I closed myself off to the woman that could be my Queen.

I turned to exit the bathroom when Tarin walked in with a pitiful look could her face. Not wanting to have another exchange with her, I attempted to walk past her to grab the door. Wedging her body between me and the door, she locked the door and began to relentlessly apologize for what she said to me at the bar. Turning from her, she hugged me, pressing her breasts on my back. Pushing her off, I walked to a stall and leaned on it as to relieve the pressure my body and mind is feeling.

She tried to kiss me, but I turned my head. She tried again, and I let her. I didn't encourage her, but I hadn't tried to stop her either. Before long I had succumbed to her persuasions and kissed her back. I can't deny her body is what wet dreams are made of, and I didn't want little Jay to respond to her, but he did anyway. I had become enchanted with every stroke of her lips. With all her boasting just a short time ago, no one would believe Tarin was on her knees, on the dirty tiled floor of a club men's room.

Finishing as abruptly as it started, we left the club in a silent cab ride home. The night ended with the most emotionless sex I've ever had in my adult life. We went through the motions without the emotions of what we were doing. The only thing I came away with was the certainty that I had no longer loved Tarin. What I loved was us beginning again. Our relationship had become a job; something we did mindlessly without having any passion for the act, but doing it out of necessity. Sometime in the night before dawn could pierce the night sky, she gathered her already packed bags, and I presumed left to catch her flight to London. I lay there listening to her shuffling, hoping she didn't attempt to wake my false sleep. When I felt her get close to my face, I tried hard to steady my breathing and relax my eyes so they didn't flutter.

She kissed my forehead, and a few seconds later I heard the front door close. I breathed a sigh of relief when I heard the door click. Opening my eyes, I mulled over how I would get Chloe back. As I thought over and over about how much I missed the curves of her body and kicked myself for pushing her into the arms of Hennison Black, I had dozed off; my scheming would have to wait for proper waking hours.

The days had passed in a flurry of meetings, calls, floral arrangements, cake tastings, and décor formation; with endless, mind numbing backpedaling by the bride. Through our conversations I've realized that her mother- and mother-in-law have a parade of guest coming to the wedding if for nothing else but to help further their husbands' businesses. Common among wealthy families like this one, it was common practice to further your parents or even future husband's financial agenda by gathering potential business associates together; indulging them with the finest wines, food, and entertainment in the hopes that they will recognize you as a caring and generous person when really the partygoers can scarcely remember the name of the bride or the groom if they're not in direct relation.

Delphine Errol is a woman with a very long social calendar. Socialite extraordinaire, Delphine had been born into one of the oldest and most elite families in New York. Her father Will Errol had inherited his money from his great grandfather whom had made his money bootlegging alcohol during Prohibition; what the rich and privileged consider being "new money." Delphine's mother is Caroline Errol, formally known as Caroline Boudreaux. Her mother being of French Creole decent, her lineage stretched as far back as the Civil War; I'm not sure how her family came into their money, but it's safe to say it is old and generational.

As the big day approached, I thanked God I hired Fallon. He took care of every task I assigned him and more. My company had been hired for the reception portion of the wedding, and they had expected for it to be the most over the top spectacle money could buy. We wasted no time getting everything in place to impress partygoers; if we played our cards right, this event would put us on track to expand the business.

The little comment Tarin made hadn't gone unnoticed; I know Malik had been doing his numbers around town and in the process dragging my name through the mud. Nonetheless, JayShawn's Signature Events continued to thrive. Malik has a big mouth, and his big mouth gets him into a lot of trouble. My reputation is impeccable, his is still in its infancy. The only thing he has on me is that he provides entertainment or what he passes as entertainment these days; in time that will change.

The reception is due to start at 4pm, with a Cocktail hour, followed by seating and appetizers, then dinner. Like every wedding, it didn't start on time, which gave Fallon and I time to fix all the messes the catering staff made. Between the inexperienced servers breaking dishes, and screwing up the food prep, the bakery hadn't delivered the cake; everyone knows how bad the traffic can get, it's possible that the cake would arrive hours after the happy couple boarded a flight to their first exotic destination on their wedding tour. As I corrected all that had gone wrong, I had Fallon do all the legwork, catching cabs across town to handle whatever daunting task I had no mind to do.

By the time the wedding party arrived, we gave the impression that this job had been so easy we haven't even bothered to break a sweat. Just as we had breathed a sigh of relief; the bride had gone M.I.A. before the announcement of the couple. Delphine's bridesmaids searched the building from top to bottom, trying to find where she'd gone, but it was Fallon who found her in a storage closet on another floor of the building. She had a bottle of wine in one hand and a cell phone in the other when Fallon had texted me his location. Rushing there as quickly and inconspicuously as I could, I saw huddled in a corner was the most beautiful bride I had seen. Standing in her white, strapless, Elena Rose Trumpet Gown, she glistened as her body trembled.

Through her repeated sobs, I somehow had made out not so refined descriptions of her now husband having relations with several women in the wedding party along with a longtime lover he once had before their courtship had begun. This is not my area of expertise, so I offered to get her mother when she broke out into hysterics again. She hadn't wanted her family to know what has been going on, to bring this level of embarrassment to the family with that amount of people to witness her breakdown no amount of donations to the attendees charities could cure the level of scrutiny that would be endured. Offering his help to the situation, Fallon asked me to leave the room while he tried to talk to her.

I had waited in that hall for what seemed like an eternity. My phone vibrated relentlessly from text messages I had assumed had been from Delphine's family, I muted the tones without looking at who they were from. My only concern was getting that woman out of a damn closet and to her reception table so I could be done with this shit show. A few more minutes passed before she and Fallon emerged from the closet. She looked like whatever he said to her worked; her breathing had returned to normal, he had helped her clean her face and straighten her hair; she had been finally ready to greet her guests and husband. Putting in a quick call to her father, I informed him we were on our way to the venue.

We walked down the hall together, Fallon and I at her side towards the double doors of the reception area where guests waited patiently for her arrival. As we neared the doors, I became overwhelmed by the moment. I felt like a man who had my beautiful bride on my arm and I had been leading her into our reception to greet our closest friends and family; the problem was I couldn't imagine who would be behind the veil, Tarin or Chloe?

This was the first time I had allowed my mind to drift to the subject since my botched proposal to Tarin some years before. Approaching the doors, they swung open, and a man came charging down the hall towards us. As he got closer, the bride let us go and sprinted into his arms. Clutching her to his chest and placing kisses wherever he could as quickly as he could, he walked Delphine the rest of the way as the partygoers gathered at the door and clapped wildly for them. Before entering the room he turned to us and mouthed "Thank You."

The rest of the night went as planned, and the happy couple had been overly celebrated. After saying their goodbyes, the two left to the airport. While cleaning, I checked my phone and noticed that all the texts I received had been from Tarin. Not wanting to make tonight any worse, I opted not to look at them. I thanked Fallon for everything he had done, not just as my assistant but as a good person; he basically saved the day. For maintaining the integrity of my company and preventing a catastrophe, I would be in his debt. I made sure he could handle the rest of the cleanup before I left. I walked practically bow-legged to the ground floor of the building. The crisp night air hit me hard, and I nearly passed out from exhaustion on the cab ride home. Whatever nonsense Tarin had going on would have to wait until the morning.

Dominique

Going into the office after embarrassing myself in front of Elgin is like pure torture. I don't know how I'm supposed to act in front of him. Am I supposed to avoid him like a bill collector? Or am I supposed to walk into the office, nose to the sky, and pretend like the moment we shared in the bathroom never existed? I wish I had my best friend to confide in, but she's off living the dream.

Elgin avoided me like I was a stranger on the train that grabbed the hand railing in front of him without giving a second thought to personal hygiene. I hadn't expected him to fall all over me, but I expected to get some kind of common curtsey or at the very least acknowledgement. He went about his normal routine of flirting with every skirt that bounced in his direction, and I did that same by catering to Hershel's every whim; this cannot be my path in life.

On the way home, my thoughts shifted slightly to Chase; for a second I thought seriously about stalking him again. After showering and putting on my favorite faded sweatpants, I camped out in front of the t.v. Being the glutton for punishment, I picked up my phone to text Chase; maybe in a last ditch effort to rekindle what we had. Stuffing my face with popcorn with one hand as I texted with the other, I half expected for my effort to be yet another rejection like all the others; this time he answered.

DomRich: Hi Chase, I know that I've been calling and texting you on the regular since our breakup and I know that you're still mad at me, but I just really wanted to tell you (again) that I'm sorry for how I treated you. You don't deserve that. Look, this text may go unanswered like all the others, but I want you to know that knowing you changed me. I'm not the same confused girl you met in the club and again at a hot dog stand. I'm becoming better, although I don't know what my next move is; know that I think of you often. I won't try to contact you again (I finally got the hint, lol) until you reach out; if ever. I'll miss you forever.

ChasinDaDream: expect nothing out of this, but I'm on the road to forgiving you. I tried so hard for so long to convince you I was different from other men, only for you to show me you are exactly the type of woman men like that do those kinds of things too. I'm glad you think you changed, and I'm content that I could help with it, but I haven't changed. I think about you too, but when I do it makes me feel like all the time we spent together was a lie! Every touch, word, and embrace. Good, you should miss me, but I don't miss you. Please don't contact me anymore. And don't sit outside my apartment, next time I'll call building security.

Reading his text shook me to my core, as happy as I am to get a reply it didn't cross my mind that he would continue to rip me to shreds. As for my armature stalking, I didn't know that he knew I was there; so much for me being discreet. I tried to send him another text, but it wouldn't go through; I guess he blocked my number. That made me feel like more of a prize idiot. He let me bare my soul and confess to him in all my text messages, reading them all and never replying, which left me in limbo. He knew I would reach out again and when I did that was his chance to demolish my ass for a final time. I sure know how to pick a man.

I've had restless nights before, but none like the one I had last night. Groggily dragging my ass into work, I no longer cared what I looked like; which for me is like the world coming to an end. My hair isn't styled; I just put it in a low ponytail. Not a stich of makeup to be found on my face; yes, I showed up plain faced, not even a good bronzer to add glow to my usually contoured appearance. Where a diva once stood, a hideous woman now took her place. Wearing black pants and blazer, white top with a square neckline and no statement jewelry, I had the exterior of any other secretary with a poor sense of superior fashion trends; at least I had on the proper footwear and that's only because running shoes are not proper work attire.

Sadness must have radiated from me as I passed through the corridors of the office as almost everyone who glanced in my direction had the look of pity on their faces as if to say "*girl, keep your head up.*" Hell, even the office pervert offered a sympathetic look in my direction instead of the normal banter of when I will let him take me out. I had been so absent of mind that Elgin's million-dollar smile couldn't wash away the stench of a thousand whores feeling that I had been dragging. Some men sure knew how to put you on a pedestal when they want to fuck you, and in the instant you don't or can't live up to their high expectations, they discard your sorry ass like a spare change in a crack head's cup that stands outside of a 24 hour pharmacy. Ah love, isn't it grand?

As the days wore on, I tried to pull myself together. Yes, everything that happened thus far had been of my doing; but I didn't think the dull ache would linger this long. One day in particular, for no reason at all, I walked into the office and saw a cup of coffee sitting on my desk. Leaning against the coffee was a small handwritten note that said:

I saw that you needed a pick me up, and I wanted to be the person who did it.

There was no signature or initials to identify the person who left my deliciously caffeinated drink, so there was no way I could thank them. While I sipped and worked, I tried to imagine who could have been so kind as to do something like this; maybe it was Hershel. His ears must have rung, because seconds later he called me into his office. In his more than normal authoritative voice, he aggressively barked orders at me and demanding that I stay late to help him close a deal with a firm that had been holding a property hostage that my dad and his cronies wanted. I do not understand what the hell they would do with the land once they got it, but whatever it was it had to boast a lot on money or they wouldn't go through the trouble of negotiations. Leaving Hershel's office with a heavier workload than when I went in, I looked over a takeout menu, because leaving the office on time tonight is out of the question.

Five o'clock came and people started exiting the office. They all hurried out like if they hadn't they too would have to stay late with me. Some were going home to awaiting families, some had significant others to soothe the pain of a hectic day, others had side pieces that made ending a work day worth the wait of brushing skin to skin worth the stress. It really didn't matter to me where the hell they went. Anywhere is better than being here after hours.

After taking care of a few mediocre tasks I'm sure Hershel could have done, I sat at my desk and played with office supplies until I was summoned again into the lion's den for yet another round of foolishness. The next call I got had been from Jamie, the night security guard explaining that someone left a delivery for me. Curious to as what it could be, I caught myself nearly skipping to the security desk. When I got there, Jamie gave me a bag full of Chinese takeout. What the hell was I thinking? What had I expected to be at that desk waiting for me, flowers, from who Chase? I set myself up for that one. Taking the bag, I returned to my floor expecting Hershel to talk shit about his food being cold. When I got to my desk Elgin was waiting, not really wanting to deal with his bullshit, I attempted to walk past him into Hershel's office.

"Hold on sweetheart, where are you going with our food?" he asked with playfulness to his voice.

"Our food, did you order this?" I questioned. "Why didn't you just go get it yourself? I'm not your damn secretary; I don't run errands for you!" I throw at him as I dropped the food in his lap.

"Wait, wait, wait. When I said our, I meant yours and mine, not those guys. Look, I'm sorry I just thought you needed a quick breather, so I gave them your name for delivery. Let's start over, Ms. Lawrence would you like to have dinner with me." He asked.

I felt the flush of embarrassment over my body. What was I supposed to think? The man hadn't said a word to me since the party and had on more than one occasion gone out of his way to avoid me. What happened between us I choked up to a fluke that would ever repeat. He sat on my desk waiting for an answer and I didn't want to say yes, but that food started smelling all kinds of good through the bag, so I nodded in agreement instead.

We went back to his office where he cleared a space on his desk for us to eat on. Hurriedly, he gathered papers and piled them up. Taking the bag from my hands, he pulled out the cartons and asked what I wanted to try first. Looking over his selections, I saw that he ordered nothing unrecognizable, so I picked up a fork and went for the Lo Main.

We sat in awkward silence for a while just eating around each other, going from our own cartons to each other's and whatever else we had a taste for like we had been doing this dance for years, occasionally getting our forks entwined. I couldn't take the silence anymore, if he would not address the elephant in the room I sure as hell was going to.

I caught him in mid-chew when I asked, "So why the dinner?"

Between chews he managed to say "I heard Hershel ask you to stay, so I thought this would be our opportunity to clear a few things up." Then he chewed again.

"And what needs to be cleared up?" I asked sarcastically.

Finishing what had been in his mouth, "How we left things at your parents' house." Then he gave me a knowing look as if to say *'you know exactly what I'm talking about.'* "Before we discuss what happened between us, how about you tell me what caused that scene to begin with?"

I thought quickly about what I would say. Do I tell him the truth? Lie and say that the holidays always make me sad? Or do I chuck it up to being drunk? As I pondered what to say, he sat behind his desk patiently awaiting my response. I struggled for a second to get my wording correct, then I decided that having a conversation like this, with him, at the office is not something I wanted to do. I offered a lazy apology and explained that I wasn't ready to have this talk with him. As the words left my mouth, he hurriedly came around his desk and pulls a chair up to mine and whispered, *"We don't have to talk about this now, you'll tell me in your own time. For now, how about I show you something about me that no one else here knows about?"* With a Halfcocked smile, I agreed to follow him.

Leaving the office without so much as a bye to Hershel, we jumped into Elgin's town car to a designation unknown; well it was unknown by me, anyway. Twenty minutes later we arrive at a factory building. With my eyebrows raised high enough to touch my hairline, I asked Elgin where the hell he was taking me; perhaps I should've asked that before I got in the car? With a panty soaking smile, he tugged at my hand, insisting I was safe with him. As we walked to the freight elevator, I wondered if this is one of those upper crust sex parties or what we call in the hood a "Lock Door Party." If it is, I'm not down with this shit and I'm not above knocking his big, sexy ass out and getting out of here in his car.

Expecting so see black lights and bodies in every nook and cranny, I saw gigantic steel doors in a dimly lit hall. Elgin leading the way, I followed him until he stopped at the door on the furthest end of the hall. Taking out a set of janitor keys from his briefcase, I casually observed my surroundings just in case I had to describe it to the police later; as my eyes were roaming, they landed on a small camera outside of the door he unlocked. It also didn't hurt that my eyes grazed his beautifully sculpted ass; if this turned out to be a Lock Door, he would be the only ass I would be interested in seeing flex in different movements.

The door making an echoing and scraping sound when it opened would alarm anyone inside that someone is coming. Holding the door open for me, he gestured me inside. Hitting a switch on the wall, the once blackened space had lit up with life. It wasn't what I expected at all; similar to Chase's condo, Elgin had a huge loft apartment. Walking in I saw a beautifully decorated sitting area, To my right sat a decent size kitchen with a breakfast bar, in front of the seating area there are three huge floor to ceiling windows, to the left and right of the sitting area were two wood and frosted glass sliding doors with what looks to be the original wood flooring throughout; no sex party here.

"Do you live here?" I probed.

"Only when I'm in New York, let me take your coat." He answered.

Taking a seat on his plush sofa, I saw that everything had been brand spanking new. We are past pleasantries, so I didn't feel the need to bite my tongue. "How many places have you lived or are still living?" Handing me a glass of Red Wine, he replied, "A few. The apartment isn't what I wanted to show you, follow me."

Following him to the first set of sliding doors, he instructed me to stay in the doorway until he turned on the lights. '*This room is messy and I wouldn't want you to fall and hurt yourself. How would I explain to your father you got hurt in my apartment where we were all alone?*' He put emphasis on the alone part that I couldn't help but chuckle a bit. Seeing the light flicker with a soft clicking sound, the rooms illuminated and littered across the walls were canvas's with paintings that were familiar but striking. In the middle of the room was an enormous makeshift desk and near the only window, which had been the same size as the windows in the seating area, sat a stool and easel. Atop of the easel sat a painting that Elgin had been working on. I entered the space and gazed at each painting to realize they were of some people we worked with in their casual moments when they think no one is watching. When I approached the easel near the window, a cloth block whatever had been hiding underneath, as I grabbed it Elgin held my wrist to stop me,

"This one isn't finished yet, it's very special to me and I haven't perfected it; I'd hate for anyone to see it how it looks." He explained.

Letting go of the cloth, I allowed it to slip through my fingers until it had returned to the position in had been. Funny thing though, Elgin had not let go of my wrist. He let his hand cradle it in that position as if to let the touch linger a bit longer. I was taken back by his reluctance to let me go. Twisting from his grasp, I returned to the seating area.

"Is that what you wanted to show me?" I questioned.

"Yes, well, not exactly." With a brief pause to get his thoughts together, he continued. "I know that the past few weeks have been rough, I just wanted to show you that when life just won't give you a break that there are creative ways of coping."

"How did you know that I've had a hard time, it's not as if we are friends and have long drawn out conversations about life, love, and happiness?" I retorted. "Listen, that whole scene at my parents was a fluke. I get super emotional around the holidays." I attempted to clear up.

"A fluke" He repeated.

"Yes, a fluke! Is there an echo in this place?" I attempted to be sarcastic.

"Ok." He uttered with a condescending tone. "Is it also a fluke that since you've been in a stupor that your fashion sense has taken a nosedive? You are not the same woman I met months ago. You seem smaller to me, nearly broken." He recalled so quickly in a fit of annoyance that he couldn't catch the words as they left his mouth.

"Wow. I didn't realize that changing my look to be more serious about my job put me in the category of being an old maid… spinster if you will. I didn't think women in the workplace were still being judged on their outward appearance." I began to go through every Women's Liberation declaration I could search my mind to throw him off the scent of him being absolutely correct about what he has observed.

"No, that's not it and you know it!" He accused. "You never struck me as a woman that could easily be brought down. And I've noticed that your aura has changed."

"My aura, what are you, a Palm Reader? What is my aura giving you now?" I asked with false annoyance.

Staring deeply into my eyes, I thought for a second that he saw me, and what I had been trying to do to deflect from the storm of emotions I've been trying so desperately to hide. Taking a deep breath before he spoke, he explained that he wanted to show me what he does to help settle his mind when it's troubled. Not just for working issues, but everything in between. Expressing that I understood his meaning and apologizing for my behavior, we ended the night on a weird note.

By the time I arrived home, I could have kicked myself for the behavior I showed him. In truth, I don't know why I behaved so badly. Ok, that's not true; I know. I don't want the next good looking man with a Black Card and Magic Mike body to set me back emotionally; it's hard enough to bounce back from the last one. Ending the night like I had done so many nights before, I checked my social media to see all the happy, smiling people having a good time. Cursing profusely at my phone before switching it off, I slid my salty ass to bed.

I had become anxious at the thought of work the next day. I had hoped that the minor episode of The Mixed Signals Chronicles Elgin and I had the pleasure of performing last night would be water under the bridge. I went in as usual; being mindful of my appearance, I amped up my game a little, not to my former level but a step up nonetheless. I didn't want to make it obvious that what he said had struck a chord.

Stepping quickly off of the elevator, I attempted to make it to my desk undetected; I practically skipped there. As I settled in for the day, Elgin emerged from Hershel's office files in hand. Damn! Is all I could think. I looked everywhere but in his direction. In a deceitful endeavor to look busy so I didn't have to engage him in any way; it would have worked too, but he had to acknowledge me in some capacity.

"Looking beautiful today, Ms. Lawrence. Is that a new dress you're wearing?" He quizzed.

"This old thing, it isn't but thank you for noticing," I uttered as evenly as I could.

He smiled and continued to speak with Hershel; so much for keeping a low profile.

Chloe

If you have to travel anywhere, I suggest it be by private plane. Flying in Hennison's private plane has had to be the most luxurious seven hour plane ride in history. There was next to no turbulence, and the amenities are nothing less than stellar. But if I could add anything to the flight, it would've been better company. The entire flight had been more like a group of traveling strangers; the only people on the flight that had been an unfamiliar to me had been Gavin McClarin and his assistant Phoenix Alexander. I had been getting strange vibes from them the moment I stepped on the plane, and the *'I'll cut a bitch with a thousand switch blades'* look Clair was throwing in their direction had been a dead giveaway that something has been brewing and it sure wasn't the French Vanilla Coffee the stewardess was serving.

Through the lengthy flight we all had plenty of time to synchronize our schedules. They had stuffed everyone to the brim with appearances, meetings, dinners, shows, product launches and beating the competition that would also be in attendance. This visit had the potential to stretch me to my limit, not only did I have to be at Clair's beck and call during the day; but I also had to fulfill every desire my boyfriend had at night. Wait… not a boyfriend, but the guy I sleep with every night and have dinners with. Yeah, that's it.

As we pieced together the engagements we had to attend as a group, I noticed that every suggestion Phoenix proposed Clair undercut with the sharpest of retorts. She had been painting Phoenix into a corner and enjoying every moment of watching her squirm. It wasn't until Gavin took notice of what was going on that Clair eased up. Could this be a *MAN* had put Clair Winters in her place with a single glance? If it had, consider me impressed. She listened to no one other than the sound of her own voice, and occasionally the reasoning

Cassidy would give on the subject of her rage. I almost starred at them both like I'm watching a movie while not so patiently waiting for the climax.

Aside from that minor tiff, everything went smoothly. When the dinner is served I couldn't have been more taken back by the restaurant quality food that's placed in front of me. Everyone quickly dug in as if this is the norm for them and they would discard anything less as trash, I had to take it all in and appreciate the position that I fell into; if this man hadn't perused me as relentlessly he did I wouldn't be with him and some of the most accomplished people in the business enjoying a five star meal, they would cram me in coach seats with the other subordinates scraping for arm rests and leg room. In that moment, Jayshawn quickly passed through my mind.

As my mind slowly came back to reality, I caught Hennison making eyes at me. Immediately, I knew what that meant. Over the past few weeks of us doing this little dance together with no real titles involved; only implications, I grew to understand the coded messages he sent me with his eyes. If we were alone, I know that without hesitation we would have had sex on every inch of the luxurious leather seats in this plane, or at the very least had a quickie in the bathroom. Too bad for Hennison, he won't be able to have his way with me for the entire week we'll be in London. Unfortunately for us, shortly after takeoff aunt flow had come to visit and brought with her all the rags that would keep me from getting unwanted stains on all the beautiful clothing I would wear on our visit; at least we had a quickie in the car.

When we landed, cars were waiting to take us to the hotel and I couldn't wait to unwind. Clair had her own suite, Cassidy would share a room with Ingrid and one of the photo editors that would arrive on a later flight, and Hennison and I had the Penthouse Suite; I'm not sure about the sleeping arrangements of Gavin and his assistant, but I'm sure Clair would make it her business to find out before her stilettos touched pavement.

Settling into the softest cotton lined bed, the world faded. For all I knew I was still in New York because all my body craved in that moment was a good night's sleep. When my body recharged, it must have realized that I wasn't in a familiar place. My inner alarm clock must have sensed evil calling, not even rubbing sleep out of my eyes a message came through my phone. Finding Hennison in the lounge area, he had several designer suites laid out. After helping him make the perfect selection, I hurried to get ready for the day's events. I wish the most critical decision I had to make today is picking wardrobe, but that's a rich person's problems. Working stiffs like me planned weeks in advance in order not to make a poor impression with crucial people.

LET THE GAMES BEGIN! As soon as I entered Clair's suite, it had been like entering the Queen's lair. With not so much as a curt nod, Cassidy hands me a clasp envelope with the week's itinerary inside with an expressive mini speech with emphasis on time flexibility. Meaning we had to be flexible in our time so if we needed to work later, harder, and more diligent we did. Clair is on a mission to crush whatever Hennison and Gavin had going on, with the bonus of trying to one up Isabella. With a lite breakfast of fruit and assorted cheeses, we hurried to the first of many runway shows.

The theme of this season's fashion week is Elevation Meets Innovation. Designers work tirelessly to complete their collections, hoping it could land them in major retail stores or on the most prestigious magazine covers with their items draped on the hottest celebrity of the moment. As we took our seats for the first show, the diva herself had to be front and center where the photographers could capture her good side. The photos they take today will be on the covers of New York newspapers in a matter of hours. So of course she had to look her best. Dressed in magnificence from head to toe, she wore an Emery Santana silk amethyst blouse and ivory castle trousers. Looking as if she had been a member of the Royal Family, she turned heads as she took her seat, and the whispers were so hushed that it scarcely seemed to break the surface of sound. Clair knew how to kill the game, which was until Isabella walked in with a form fitting red dress that would hold up traffic better than any red light in New Jersey.

Isabella sauntered in and took her seat on the other side of the stage in the seat directly in front of Clair. These two juggernauts would come to blows; I just hope that aftermath didn't affect the magazine. The lights deemed slow, and the music began to play. On the loudspeakers the announcer introduced the Sun and Moon Collection created by Lotus Sun and her partner Jacob Moon.

The designers had to have had open casting calls for weeks in order to find the perfect size appropriate models, as there aren't many curvaceous Asian models in the industry; though the few they found were fantastic in my opinion; I'm sure Sloan consulted them in some way. Each model had been the perfect frame for their garments. The show started subtly with dainty everyday ready-to-wear garments and then transitioned to more dramatic pieces. As the designers brought the drama, the music accompaniment changed to create a mood for the show. This is not something new that designers haven't thought of before, but the transitions had been so seamless that if you were caught in the sheer beauty of what you had been selected to see, it could have easily been missed.

As the final walk began, and the designers followed the last model, Clair leaned to whisper to Cassidy. Nodding her head in agreement with whatever had been said; Cassidy then rose from her seat and left the event. As I followed Cassidy with my eyes, Clair caught my line of sight and starred at me through her dark Ellie Rose shades. Resuming my previous position, I wondered what the hell was going on. The game has gotten harder and harder to figure out by the day. Also, it seems like there is more bad blood than I thought between the two magazine Editors and Chief.

Leaving the show as quickly as we had come, the next show is being held across town and featured designer Attali Santiago. This Philly born designer started off creating airbrush designs on T-shirts and boots, then later branched out to making Men's wear. In London

Attali is premiering his newest endeavor of men's wear called the "Soulful Savage Collection" that comprises big and tall ready to wear, street wear, business wear, sportswear, and some grooming products. Of all the new designers that have travelled here to show their collections, Attali has to be my favorite.

The man literally turned his life around through fashion. In his bio, it explains how he got caught up in a shady crowd of people (as most of us do) and as a result did some things that landed him in jail for three years. Upon his release, he created his brand High Conviction. Beginning his empire in his mother's dining room, he quickly realized that men want to look good too. Working in retail for a few years as to get an unorthodox education in fashion, Attali realized that men's wear can be a one-trick pony; so he revamped what the masses conveyed men's ready to wear to exude. Men aren't just wearing either business suits or jeans and boots anymore. The modern man is into a well-groomed appearance, and in the current decades some recognize that all men regardless of orientation want to look and feel just as good as women do when presenting themselves on the world's stage. He's had some local success in the states, but being here will give his brand the much needed international recognition it needs.

Arriving in what looks to be a local art studio, we took our seats and waited for the show to begin. As we waited I curiously looked at my phone to see if I had any text messages or emails, with none to be found I looked over our event schedule for the day. According to Cassidy, we had time for one more show before a quick R&R (rest and relaxation) before returning to the hotel to meet with Gavin and Hennison. As I looked up to scan the room, all the who's who of the Plus Size Industry had been in attendance and vying for the attention of Clair. Clair ever so cleverly mingled among the attendees, while Cassidy loomed at her side running interference for the undesirables; when in walks Nevelynn "Nevie" Porter.

When Nevie enters a room, she shuts it down! Being a curvaceous five foot nine powerhouse, she has a smooth chocolate completion, a body made personally by the Gods, with shoulder length hair so sharp that it could cut the wind; it was so scared it wouldn't dare blow when she entered or exited a building; she's my girl crush. Nevelynn is more than a beauty she's the creator and CEO of Corporate Solutions, a company that finds, connects, and relocates employees with the most elite credentials to employers that will meet their particular needs; in other words Nevie is a Headhunter.

She finds talent in the most unlikely places or in well-known companies and places them in prestigious firms around the world. I heard through the grapevine that she is in London to poach another potential employee to bring to her exclusive clientele. No one ever knew who her clients were, they preferred to be anonymous; but it's known that they spare no expense when selecting potential employees. I wonder if she's here to poach Kelly. If she is, she can have her for free; hell I'd pay her to take Kelly's lazy ass off my damn hands!

Noticing Nevie's arrival, Clair sends Cassidy to greet her and offers her a seat in the front row next to her. Annoyance taking over me, as I stood in the back of the room, because the seat Clair offered her had been mine; only standing room left. If anyone had to stand for a fashion show, you know it can be excruciating on the feet and calves. The shades in the studio were drawn, the lights dimmed, and the stage illuminated as the music played. Attali greeted the attendees briefly saying a few words and then returned backstage. Staying true to this year's theme of Elevation Meets Innovation, the designer began the show with garments that launched his career, and as each of the very handsome male models entered and exited the runway, the crowd marveled at the elevation in his designs displayed and became excited by the innovations he's made when addressing the needs of his niche market of men.

Like fuller women, husky men have been largely ostracized in the fashion industry and have long waited for designers and companies to recognize that their money spends just as well as anyone else's. Largely neglected, the market for dressing stocky men has brought us designers such as Julius Banks who's been dominating for over a decade; he now has some competition with newcomer Attali.

The conundrum isn't different when it comes to men and women; the only difference is the gender. Both have goals, strategies, connections, and a hint of underhanded dealings in their business with competition. Some embrace the challenge, others fold under the pressure, and a small few continue to thrive. In my opinion, in order to thrive as long as the successful designers and insiders have is to be authentic with a side of cutthroat. Recklessness is a luxury that isn't permitted; words on contracts with dry ink is what matters, in other words it's what you can prove; and if you're fool enough not to look at the fine print or the innuendo of the situation, then you've already lost the game.

Mingling with the crowd when the show concluded, I walked within earshot of Clair cozying up to Attali and his Marketing Director Quincy Ross I overheard her offer him a featuring in Indulgence's Latin Flavor Issue. When Clair recognized a money maker, she pounced, and sweet-talked them in such a way as to get them to agree with whatever she offered. By the end of the conversation they would feel like it had been their idea to be in the issue and would be delighted to by ad space to ensure a profitable marketing campaign. That's when I realized that this is the game she and Isabella had been playing.

They both had been attempting to secure advertisers to bring in money. That's why Gavin McClarin had accompanied us here and why when he shut Clair down on the plane she conceded; she didn't want to rock the boat and cause Gavin to shift his support from her to Isabella, though that still didn't explain the hostility towards Phoenix. As I pondered the evidence I had been mentally gathering, it left me with one lingering question… Why did they need to fight for money in the first place? Is Black Enterprise in trouble? Could all this be in relation to the late night call I caught Hennison on? For now, I would keep this speculation to myself and watch for more indication to the contrary.

Grabbing yet another glass of Champagne from the small refreshments assortment, I sipped a little more quickly than I had with the previous two glasses. The bubbles tickling my nose as I had been a little too eager to wait; I had been so overwhelmed by my thoughts I didn't feel someone sneaking up behind me, but I caught the scent of Nectar Blossom Perfume by Joy Riley. Not giving the beautiful scent a second thought, I continued to glance over the appetizers for something edible when I felt a soft pat and a quick rub on my ass. With the adrenaline pumping through my body, I felt the muscles in my jaw tense up and my body temperature rise quickly as my head flew around my body so fast I spilled a few drops of my drink on my top, only to find Ingrid behind me laughing hysterically at my reaction.

"What's the matter girl, thought I was Hennison here to steal the booty in broad daylight?" as she snickered.

"No, I was about to pop you right in the forehead for trespassing. I know how these European men act towards women. I'm like the MTA; no one touches me without paying the toll." I cackled at my joke.

Grabbing the glass from my hand, she gulped in down in a swift motion and looked exhilarated as she did. I could tell she had something to tell me; the whole time we were on the plane she had been giving subtle nods in our fellow travelers directions.

"So, Chloe, have you been hearing the gossip about the re-organization of the company? I'm sure the love of your life has clued you in on what he's been up to?" she whispered as a warmup to letting the cat out of the bag.

"No, when we're together we don't talk business. We keep that part of our relationship at The Black Building. Why, what have you heard?"

Leaning in close so that none of the nosey partygoers could hear us, she explains the reason Clair and Isabella had been in so much competition with each other more than usual. Tugging my arm to pull me into a lonely corner; she told me what office chatter had been brewing.

With a hushed voice she says, "Well, apparently that knob head Hennison and the other board members see no reason to have two fashion magazines in rotation; something about saving the corporate dollar or some bollocks. Remember that meeting some time ago in the Indulgence office between the three of them?" I nod in remembrance, because I had to schedule that meeting. "Well, it seems he broke the news to them in that meeting. So, to figure out which magazine is more profitable, they must compete with each other to see who will be the last one standing. And that Gavin McClarin, we need to watch that one; he's one of the guys Hennison brought in to influx money into the company, and in return he'll get a stake in Black Enterprise. Depending on which way the board swings he may acquire controlling shares, but I'm sure Hennison's clever ways will outwit him." She concluded.

With eyes as wide as the economic divide in the U.S. I couldn't believe what I heard. Both women had been legends in their own right in business class, and industry connections to name a few. Now Hennison has them both competing to keep their jobs; maybe that was the reference Clair had been alluded to the night we left New York. I quietly wondered what tricks she had up her sleeve to save the only baby she has; Indulgence. She breathed that magazine, every issue, photographer, model, and columnist, had been hand chosen and groomed by her. Surly if she was pushed out they would follow her, but then again people are only as loyal as their next paycheck so it's very possible that she would be out on her well-toned ass if the board members voted against her in favor of Isabella.

Isabella St. Scott is a well accomplished, perfect size 4, fiery red head from Westminster Abbey. Approximately ten years Clair's junior, she joined the fashion world at age twelve, modeling for the most exquisite designers the U.K. birthed. She's been on every cover known to man and some that I have never heard of. Being a major player in entertainment, she's done everything from movies to a very brief stint as a singer; though she quickly realized her singing career would never get any traction due to the fact that she never sang a word of her own songs. YES GOD! Rumor has it she pulled that all too well known lip synching move; allegedly (side eye). After she got too old (by fashion standards) to walk the runway, she had to find the next best thing to stay relevant. You got it! Editor and Chief of Rouge Magazine, at the time of her hire, Indulgence had been the breadwinner for Black Enterprise's new publishing empire. Paul Black had the vision to turn his profitable company into a publishing juggernaut. First starting with a men's magazine, then quickly realizing that women are a more profitable consumer and the rest is history.

Just as I was about to bombard Ingrid with an assortment of questions she turned to the door, following her gaze I saw my favorite train wreck Kellendra walk in. Honestly, I couldn't tell what Cassidy saw in her. I mean, I'm no hater, but she looked like a well-dressed number two pencil.

"Oh bloody hell, look what the cat dragged in." Ingrid breathed heavily.

With a slight eye roll, I replied, "What happened to her body? I guess it didn't clear customs or maybe she just left it at home." I chuckled.

"No, I think she left her body in that gutter she rolled out of." Ingrid quipped. "Ok darling, I have to go. I'll meet in the hotel pub later, yeah?"

Agreeing to meet later, she took one last swig before exiting the gallery. Kelly passed me quickly with a slight nod in my direction. Walking to Cassidy, she touched her ever so softly on the small of her back, Cassidy smiling as she turned and saw her. I don't know what it is about her that really makes my anger rise about ten notches, but I know one thing; it has never steered me wrong.

Jayshawn

Fallon made it through his first event with me unscathed, and I must say that I was very impressed with how he handled himself. I'm not so confident as to leave him to his own devices, but at least I know that he's capable of getting the job done. It was unsettlingly slow in the office today; I concluded it was because New York Fashion Week is over and most events that had been lingering were winding down; at least until spring. Exiting my main office, I crept into the seating area where Fallon had been diligently typing some report. Asking me if I needed anything without missing a beat on the keyboard, I advise him to wrap up whatever he had been doing because I was ready to close up early.

With a quick text to the fellas, I told them I would be able to stop by the card game tonight. Tarin being gone had been a major pro because now I can hang out with my friends without her constant nagging and texting. She never liked my friends; she always found something wrong with them. Dane is too into the saving the baby thugs as she referred to them, Saddiq is too righteous, Griff is too thuggish, Zuri has too many women around, but Kelvin is just right because he married his college sweetheart as soon as we graduated. These are my boys, they keep me grounded when the women in my life try to drive me to the closest liquor store.

Waiting for Fallon as I stood outside of the door, I wondered what he would do after leaving here. As I thought deeper, I realized I don't know anything about the brother. I know I have to keep an employer/employee relationship, but he seemed like a cool guy so why not give him the benefit of the doubt.

"Hey Man!" I blurted out at him without warning. "What are you going to do with the rest of your night?" I inquired.

"Nothing, maybe just go home, kick my feet up, and share the evening with my good friend Vodka on the rocks and invite ratchet tv to come and join us." He chuckled. "And you?"

"I'm meeting up with some friends I haven't seen in a while to kick it, you know? Play a little cards and chill while my girlfriend is out of town."

Continuing the conversation on the elevator, "I didn't know you had a girlfriend." He uttered in a flirty tone as he looked surprised that I had a one. I know the floodgate of questions were headed my way. Luckily, there isn't much to tell that everyone else doesn't already know.

"So tell me about this girlfriend. All the time I've been working here, I have seen no evidence of a woman in your life. Are you keeping secrets, Mr. Thomas?" He questioned in a fake accusatory tone.

"No, no. There's not much to tell. She's a model working in the London Fashion Week shows, she's stunning (and a major pain in my ass), and the relationship is new; so we're just taking it slow." I tried to answer quickly. "Do you have a significant other in your life?"

Stepping off the elevator, I could tell that my question made him uncomfortable. His usual confident demeanor had faded slightly as his shoulders slumped and took a deep breath before he could answer.

Not looking directly at me, but at the floor he answered by saying, "I had someone for a long time, but it didn't work out. He wasn't ready for a public relationship, and I'm not prepared to continue to wait until he is." He recalled as his entire body expressed melancholy.

As we walked to the doors to exit the building, he walked slower and dragged his feet. On his face it looked as if he had been replaying a scene in his mind over and over, and the light in his face sort of dulled.

"Hey man, I didn't mean to bring up sordid memories. I just thought we should get to know each other, maybe converse with each other about things other than work." I offered as an excuse.

"No, Jayshawn. I'm not upset with you at all. It's just that... well, I've tried to forget him and move on with my life. And as bad I want to do that, I still care deeply for the guy. My mind and my heart are in constant war about if I should call, as him to dinner, stop by his place. But I know if I pursued those actions I would end up in his bed, hopeful that we have an understanding only to realize that it was just a quick nut and I'll be the one to get hurt and regret it; you know?" he explained.

Nodding my head in agreement, I completely understood what he was saying. Though slightly different in situations, I suspect that's how Chloe felt about me and why she's distanced herself; not that I blamed her, it was foul how our situationship ended. Nonetheless, my thoughts always drifted to her; wondering if she's happy with her current surroundings. In that moment, I realized both Fallon and I needed a pick me up. Maybe he would want to chill with the fellas?

"Fallon, I know this is spur of the moment; I don't want you to be uncomfortable or anything, but I think your friends Vodka Rocks and Ratchet will be ok without you." I attempted to lighten the mood.

"Oh, I don't know Jayshawn. I'm not sure your friends will be comfortable around me." He assumed with a question in his voice. "I'm not exactly one of the homeboys."

"No, my friends aren't like that. I'm not going to lie and say it won't get awkward from time to time, but I will let none of them disrespect you. You have my word, ok." I offered to him as some sort of reassurance.

"Well, I'm not sure my friends will be ok with me canceling our plans so last minute." He laughed as breathed heavily at the same time. "But, sure why not? Those hoes don't have any conversation for me, anyway. Maybe playing a little cards with the boys will give me some insight as to how you manly men think. And who knows, statistics say one in every six males are homosexual; I might find my prince charming at the game tonight." He laughed with his entire body.

"Those aren't real statistics, Fallon!" I laughed with him.

"It doesn't matter. Hell, I'm willing to make my luck and tilt the odds in my favor whenever possible." He offered as a retort.

Understanding his unique humor, I have him a pat on the back and we walked to my homie Zuri's latest business endeavor called The Juicery. I promised Fallon he would be ok, so on the walk I sent a quick group text to the guys explaining that I would bring a friend and not to make things awkward when we showed up. They all replied back not really caring who I brought, they were just happy I was showing up at all especially since being back with Tarin; also they knew that I would never bring anyone around them that wasn't in some way, shape, or form cool. Also, as my punishment for ditching them, I wouldn't be let in unless I had with me minimum four cases of beer and or their favorite spirits; of course they had to include the entry fee for Fallon, so his two hands counted as being able to carry the miraculous liquid that will aid in plenty of laughs and good times for the night.

Standing outside of The Juicery while the icy wind beat on us mercilessly; I almost didn't want the heavy boxes of beer I had been holding. Just when I was about to ask Fallon if he wanted to leave, Griff came running from the back to open the door. Relief and anger washed over me all at once as he unlatched them.

"Man, what took you so long! It's colder than a mutha out here!" I threw at him as Fallon and I hurried in, and Griff re-locked the doors.

"My bad, my bad Jay; see what had happened was ya boy Kelvin is back there trippin again and Dane is trying to calm him down." He offered as an excuse.

"What do you mean?" I probed.

"Jay man, you know how he is; soon as he gets here, we tell him you on the way to finally chill with us. He's all hyped, then old girl calls and tells him that the kids miss him and want him to read them a story or some shit like that. I'm telling you she must have some MVP, cause he's ready to run as soon as she hangs up." He says as he leads the way to the stockroom where I'm sure Zuri has everything looking like a man cave.

With a confused look on his face, Fallon turns to me and repeats, *"MVP?"* I forgot for a second he was there; I let Griff get a little further ahead of us when I explained, *MVP means Most Valuable Pussy."* With his eyes rising to his forehead and quick twist of the neck, I knew he had now understood. Pass the kitchen into the stockroom, Griff announces that I arrived. With a chorus of "Hey" from everybody, they look past me at the impeccably well-dressed man behind me with a questionable look on all their faces.

"Guys, this is Fallon, my new assistant. Fallon, that stocky one over there is Griffin, the brotha with the nappy beard is Saddiq, the dude that looks like he drives a minivan is Kelvin, the guy who looks like he sells Bibles is Dane, and… Yo where's the ladies' man?" I asked.

"You know that fool, he's in his office, probably talking to some female." Dane offered.

"So ugh, you're playing cards with the men tonight? No paint and sip with the ladies?" Griff said sarcastically.

"Oh, you're talking to me, Thickums? No, no wine with the ladies; but if you girls don't mind me whooping your ass in cards and taking all your money down to the Aiden's Palace to fill my favorite strippers G string, I'm down. So, you ready to get that ass spanked big boy?" Fallon retorted as quickly as it took Griff to swallow a swig of beer.

With a smile on his face, "Oh, so you think you can take my money? We gonna see." He replied as a lame comeback.

Taking our seats, I dealt the cards. Starting from my left is Griff, Fallon, Dane, and then me. Playing partners with someone who I wasn't sure could play the game is risky, but I can't leave him hanging. I wonder if Fallon would be mad if the money he made me lose tonight I could deduct from his paycheck; just kidding... maybe.

As we played, I noticed Kelvin in the corner sitting on a stool texting frantically on his out-of-date flip phone. Shaking my head at the sight, I kept playing. Since everyone had been concentrating on the game, I took it upon myself to ask Dane how his outreach program had been doing. He started a platform known as The Urban Male Youth & Development without Boarders program, together with some community leaders and members he has also constructed The Urban Male Youth & Development without Boarders Basketball Team.

With the help of volunteers, the men mentor and groom boys into become young men. More often than not children particularly young men fall victim to the streets, and by the time they become old men... well if they're lucky enough to make it that far, become lost or have no direction and look for help from a government who couldn't care less if they lived or died just as long as they stayed incarcerated long enough for the system to make money off of them being inmate number 97313A86201609 or some shit like that. Dane's program help disrupt that pattern before it starts.

"The program is superb. The kids are thriving and I couldn't be more proud of the work we're doing. Just this fall we implemented a girls' program, and it's been really making a difference with the young ones. The parents have been more receptive and through the program we've been able to help them with jobs, housing, after care; it's a beautiful thing." He proudly spoke.

"When are you going to come and speak to my youth group? It'll be good for them to see a person like themselves owning and operating their own business; even Zuri is coming to speak on Saturday."

"Zuri man, you better hope his speech is scheduled between meeting women; no pun intended." I retorted.

"I know that isn't Jay throwing dirt on my name." Zuri said as he came out of his office and came towards me for a quick dab. "Look who's finally here with the fellas; Tarin finally took that leash from around your neck or she let you come out for good behavior and a designer bag?"

"Don't worry about all that, the only thing that matters is that I'm here." I dodged. "And this is a friend of mine Fallon, Fallon this is Zuri."

Shaking his hand, we all continued to talk and play cards. By the end of the first round Fallon had done exactly what he said, took all of Griffs money. Getting up so that Kelvin and Zuri could play the next round, we continued to drink, eat all of Zuri's inventory and talk; it felt good to just be around the guys and not having to worry about how my business is performing, if Malik is trying to cut my throat, if Hennison is fucking Chloe, or if I missed the way Chloe's lower back curved into the top of her ass; damn, that girl knew how to maneuver her body.

Saddiq finally chiming in, he asks, "So Fallon, where you from brotha?"

Looking up quickly, he answers, "I'm originally from New Jersey."

"That's it, you from The Garden State. Come on, man, we ain't as closed mind as you think, don't be shy brotha. If you with Jay I know you're good people, we just trying to get to know the man who paid his entry fee in beer to get in here, that's all. If you were that sucka Malik, you wouldn't have made it down the block." He laughed.

Visibly hesitant as he tightens his grip on his cards, Fallon opened up to a strange group of guys he's only just met. "I grew up in a two-parent household, my mom and dad is still married to this day. I have two sisters and an older brother…"

"So when did you tell your family you're gay?" Griff interrupted as Fallon had gained a little confidence and with that interruption had shifted himself uncomfortably in the hard folding chair.

"Shut the hell up, Griff," Kelvin shouted. "Let the man speak."

Cutting his eye sharply at Griff, Fallon continued. "My family had always known that I had a partiality towards things more feminine than masculine. It was never something I had to hide or be ashamed of. They made it very clear to me they loved me and anyone who had a problem with me would get fucked up with the quickness. My dad in particular wasn't one to tolerate any disrespect in any way and that was double for his wife and kids. So, I never felt like I had to be closeted." With the men nodding their heads in agreement, he continued. "It was difficult in grammar school, because you know kids can be cruel; but my older brother handled anyone who had an issue with me, and if a female had a problem, my sisters shut them down. My parents had raised us to stick together and be strong, so I carried that with me into adulthood." He concluded.

"What brought you here to New York?" Saddiq asked. "You could easily have made the commute."

"That's a more complicated situation. I originally came for work. I had been an assistant for a few designers, while part timing as a showroom coordinator and working retail at the same time; the rent here is no joke. But when it all boils down to it, I stayed in the city for love." He finished.

"Is it that the guy we talked about?" I questioned.

"Yes, it was. Before him I just dated, nothing serious. I guess you could say I was a typical man, going from one conquest to the other until I met him. But he wasn't ready to take our relationship public, and when he did want to be public, it was at the most inopportune times. He wanted to be with me behind closed doors, but he had a jealous streak that was unfathomable and would make a scene regardless of where we were; and I'm too good of a partner... man to be forced into being in a situation that I had never been in, because he felt uncomfortable about his sexuality. So, I ended things with him."

"Wow," Responded Kelvin. "That sounds like ya boy over there with Tarin."

"What do you mean?" Fallon asked Kelvin as he looked at me with confusion.

"What he means is your boss over there left a sexy, thick girl for a thot." Griff chimed in.

"Come on, Griff man; don't put the man's business on the street like that. Besides, you were in the same predicament with Yvonne, remember?" Zuri accused. "Check this out, Yvonne threw him a little ass, and he was sprung on her. She had him paying the rent, daycare for her twins that ain't his, and footing the bill for shit he couldn't even pronounce." Zuri ran down as he burst into a fit of laughter.

"Yeah, I might have been paying a little bill here and there, but baby made up for it with her head game." Griff tried to justify damn near going into bankruptcy.

"Fuck outta here, she had you wide open, just like Natalia has Kelvin ass open. But at least he married her, and his kids are his... we think." Saddiq finished as Kelvin gave him a screw face.

"Stop playing with my babies' man." Kelvin snarled at Saddiq.

"You know I'm playing man, Jr. looks just like your ol biscuit head ass." He laughed. "You know I love my God kid's man, chill you know I'm fucking around." Saddiq offered as a half ass apology.

"Naw, but for real we all have been there before; even me." Zuri expressed. "I had been with a girl I dogged out, and by the time I realized I was in love with her she had moved on with a guy that I sort of pushed her on to, so I get it."

"How did you push her to another guy?" Fallon asked Zuri.

"Aiight, so we met working together. This was back when I was at Savage Mind Advertising. Remember Jay?" he asks as the statement had jolted my memory. "It was a small ad company that was startup. So we were both interning trying to get our feet in the door. We worked on damn near every project together. If I wasn't at her spot, she was at mine. We eventually became good friends, and as we got more comfortable with each other we got more comfortable, if you know what I mean. We didn't exactly date, but we were with each other every night. I cared about her and I could tell she wanted to put a title on what we had been doing, but me, I can't be tied down; I just want to make paper and grow my own endeavors. So, when the company we worked for partnered with a bigger agency that eventually took over, the headman in charge started taking an interest in her. So when she demanded that I make a decision about the status of our relationship, I passed on her and she ran into the boss man's arm and has firmly been in his clutches ever since." Zuri concluded.

As Zuri finished his story of lost love, the room fell silent. I could tell by the looks on all them men's faces that they too had been remembering the moment where they found the person who could've potentially been the one, but for one reason or another they fucked it up. I knew Zuri's story and at that time Tarin and I had been thriving, in truth what had been going on with him had motivated me to propose to Tarin in the first place. I knew that I loved her and that as her career grew, I had to cement our relationship to prevent anything from coming between us; but I had a rude awakening when I went down to Miami to surprise her.

Shifting subjects, Dane asked if Fallon wanted to come and speak to his youth group. He expressed to Fallon that there were some young men there that could benefit from seeing a positive, male, and unapologetically gay professional giving advice. In our society if you don't fit the mold or whatever box you're put in that automatically you are a rebel, a problem to be solved, or a disease to be eradicated. The children need to see and hear that they matter and that they are valuable; what better way to get that message across than to invite reflections of themselves to submit ideas, make connections, and to uncover skills that they never thought possible coming from their types of backgrounds and to show them their potential by way of positive male role models from all aspects of life.

Agreeing to the offer, Fallon then excused himself as I guess they had worn him out from our banter. Before he could stand to put his coat on, Griff ran over and apologized for his behavior and expressed that he didn't mean to be abrasive, but that was how he got to know people. Not one to hold a grudge, Fallon accepted, and they shook hands as Griff whispered to him, *"You have to come to the next game and give me a chance to win my money back."* With a slight laugh, Fallon agreed and headed towards the door.

Walking him out, I quickly asked before we could be interrupted "I hope it wasn't too awkward in there for you? I'm sorry about Griff, he doesn't mean to be an asshole it's just a birth defect you know?"

"It's ok; I've gone up against rougher characters and have lived to tell the tale; so I'm not worried. He actually just invited me to the next card game. Your friends are decent guys, they're cool with me. But I wasn't expecting that story from Zuri, though." He whispered. "And what did Griff mean about you leaving a cute, thick girl for a thot?" he asked.

"Well." I hesitated. "Similar to Zuri, there was a woman in my life that we started as just friends. Really, she was the girlfriend of my rival, and he dumped her in the worst way possible. We had always had a connection since we met, but in the very beginning I pushed her to him and when they broke up, I felt like it was my fault. So in the mix of me trying to ease her pain and my conscience, we had a situationship. I didn't expect to fall for her, but I did, and when my ex made a reappearance, I tossed her to the side for Tarin; who's my ex, I suspect you've guessed. Now she's with another rival of mine, and he's the owner of the company she works for." I concluded.

"So, your story is just like Zuri's the only difference is… (He stood for a second to ponder) There is no difference really. Why do we men find the person we could see ourselves with and then leave them because our brains tell us there might be something better out there? Then get mad or regret what we've done when the person moves on. Do you still care about the girl?" Fallon asked.

"Yeah, I do. But she won't speak to me." I expressed.

"I wouldn't speak to you either after you cast me aside for some broad who appeared out of nowhere." Fallon sympathized. "Maybe after being hurt first by the man she loved, and then by the friend she cherished it was just too much for the girl so she disconnected and let herself get caught up in a man that she wouldn't allow to hurt her the way y'all two fools did, and now that she's gone you miss her."

"Yeah, I miss her. Every time I try to reach out to her either I get blocked or I just can't summon the courage to face her. And it's crazy because I can't stop thinking about her. It's like every free moment I get I let my mind briefly remember our time together and I wonder where she is, or if she's happy." I admitted.

"Are you sure she's not the one you're in love with and not this Tarin? Have you considered, that the woman you've could build a life and relationship with has moved on to someone who most likely couldn't or wouldn't be able to not only appreciate what she brings to the relationship but what she gives to you as a man?" Fallon conveyed inquisitively.

I didn't have an answer; JayShawn Thomas, the man who could solve any business problem, couldn't answer this question. As I stood there, I knew that I had been lying to myself. This so-called relationship with Tarin is over; matter of fact, it was over before it started the second time around. I don't know why it had taken me so long to realize that I had been clinging on to an idea of what was, instead of what's real. Because of my lack of answer, Fallon gave me a knowing look as he spoke, *'Think about it.'* In a hushed voice as he was about to walk out of the door into the icy wind covered streets that waited. Before the bells on the door could ring, Dane came rushing from the back of the café.

"Hold up, hold up!" Dane shouted as he approached us. "I need to ask you fellas, are you really coming to the conference Saturday? I really need the young men to see brotha's like y'all being successful; it will give them something to aspire to becoming." Dane tried to convince us.

Without thinking, I turned to Fallon and asked, "How's my Saturday looking? Will there be time?"

Looking towards the ceiling for a moment, Fallon answers, "Yes, you have a few blocks of time available to speak at the conference. That sounds amazing think of all the boys that will see you and see more than the rough neighborhoods they've grown up in." he concluded.

"Fallon, brotha I would like you to speak as well. There are so many young men like you out there with no guidance, and with the stigma the community places on these kids regarding it can be detrimental to their growth as they become men. If you speak to them, it may give them the confidence to live, and walk in their truth without fear." Dane persuaded.

I watched Fallon's facial expressions as he rolled the idea over in his head about speaking to a bunch of kids. Finally, after a few moments, he agreed. After locking the door behind Fallon, I returned to the den of brothers trying to imagine what I would say to a group of adolescent boys which also included my nephews.

Playing a few more hands of cards before leaving, in the moments where the guys were completely concentrated on the game my thoughts drifted. My business is doing well, but it can always improve; what are services I can provide to elevate to the next level? Mentally taking notes, that is one subject I want to tackle when I talk with the kids; not to be a one-trick pony, but find other facets to tie into your main passion to continue to thrive in your particular niche market. I never stop thinking of ideas, or making plans for plans. Keeping my mind occupied kept me from considering the possibility that I made a monumental error in judgment and no one is immune from being human.

As the lateness crept up on us, each of the guys left one by one. Before leaving, I asked Dane about my nephews and asked if my sister had been complaining about me not being around. Blowing air out his chest quickly and giving me the *'you already know'* face, I could only imagine what she had been saying to not just him but to the family. Assuring me she and my aunties would be at the conference I knew I was in for more than just my head spinning from all her reckless talking, but the side comments from the rest of the family as well; Tarin leaves a foul taste in most people's mouths after the first few times of meeting her, and my family is no exception.

The days flowed effortlessly into another, and before I knew it Friday (or affectionately called pre Saturday) had strolled onto my calendar. I tried to talk to Fallon about what I should say to the kids. I hesitated to get his input when I saw how he also contemplated how he would tell a group of adolescents he was a successful gay man. Would the children understand? And most importantly, will they receive the message he would give?

The last few days have been rarely slow; the wind down period after all the major events came to a halt, and the next round of crazy begins. This is normally the time when Makayla and I would have re-cap meetings outside of the office to get a fresh perspective. Our meetings would comprise all the events we've done up to that point, the type of project, cost, profit gains/losses, improvements, and additional options to consider. I would now have that meeting with Fallon this year, not that I didn't want to have these discussions with him; after all its apart of his job.

I hesitated to ask him to block off time for us to have this powwow is because I missed my friend. Yes, Makayla was my employee, but we have worked together for years before she betrayed our business relationship. She wasn't always irrational; it developed slowly. People come to the city for various reasons, though mostly for success and fame. Others who are born and raised here want the same things, but on a different level than a person who is from out of state. The people here want respect for their craft (whatever it may be), recognition, someone to believe in a cause or purpose, achieve a dream; or what we refer to as leveling up, Makayla is no different. I think she got lost in the hype paired with the work that we do, and she is a personal witness to the money people throw away in the name of having a good time. Those things coupled with her personal ambitions impaired her judgment. Nevertheless, I had to let her go.

Gathering up most of the materials we needed, Fallon and I left the office to have our meeting in a hole in the wall café that had great grilled cheese and bacon sandwiches; which I'm in the mood to eat. Setting up shop in the back, the waitress took our orders and then we dove head first into file after file of vendors, number, issues, etc. After about an hour and a half, I needed a break; Fallon had become so exhausted from the small tasks we could accomplish he took off his blazer and loosened his shirt, as manicured as he normally is in the office I didn't expect for him to alter his continuously polished appearance; stress gets you every time.

Going to the counter for the umpteenth time for coffee, I realized that I hadn't had a single thought of Tarin; which is oddly comforting. It felt good to get back to what I loved to do without her interference. I mean, I'm sure I love her, but she can be very demanding and needy of my time. I know she understands how difficult it can be to have your own business and run it as successfully as I have alone for so long, but at times I get the impression that she doesn't care about my work, only the benefits of it.

Nearly working through lunch, Fallon and I called it quits for the day. We ordered some food for the coffee in our stomachs to eat on. Placing the cup in front of him, I noticed that he had been slumped in his seat; I know I tired him, but it looks as if more is weighing on his mind than what had been in front of us.

"What's up, man? I'm not working you too hard, am I?" I sarcastically asked.

"Oh what... No, I just have a few things on my mind." He answered with aloofness in his voice.

"So what's on your mind?" I continued to pursue.

"It's just that I have been in contact with some people from my past and conversing with them again is causing me to examine if the decisions I made were the right ones. I'm unsure of what to do." He confessed with exhaustion, as if he'd been carrying a huge weight.

"What people? Is there someone who's harassing you or something? Let me know and we can take care of it ASAP!" I hurdled with urgency.

"No Jayshawn nothing like that, remember the guy I told you I was involved with? Well, he's trying to come back into my life. I feel like as soon as I got over him and our chaotic relationship he is trying to disrupt all my progress by reminding me of what we had together and feeding my mind ideas of how much better we can be if I allowed him to occupy a spot in my life; I just don't know what to do. Also, Nova has been texting me about wanting to have lunch or dinner."

"Are you going to have dinner with her?" I inquired.

"I don't know. I've thought about it…" he trailed off.

"I wouldn't think less of you if you took a meeting with her. You've worked together for a long time and it would be irrational to think you can forget about your relationship together; business or otherwise." I tried to sound cordial.

"I'm not thinking of going back to work for her if that's what you're thinking." Fallon insisted. "That thought hasn't crossed my mind at all. Nova and I have several issues I think we can get over as friends, but not as lovers."

As he spoke, an air of disbelief washed over me like the shock of a cold shower. Did my ears hear him correctly? Did I hear him put the word lovers and Nova in the same sentence? I had never been the person who's been interested in coffee shop gossip, but I'm intrigued. As he told the story of his love triangle, I couldn't stop my thoughts from reflecting on my crisscrossed love affair; it's crazy how nearly every situation I find myself in always brings me back to thoughts of her. I wish I could see her face, not on social media; in person. See her smile that brilliant smile, especially when she's not trying or when she's being funny, I remembered as I reined in my drifting thoughts back in to focus on Fallon.

"It started about a year ago, my boyfriend and I had been going through several rough patches for a long time about how he handled our relationship, and she was the friend I confided in. Because of the industry we're in, he would always become jealous if Nova and I had an event to attend or even if we had to entertain industry insiders to get funding for whatever project she had. As much as he wanted to keep it under wraps he was jealous at the same time and didn't want me to be around people he knew I could have an attraction towards. He would show up and show out wherever we were. I used to bring him as my plus one to ease his mind, but when he embarrassed me in front of people who had the potential to elevate my career, I stopped inviting him with the quickness. It even got to the point when I had to let the bouncers or security know that if he showed up not to allow him entrance." Fallon stated.

"So, at what point in all this did you and Nova sleep together?" I probed.

"I'm getting there," he insisted. "Nova had become inspired to create an exclusive lingerie line, to launch it she wanted the party to be very gauche, so she held it at the Stiletto Club. You know, that high end strip club all the power players go; that one. Who better to launch a lingerie line, but the women who inspire insatiable sexual appetites but the ladies of Stiletto? She named the party The Hips and Tits Party, and as the mistress of ceremonies she had saved her best creation for herself. She wore a head to toe sheer mermaid style negligee with thin straps that lead from the shoulders down to her breasts and then continued down her torso to embroidery in the crotch area that resembled a blooming Lotus. In the back there was a sweep train; she looked marvelously arousing." He finished.

Giving him the 'hurry up' look he snapped himself out of his self-imposed stupor and continued, by the look on his face I could tell the story was just beginning, the real story is yet to come… or did they both cum? I would soon find out.

"To prepare for the party I had instructed security to be on the lookout for my boyfriend; at this point they knew him well. So party went smoothly, the girls modeled the line, and it was a huge hit with all in attendance. After the show we partied a bit it got a little wild, and the next thing I knew my boyfriend had slipped pass security and had gotten on the stage and yelled at the top of his lungs for me to come to him and stop getting my dick rubbed on, and just acting an entire fool with his carrying on; the cat was out of the bag about us now, and he couldn't put it back if he tried. He would have to come clean to the people in his life about the double life he'd been living. Disgusted by his constant behavior, I decided this had been the last straw for me and I just broke it off with him in front of a club full of half-naked partygoers. Jumping off of the stage, he walked to me and slapped me across the face so hard I saw stars; so you know I was mad and embarrassed, so I hit him with a right hook out of reaction to what he'd done. Needless to say he fell over a small table; his legs went into the air like a cartoon character. When he composed himself enough to stand he tried to fight me, but by then security had come out of the crowd and snatched him up." Fallon finished.

"I hope you guys weren't living together." I stated.

"No, thank God, but I had some things at his place that he destroyed. Anyway, after clearing out the club, I was in no mood to be alone. Taking a few bottles that were left over, Nova and I slipped into one of the private rooms and recapped the night. We talked, drank, laughed, and cried; she was not just my employer, but I considered her a good friend." Fallon reminisced. "The more we drank, the bolder we both got. I confess I found her attractive; I'm not exclusive to boys, you know; but you can guess that's why my ex had been so upset, I enjoy the company of men and women. But still she's my boss and some lines shouldn't be crossed but that night we crossed them all."

"And," I asked, looking for more information.

"And that's it. I'm not going to go over all the explicit details of our escapade, just know that it was amazing and by the end of the night her outfit was in shreds and she had to wear one of the club's bathrobes home and several of her hair extensions had been loosened. We had a few rendezvous nights after that, we had fallen into a regular routine of work and sex and it was ok, until it wasn't ok. When I explained to her my position, and that I wanted to stop our trysts, she become enraged like any other woman would. That's when I quit and took time to myself when I came across your online ad for an assistant."

Completely blown away by Fallon's story, I couldn't believe what he had just told me. If someone like Griff told me something like this, I would have assumed that he had exaggerated it somehow, but with Fallon I knew it had to have some truth to it. His body language told the tale of being tired and stressed and this physical reaction you can't fake. Your body will tell the tale of how you are physically, mentally, and emotionally managing things even when your mouth says something totally different; Fallon looks to exhausted from the internal struggle. Clearing the table of our belongings, we stopped working for the day to prepare to speak to the kids at Dane's event the next day.

Arriving at the recreation center where Dane is holding the Without Bounds Youth Conference, it was an amazing sight to see all the kids and their parents that showed up to support; I secretly wished someone had a program like this when I was growing up. My parents worked from sunup to sundown when they came to this country to provide for my sister and I. My father was an amazing man, but giving us the life he thought we deserved rendered him unavailable at times, and caused him to become ill just as he saw the sacrifice of his hard work take root. This program would have been a welcome buffer for those times. Nevertheless, I've been taught well; or so I thought.

Taking my seat on the stage next to the other speakers, I looked around for Fallon when Dane walked up to me explaining how they laid out the program. After speaking, he quickly asked where Fallon had been, expressing concern I admitted that I didn't know. A few more minutes passes when he finally shows up and one of Danc's assistant's points out his seat on stage next to me.

"For a minute there, I thought you weren't going to show up." I whispered to him.

"For a moment there, I thought the same thing. But I can't do this to the kids, you and Dane. I made a commitment and I intend to see it through." Fallon replied.

Starting the conference, Dane gave his introductions to the audience members about the programs and its humble beginnings, then introduced each speaker and their industry expertise before inviting each one to address the audience. Each speaker went to the microphone and gave their best rehearsed speeches to the crowd; some of them you could tell had given the same speech over and over, only changing the title or key phrases using Without Boarders Youth Development. Hell, even my speech had been pre-written and generic for such an occasion; you can't play a player. But when it came Fallon's turn to speak, I hung on his every word.

He spoke of his upbringing and growing up having an innate sense of self. He spoke fondly of his family and the strength they instilled into him, his love of all things creative and artistic, his faith that humanity will one day practice what they preach in the realm of love and support all people fairly, and regardless of social-economic status, gender, color, creed, and/or sexual orientation and identity. By the end of his speech, perfect strangers applauded him and nodded in approval.

It had almost mimicked a church parking lot at the end of a service by how people stood in the lobby of the Youth Center waiting for the next round of workshops to begin. A few pockets of people approached the speakers and inquired about the inspiration for their Enterprise. I spotted Fallon speaking to a few adults mostly made up of women; when I took notice of a young man that slowly approach Fallon. I almost deserted the group I was speaking with to offer some assistance.

As I walked in their direction, my feet became heavy and I couldn't move, it felt as if something had been holding me in that position forcing me to stay where I was. I saw the two sit on chairs a few steps away from where I had been. It looked as if the young man had been explaining something to Fallon, and instead of responding he just sat back and listened, occasionally nodding his head at the kid. The young man had reached up to wipe his eyes when I saw Fallon's mouth move. I watched this exchange between them for what had seemed like hours. At the end of the conversation, the two shook hands and the young man walked off towards the group of children that had been calling for him to come over.

This had been the longest day of my life and I couldn't wait to get back to my office. Leaving the event Dane stopped by to say thanks for bringing with him his wife, my sister Talia and their three boys Jacques, Joaquin, and Jaquill. Introducing them, Fallon realized he had been speaking with Dane's son and my nephew Jaquill. After my sister suggested that she, the boys, and I enjoy the food she and my aunts had prepared from their family established restaurant Down Home Decadence for the event.

I air hustled Dane thank Fallon for speaking to his son on a subject that he had no experience in and hoped that he would be open to speaking to him again if the occasion arises. I want to turn back and intrude on their conversation, but I knew that this was not a dialogue that I needed to be a part of. This was a conversation between two men, a parent and a mentor about the welfare of a child, and I had no place to intrude on that. Even though the child is my nephew, I don't want to bring the wrong attention to all parties involved. I'm happy that my nephew could have someone to talk to, and I'm especially happy that person that can help guide him is one that I have in my employ; I guess my poor judgment has finally turned around.

Malik

I can't believe shorty got me looking for her. I went back to her place and waited for her outside, only for her not to show up. I had to wait for someone to get buzzed into the building, and then followed. Once I arrived on her floor, I knocked repeatedly, nearly to the point of possibly denting the door; I stood there for a while until I realized she wasn't there. Walking towards the elevator to leave, I saw a neighbor and asked if she had seen her. The elderly woman told me she had been gone for a few days, but that's usually because of her job. This girl had been slowly becoming more and more intriguing by the minute; maybe she didn't have a rich daddy like Dominique, perhaps baby had her own money that she is just waiting to spend on a man like me. I hit the jackpot this time! Every chick I had been meeting in the past year has been a come up for me and with each new coochie came a better opportunity and this one would just be adding to my growing list of investors.

I normally would probe the neighbor for more information, but today isn't the day to entertain a future conquest. I have a podcast interview with Tesserae Scott, one of the most promising up-and-coming Music and Entertainment Journalists in the game. In a short time in the industry Tess has made important connections and broken down doors that were once closed to women; if she wasn't as well respected as she is, I would have slid up in her real quick and added her to my roster of ladies.

Opening her own Music and Arts Academy for children, Tesserae has been awarded the local community leadership award which has simultaneously opened her up to endorsements, and donations from celebrity artists from all walks of the entertainment industry wanting to contribute time, currency, energy, etc. to the cause she began. To have her as one of my allies is a much better use of her than to have her as my dick warmer.

Arriving at the space Tess used for her Academy, her assistant lead me to the area she used to film and record her podcasts. Greeting each other quickly we jumped straight into the interview, with the Montreal Music and Arts Festival around the corner I had to be on beast mode promoting my artists that would have a showcase and generate support for my other artists projects. Naturally, Tesserae asked me about TNT first, mainly because he's the pack leader in the underground music game right now; second, because he's also one of the most eligible bachelors on the rap scene. The man has children, but he's not romantically involved to any women; at least, not publicly, and I mean to keep it that way.

If he keeps up the persona he's available, women will come clamoring for him; buying every EP album, concert ticket, t-shirt, everything. When he does finally select a lucky lady to be his woman, she has to be a top-notch cutie with ties to the industry herself, but not too much as to outshine him. Once their relationship is solidified we can expect the endorsements to come pouring in. Men and women alike will buy their music, wearing what they wear, watching their reality tv show, drink the same brands they do, and even naming their kids after them. And if the plan doesn't work; you know I always have a Plan B, right? I'll just have them put out a sex tape and accidentally leak it to Eclipse Celebrity Gossip online site.

I promoted TNT's newest mix tape while reiterating his past successes, and then gently slid into promoting the women on my roster; China being one of them, but if she doesn't get her act together and fall in line, she will find herself without a man or a manager and I'll toss her ass back in that strip club I found her in and pick Chloe's ass right back up since I know she's had to have made industry connections of her own that I can manipulate. Meanwhile, I haven't heard from one of their family members threatening me; I'm under the assumption that they aren't aware of what transpired between us and I'm positive none of them knew China had been sucking and fucking in a strip club when I found her. When I felt like Tess was trying to end the interview, I quickly threw out some show times of the performances my artists will have during the festival.

I have to make sure all of my affairs are in order before I leave the city for any length of time by checking in on Priest the music engineer I hired to get all the music mixed to perfection. He earned his stage name as Priest because of all the miracles he performs when he turns a mediocre artist in to musical gold. I caught him in the middle of Foxy Calhoun's solo single. I found her in some dive bar singing cover songs with the other members of her group Hells Angels.

The group was ok and had some success, but they had no direction; that's where I stepped in to provide them with a little guidance, show them how the game is really played. Divide and conquer, baby! That's exactly what I did to Hells Angels. Foxy had been a hard core lyricist and the other girls were just too soft to keep up with her esthetic; so I divided them into two groups, Foxy being the solo artist and with the other girls I formed a Neo Soul group called Legacy. Foxy's debut single Angel Unleashed would pave the way for her album Inferno to climb the music charts while allowing Legacy to ride her coattails to the top and line my pockets, enabling me to build my empire.

I had been creeping out of the event planning game and into musical management. I'll still keep my money coming in from all angles, but management is my primary goal; perhaps I'll move Makayla from being TNT's background singer back into event planning. Things have been heating up between them on the road. The Road Manager Jerry had kept me well informed of their late night sessions, and I don't need her distracting my number one artist just at the time when his star is rising higher, elevating us both; I'll keep a lid on that situation until I can safely get rid of her. Of course I would need to put a team in place to ensure my interests. I'll never forget those dirty little tricks we played with Jayshawn's business and how quickly she was willing to jump ship and watch him drown; she'll just be an assistant to the office manager until I figure out what to do with her.

After checking on my artists, I had to make a special visit to the number one woman in my life, my mother Marion. No one knew about my mother; if she had been living or dead, in New York or somewhere else in the world. She raised me alone after my father Cecil left when I was still a little dude. They had married young and my mom gave birth to me soon after their wedding; she had been a very pregnant bride, but neither of them cared as long as we were good. My dad had a little nine-to-five job, but always (and I mean always) had side hustles to bring in extra money.

He would bootleg liquor, fix cars, sell a little smoke. He was so well respected around the way, which is why his customers felt comfortable with him making "house calls".   That's how he and Ms. Stella set up weekly visits to her house so she could get her fix, as my dad would call it. She was a beautiful smooth chocolate sister with red/brown hair. He would make "house calls" to her on Wednesdays afternoons. Her husband would be at work, and my mom would work too. After picking me up from school we would stop at her house on the way home, Dad used to make me wait outside her house while he was handling business, and when he was done he would take me to the bodega and buy me an icy. Also on the walks home he would school me to the money game, then ask me questions. If I got the right answer, he gave me a dollar, if I got it wrong I had to run laps around the block until my heart felt like it would come out of my chest.

On Saturdays my mother left early to the clinic where she worked as a nurse, my father and I would work out a little, and I helped him tune up a few of his friends' cars; I would get beer and cigarettes for them as they waited. When that was done we would stop by a few bars and drop of batches of his homemade liquor. One Saturday when mom was gone, my father woke me up early to drop off the liquor alone. He said I was old enough, and he trusted me to get the job done. He told me if I had any problems or someone tried to cheat me out of the money I was supposed to collect to let him know. Nobody ever gave me a problem, they knew my father was no joke and his hands were one the sharpest in the neighborhood.

Under my father's tutelage, I learned the art of slick talking and fast moving. That day I negotiated a five dollar increase for the product, I was so proud when all his clients obliged the increase. I gave them a story about the material cost going up and they swallowed it; I knew my dad would be proud of me. Not only had I brought home more money, I did it alone, and no one tried to cheat me.

When I got home, I ran straight into the house at full speed and went to my parents' bedroom. Pushing the door open quickly, I saw Ms. Pam, my mother's friend in bed with my father. Pausing and scurrying around the bed, my father screamed for me to close the door. I left the apartment and sat on the stoop, trying to make sense of what I saw. A few minutes later Ms. Pam walked pass me and didn't even give me a sideways glance at she walked down the street. A minute later my father came and sat next to me. He tried to give me some bullshit about being a man that helped a woman in need, and she needed his help in that moment. Basically, anything he thought would make sense to a kid. After attempting to make sure I didn't tell my mother, he asked me about the money; as expected, he was proud at the initiative to help the family business; he gave me five dollars this time.

Before my mom got home, he cooked a banquet-sized meal for the three of us, as he cooked I couldn't help but to ask him if he loved my mother. In his ramblings to answer the question and shut the subject down as to not have it come up again, he explained that my mom is the love of his life and would never leave her or his family for anyone, but from time to time he liked to "help" women who needed his assistance as he put it. It ended there, and I didn't pursue it further; none the less, my mother was thrilled with my dad for cooking dinner when she got home; at the end of the day I didn't want to be the cause of my mother being unhappy, so I kept my dad's secret, but you better believe I really studied his moves after that.

The guilt must have been really weighing me down, because my mother noticed the change in me. I became a loner and crawled inside my mind coming up with ways to make coins. She pulled me to the side before school and asked me what was on my mind, not wanting to lie to my mother and tell on my father; I threw my mood change on wanting to pass a stupid class in school; I knew she didn't buy it, but she let it go. I didn't have to live with the guilt long.

My parents loved to throw a good house party, so it was no surprise to me that the next weekend we had a house full of folks eating, drinking, playing cards, and freeloading. Everyone who's anyone was there, including Ms. Stella, Ms. Pam, and their men. Being the only kid around, my mother would make me stay in my bedroom away from the adult behavior; or so she thought. There has been a few times my parents' friends forgot I was home and came into my room with partners, realizing I was there, they would leave as quickly as they had come in; they knew moms didn't play any games with me, if anyone had a thought about how she raised me they'd never said a word. She showered me with love and whatever I wanted. It could be new sneakers, clothes, toys, bikes, whatever, just as long as her Prince (her pet name for me) was happy; she made it very clear I was her number one.

That night while everyone was in the living room, my dad and Ms. Stella eased off into the bathroom together. Not realizing that they were in there, I barged in and caught my father once again cheating on my moms. At this point, I knew the routine; I closed the door and turned to go back in my room, but not before I snuck a drink from the kitchen. There were so much of my dad's bootleg brews that no one would miss if I stole a glass. But before I could make it down the hall, I saw my mom lazily walking toward me with a smile on her face, and homemade brew on her breath.

"Hi baby, are you all right? I came to check on my Prince; do you want me to make you another plate before all the chicken is gone?" she asked.

"No mom, I just want to go back in my room." I reacted as I tried to turn her around.

"Wait a minute, little man. Is that how you treat a lady?" she questioned.

"No, ma 'am." I uttered as I dropped my head in embarrassment and to satisfy her enough to make her turn back.

"Well all right then, show me how a man is supposed to treat a lady," she demanded.

As I took her arm and wrapped it in mine, I escorted her back to the party. She was just about to tell me something when the bathroom door flung open, and she saw Ms. Stella wiping her face, and my father stood behind with a satisfied smile on his face. In that moment my heart stopped and all the breath I had was knocked out of my body when my mom pushed me against the wall and went charging at them.

Trying to run back in the bathroom, Ms. Stella tripped and fell onto my Dad, who had no idea what had been happening until the last minute. Pushing the door so hard that they both flew backwards, my mother swung wildly at whoever she could get her hands on; which was mostly Ms. Stella's wig. By the time the rest of the crowd made it up to hallway to where we were, my father had scratches all over and Ms. Stella's lip had been busted and face starting to swell; I guess it was a good thing my dad have made a delivery to her early that week, so she had plenty of smoke and drink to help her ease the pain in her face and losing a friend.

After that mom kicked dad out, my Dad had beef with the men in the area whose women he had been servicing, he lost most of his connects at the bars because none of them wanted to buy his stuff; if there male customers knew it was his, they wouldn't spend their money in that bar anymore. My Dad went from top dog to a herb as nigga in one fell swoop. My mother loved him, but she had that black woman's pride and wouldn't let him come back home. They crept around every once in a while, but eventually that stopped; I guess she figured she had to let him go. Eventually he stopped coming by at all. He and she divorced, and it left me fatherless. He moved out of state and only called, never visiting except for Christmas, but that eventually faded out too.

It was tough for us for a long while after my father left. We struggled financially until my mother could get a handle on things. My Dad leaving had been such a huge blow financially that in order to get her footing she had to stop buying me the things I had become accustomed to having. My new clothes became dated, my sneakers became worn and turned over, my hair cuts became less frequent, and she only cooked meals that would last a week or more; no more eating takeout. The only time she splurged a little was around the holidays, and even that got tougher and tougher for her to do alone. It had been around that time that I decided we would never be in this situation ever again; my mother would never have another sleepless night.

Since then I've conjured up several business ventures, not all of them have panned out; though the ones that have has become very lucrative. So much so I have been able to afford a decent apartment, buy the best clothes, party with the most influential people, and keep a gorgeous woman to warm the opposite side of the bed; life is good. Using my spare keys to get into my mom's apartment, I yelled for her, with her voice ringing back to join her in the kitchen.

"How's my number one girl?" I asked her excitedly as I gave her a big hug.

"Malik, I'm cooking now! Get away from this stove before you get popped by this grease!" She warned.

"Sorry mama." I faked mumbled is defeat as I took a seat at the table.

"I'm fine, sweetie. What have you been up too, you haven't been coming by for Sunday Dinner in a while. You haven't been chasing after those fast ass girls have you, like your daddy?" she remarked.

"No ma'am, I've been working and building up my business." I explained.

"Well, what is it now? Whatever happened to event planning?" She asked.

"I'm still doing that, but I have employees to take care of that sector while I focus on Entertainment Management." I said proudly.

"What type of job is that 'Entertainment Management' is that like finding jobs for folks?" she questioned as she put a plate of eggs and bacon in front of me.

"Now mama, how did you know I was hungry?" I teased.

"Boy, I know my son and you're always hungry. You rip and run so much I know that you hardly get a decent meal in your belly; so eat." She insisted as she made a plate for herself and sat at the table with me.

We ate in silence for a while until I spoke first. "I'm sorry I missed your retirement party mama. I had business to take care of; I want to set you up so you won't have to worry about getting by financially since Gregory passed." I apologized. Gregory is the man my mom married a few years after the divorce.

"Now Prince, don't worry about me. Between savings, retirement, and a little nest egg Gregory 'God rest his soul' set up for me, I will be just fine; don't you go worrying about me. I know it was hard before, but those times are over now and I think we have both come a long way. Ok." She comforted. "Speaking of hard times, your father called yesterday; he wants to see you."

I nearly spit out my eggs! I haven't seen my father in eight years, and I don't know how many years it had been before that; he had some nerve reaching out to my mother. When I didn't give her a physical or verbal reaction, she kept calling my name to get my attention. Gobbling up the food left on my plate, I kissed her on the cheek and left as fast I could. I hated to disrespect my mother that way, but Cecil is a sore subject for me and I'm not dealing with this now right before my trip. Sending a quick text to all the talent that had been invited to attend the festival to be ready in the morning, I followed my own directions and went home to pack. I have no time to entertain the past, especially since I have so much to look forward to; when this festival is over, I'm sure the offers will come pouring in for one of my artists to get a deal, if not I always have a Plan B.

After arriving in Montreal, the first stop is the hotel and the next stop is the nearest bar. I can't believe I'm nervous, me; of all the things I've done to get here, nerves should be the least of my worries. Repeating my new mantra of 'It has to work' over and over, one of these artists has to get picked up; to put in more effort into them by implementing a 'Plan B' would be monetarily risky and mentally draining.

The festivals events wouldn't start for a few days but anyone with an ounce of common sense would be here as early as possible to ensure that all requirements and/or demands have been met, staging, lighting, and sound are all prepped, security briefed, media presence established, interviews scheduled, and money from ticket sales collected before any artist hits the stage. Yara Webb one of the musical organizers of the event, and a host of this year's EPIC Awards can be very meticulous in her planning and went over the details of each performance with a fine-tooth comb as she gave investors a behind-the-scenes tour of how the workflow of the event would go with contingencies to be implemented should a particular area become compromised. During these tours all event areas are off limits to everyone except event staff, though I had secured a distant front-row seat to the first set of tours by sitting in the right VIP bar, at the right time to get acquainted with the faces of the people that I need to be in bed with so I can make a real power moves to become influential in this business; that's when I saw her, I knew the outline of her body anywhere. That's why she hadn't been home; she's here with some older man; maybe that's her rich daddy. So I really hit the biggest pay load with this one. If the man she's with is a part of the investor tour it's safe to say that he had limitless funds at his disposal with a possible interest in capitalizing on little more. All I had to do is get Phoenix alone long enough for my charm to hypnotize her and I could elevate my company to the next level.

Approaching Phoenix would take some time, especially since I have no idea how long she will be in town, so I have to work fast and make sure that the Malik Robinson magnetism is always at max capacity. I would have continued to watch them until they faded from view; she has an amazing physique, but I had set up an interview with Elaine "Lane" Kim and Allah Supreme DJ and Radio Hosts of Infamous the most prestigious radio show in the game for Hip Hop and R&B. I called in a lot of favors to secure this interview and no one; I mean no one will prevent the 'Winning Team' and myself from making this appearance; though watching her from a distance gave me a rush of adrenaline, and for a moment I considered skipping the interview and sending the team without me in order to find out more about why she was with the group of investors and how I can ease my way into their elite circle.

As part of my obligation to work and family, Olivia or more commonly known as mother took it upon herself to have my dress made for the Monet wedding affectionately nicknamed as The White Wedding. She commissioned a white halter dress with medium train to made by Soul Dimension which had been a welcome surprise on her part; I didn't know she knew who that designer had been.

Farrah Noah daughter of Gerald and Adina Noah my father's business partner is set to wed Sebastian Monet son Calvin and Marlow Monet world renowned restaurateur. I've been drafted to attend this wedding to help Hershel and Elgin close a deal with the Monet's for a new restaurant location as a gift to the newlyweds.

It seems young Sebastian is following in his father's footsteps as Farrah is continuously being groomed to follow in Mrs. Monet's footsteps; let's just hope Farrah doesn't develop her taste for the cooking sherry as she places each stiletto strapped foot in front of the other. Maybe I'm being too hard on the couple, at least they are in love, or so it seems to the casual observer. Farrah seemed to be very involved in the planning of her nuptials, not like Rebecca when she married Hershel. Rebecca allowed her mother and all her old crone friends to make all the arrangements for the wedding, down to the honeymoon. The only time she ever spoke up was to indicate what dress she would wear and if Hershel had to return early for work that she would continue her honeymoon without him; we should all be so envious of their passionate romance, I thought sarcastically. Ramir and Kasha had been the same with the families making all the arrangements with the only thing left for them to do was show up and say 'I do'. Farrah on the other hand had let no one to dictate to her how the special day would commence.

It had been dubbed The White Wedding because every aspect of the wedding would drip from pillars to pew in white. I know, a white aspect in a wedding isn't at all mind blowing; but when you create a paradise made completely of white ambiance, something has to be said about that; she even imported white Japanese Sakura Trees to bathe the passageway as the wedding procession enters the venue; she had gone through impressive lengths to ensure that he and she would remember their wedding day long after retirement, why would she pay so much attention to the details if she hadn't truly loved Sebastian. If I had a love in my life like that, I would marry him in a Vegas Chapel just as long as we were together.

In our societal circle, women always try to outdo one another. It doesn't matter if it's a wedding or a funeral, no one is safe. At most weddings you will find that one woman who wears white (which we all know is an insult to the bride) in an effort to steal the limelight. To avoid having to compete with the envious women vying for the attention of the men in the room including the groom, Farrah instituted a dress code. Her dress as you would guess will not be the traditional white dress; no one actually knew what color her dress will be, it's a secret held between her, her mother, and the seamstress who would be in very high demand after the festivities concluded.

Arriving at the church, I felt like an old maid who couldn't pay a man to be my date; I couldn't pay him anyway because I haven't saved enough money in my 401k to even rent a date for the event. Everyone who's anyone would be at this wedding and will be sure to see me arrive and depart alone, adding to the already stirring rumor mill that had been brewing about me. People would whisper asinine notions like…

"Poor girl she will never marry," or *"I heard she was living with another woman, poor Olivia she'll never have a grandchild,"* or the more recent *"She's nothing more than an elite escort; she loves to flirt with married men. I hear they buy her all kinds or jewelry and clothing and take her on exotic trips so she can perform duties for*

them." I just hope that if Elgin ever heard any of these vicious lies that he wouldn't believe any of them.

Taking my seat in the back near the exit in case I had to make a quick and clean getaway, I noticed that all the women seemed to hold their significant others' arms a little too tight as I passed by. Adding to my already growing insecurity, my eyes caught Ramir as he settled into the seat next to Kasha. As our eyes met, my breath got caught in my throat and all the memories of the not so distant past flooded back; I hope I would be strong enough to get through this wedding in one piece.

Just as I felt myself begin to shrink under all the pressure I had been feeling, I felt the brush of someone sit next to me. My first thought had been that perhaps the person couldn't find a seat anywhere else. Turning slightly as to not immediately stare, my eyes caught the million-dollar smile of Elgin Reese. Letting out a sigh of relief as I smiled in his direction, I'm so relieved it's him and not one grooms creepy cousins. Leaning slightly to whisper in my ear I looked 'Radiant' as he put it we sat in silence sort of guarding each other from unwanted bating from the other singles that had are invited.

As the Organ cranked up and the wedding precession began the all too familiar wedding march down the aisle, I couldn't help but feel unaccomplished. It's crazy how events like a wedding or a funeral can put life's acts into perspective. When a woman accepts a man's proposal of marriage, both parties are making a promise to always hold each other at the highest regard, sacrifice your own happiness if need be for that of your spouses. Together no one ever promises to be perfect, because that doesn't exist; but having a partner that can help you carry the weight of what life can throw in your path is immeasurable.

All the Bridesmaids and Groomsmen had settled in their assigned places, as the Organist played as a signal to the Bride to begin her ascent to her alter to meet her soon to be husband. The twins doors to the sanctuary opened and there she stood wearing a formfitting,

Crimson color Grace Griffin gown with a plunge neckline. On her head instead of a traditional veil she opted for a lace a birdcage veil; she looked striking and defiantly wouldn't be upstaged by hyenas masquerading as upper crust socialites.

The pastor made quick work of the 'I do' portion of the program within an hour everyone had been arriving at the venue for the reception. Assigned seating is a must when you have two families joining and have somewhat of a scandalous past to put it lightly.

During cocktail hour, I overheard Millie Portier insinuate that Mr. Monet needs for the relationship to work because he's made some terrible business decisions and their entire restaurant chain could be at risk and this wedding could put him in a good position to sell some of his smaller restaurants to recoup his losses, but he requires Farrah's father to make all the necessary arrangements; maybe that's why Mrs. Monet is drinking every bar's inventory from here to Philadelphia, where their current money pit resides. But it's something Elgin mentioned to me about the gossiping women as he handed me a cocktail; it burned a hole in my memory and placed heaviness on my heart. He listened intently at the same conversation I had been eavesdropping on.

"So that's why they think Mrs. Monet is a lush? That couldn't be further from the truth." He corrected them without their knowledge.

"If that's not why she's boozing out, then why?" I provoked.

"The business end is true, but that's the only part Miffy has right." He mocked Millie's name as he trailed off as he took a sip of cognac.

"Well, don't keep me in suspense. What's really going on between the Noah's and the Monet's?" I insisted. I had been so overzealous for the information, because for once it hadn't been about me.

"This stays between us… I'm serious, if this got out it would be a very poor reflection on both families." He insisted sternly as he held my gaze for what seemed like hours.

"I won't speak a word of it to anyone, I promise." I swore.

"Mrs. Monet has been on edge since Sebastian and Farrah began dating; you could say she had been dreading this day from the start." He introduced. "Mrs. Monet and Mr. Noah had dated in their younger years and from what I've seen and heard about them their romance had been scorching hot. The romance ended with both marrying someone else, but rumor has it they had continued to carry on a love affair until Farrah's birth. As to not be outdone by Adina Noah, Mrs. Monet had Sebastian a year later." Elgin concluded.

"How do you know that story is true? It could be a rumor made up by anyone who has a vendetta against the families." I questioned the validity of Elgin's anecdote.

"I don't know if it's true or not; it could be she still carries a torch for Gerald Noah and seeing their children have something together that they never got close to drives her to the bottle in an effort to mask her pain… or she's just a lush and the demise of her husband's business and the thought of all their beautiful things being sold at an auction is enough to make the poor woman empty every distillery on the east coast, you decide." He concluded as he strode away to greet a business partner.

I stood at the edge of reason contemplating the two scenarios Elgin presented and pondered if either had more legitimacy than the other. As my mind drifted from one outlandish flight of fancy to another, I accidently caught the eyes of someone I hadn't expected to see at an event like this. Looking at his face had stirred in my mind all the memories of being with him; it has also stirred my body, and I suddenly felt a familiar humming from beneath my custom made dress that illuminated throughout my body. His eyes are just as I remembered, they're tender and comforting with just a slight flex of green; he still has the most beautiful eyes I had ever seen.

It was something out of a movie; we locked eyes just as everyone had been summoned into the dining area. We all sat at our assigned tables and feasted on the first course; we would catch each other's eyes every so often, as if we were sizing each other up for what would come next in this eye version of the Argentine Tango we were performing. No one here knew our history; well that had been my assumption. If they had been aware of it the room would be more fixated on us and the drama that could ensue at any second. People chatted, they made the toasts to the happy couple, the next few courses were served, then the ceremonial cutting of the cake; all the predictable events of a wedding.

Everyone joined the couple on the dance floor and there had been nothing but smiles to be seen, if anyone had opposed the marriage they were nowhere to be found as people danced together, and changed partners during the group dances; I had been enjoying myself that I had forgotten that I felt awkward at the start of the day. I even caught glimpses of my parents dancing excitedly; that's something I had never seen before, not even in my childhood, I guess weddings really bring out the best in people. As I danced unabashedly with Elgin, he spun me around and I had unexpectedly landed in the arms of my eye Tango partner Chase Greene. The music changed and like an awkward moment in a movie, two ex-lovers danced together as to not cause a scene and ruin the partygoer's good time.

We danced, and for a moment being that close to him again made me nervous. I shook a little, and I noticed that my heartbeat started to beat a little more rapidly as a wave of euphoria washed over me. I quickly realized that this would probably be the last time I would ever be this close to him. I began to make mental memories of how he smelled, the build of his body, the pressure of his hand on my waist and the other hand cradling my hand as he led the dance while we synced to each other's tempo; it felt incredible. The feeling was short lived when Elgin cut in, and I obliged him.

The evening had been draining, and after my interlude with Chase I had no energy for pleasantries, so I hid out at the bar. As I stood with a drink in hand, I replayed the dance with Chase over and over in my mind. I speculated of what I would have done if it hadn't been so spontaneous that we ended up as dance companions, especially because of how things ended when we last saw each other, and the entire text message debacle. I don't know how long I had been in the universe exploring new reaches of my mind when I heard someone aggressively clearing their throat. Turning in the direction of the sound, I realized it had been the bartender, and he slides me a note discreetly as he wiped down the counter; the note read:

"Meet me now in the room that has a vase of Mauve Carnations outside of it."

I stood in shock at who would send me such a cryptic note. It could be anyone; maybe it's Ramir or his crazy ass wife attempting to make sure I stay away from her philandering husband? It could be Elgin wanting to re-create the moment we shared in the bathroom on Christmas? Hell, it could be Hershel wanting me to go back to the office to retrieve a schematic for Mr. Noah? At this point, the bartender who slid me the note could be the person requesting an audience with me. Either way, it had sparked my interest of who would take time out of such a significant event to have a meeting with me; maybe it's Hershel.

Exiting the dance space, I looked up and down the hall for the vase of Carnations. Removing my shoes as I walked, I found a vase that looked out of place on the far end of the venue past the kitchen. Walking closer, I recognized the flowers in it as Carnations; it looked as if someone had placed it there, but who? Who would go through so much trouble as to get me into a secluded area? Upon approach, I hesitated a bit. Tightly holding my shoes, I'm prepared to defend myself if somebody jumps out at me from behind the door. Taking a deep breath, I twist the knob to find an empty lounge area; it resembled a dressing area where brides/grooms would prepare before a ceremony. Upon further inspection, I saw who the mystery person had been; I guess Chase needed to further my embarrassment. The countless text messages I sent apologizing hadn't been enough; he needed to take another dig at me in person.

"Close the door." He commanded.

I had been so shocked to find it had been him; I didn't realize I left it wide open for anyone walking by to see the carnage of yet another humiliating moment. I slowly slid to the center of the room with shoes in hand and defeat in my eyes as I let out a throaty sigh. I waited for him to say something to me; instead he stood on the far side of the room near the window with a drink in hand as watched me watch him. As I attempting to rush the interlude along by beginning the conversation, he stopped me dead in my tracks.

"No, don't say a word." He demanded. "I need you to hear a few things, and I don't want to hear the sound of your voice while I say them." He took a deep breath, like he had been trying to remember the words he'd been practicing. "I knew you would be here. My plan was to bring a beautiful woman with me and flaunt her in your face, especially when I saw that the other guy you were fucking is here."

"I didn't know either of you would be here." I said before he could shut me down.

"I said I didn't want to hear your voice!" he warned sternly before continuing. "I saw you with the newest victim, and I thought to myself the best revenge on you is to give you exactly what you want;You did always like men who've treated you like shit. Isn't that what turns you on?" he hard-pressed me.

"I don't know who the fuck you think you're talking to, or what you saw, but I'm done with this shit!" I yelled at him. "You can be mad all the fuck you want, I don't care anymore. I tried to make things right and all you can do is tell me of how shitty I treated you, as if I don't have a fucking clue of what I've done. You can't hurt me more than I'm already hurting!" I spat at him as I turned to leave.

Realizing he lost his grip on the situation, he did the only thing he could do in that moment to keep me in the room with him; he caught up to me quickly and hugged me tightly from behind as he stroked my breast through my dress and began a rotation of licking and kissing my neck. God, it had been so long since he's touched me; in truth my body craved him, I just didn't realize how much so until the moment.

I felt my body open up to him without question. Still holding me, my lips rose to meet his for a deeply aggressive kiss. Removing his jacket, he lifted me up to his waist; it felt so natural to wrap my legs around him. Losing my hair from my sleek ponytail, he cradled me as he walked over to the nearest couch. Not to be too troubled by removing all our clothes, he had unzipped his pants, lifted my dress and slid my panties to the side. The couch was so small he could only get his knee on the couch and he had to anchor himself on his leg that stayed on the floor, while I had one leg hoisted in the air and the other at his side. He held me so close I could feel the heat of his breath and taste the sweetness of his drink as he kissed me. Grabbing a fist full of my hair, he forced my head back as he took his rage out on my neck and my vagina simultaneously.

After a few minutes of aggressive sex, he collapsed on top of me. When I tried to reach out for him, he moved away quickly and tucked his shirt back into his pants. Following his lead, I put myself back together. After dressing he returned to the window to finish his drink. Apparently this is the signal that he had been done with me and I'm being dismissed. Realizing that we needed this encounter for the both of us to have closure; I put my shoes on and left the room as quickly and inconspicuously as I had arrived. When I got into the main gallery, I spotted Elgin with my coat. He explained that he had waited to see if I needed a ride home and asked where I had been. Explaining quickly, I told him I needed some air; the bartender had been over pouring the drinks and I felt a little queasy.

As we left, I glanced over my shoulder to see Chase with a mischievous smirk on his face. I just hoped that our encounter had been enough and that this game is now over between us; we (I mean me) could finally move on. Deep down I know that notion isn't true, because when I saw him glaring at me I felt my kitty begin to purr for him again. I'm beginning to hate the affect he has on me; possibly with time the feeling would go away.

I cannot wait for this trip to be over! I had been so caught up in the hype of going to London, that I forgot the work aspect of it. Clair had all the staff so busy that the only parts of London we got to see were the hotel lobby and the people as they walked the streets to their destinations. We drove to whatever back ally gallery where a show is being held. The only jewel of the entire trip thus far will be the Elevation Creation fashion show sponsored by Black Enterprise, which will also feature product debuts; I'm so proud of Hennison.

It's the morning of the show and everyone is on their "A Game" or so I've been lead to believe. Cassidy seems off, she's not her usual feisty self; it's like she's walking around in a daze. More than once during our staff meeting Clair had to call on her for whatever bit of information she had been demanding. Cassidy's mind had been adrift somewhere in the universe, and the once important Indulgence Magazine took second place to something that troubled her to where even Clair hadn't been able to bring her back. Clair also had been acting unusual. She walked and talked a mile a minute to where it had been difficult to keep up with her instructions for the fashion show. The team leaders looked at each other with confusion as they tried to decipher her instructions. When in meetings with Clair the staff did most of the talking, and she did most of the correcting; watching her now she gives me the feeling that she is in some sort of race, and how she had been reacting gave me the impression that she's losing… But if that's true, who's winning? The one person I could count on to keep a level head in all this is the one person who couldn't.

Going back to the suite before they scheduled us to arrive at the venue, I found Hennison in the seating area with a glass of cognac while wrapped in a towel giving an appearance of not having a care in the world; at this point he had every care. Many people employed by his company counted on having a job to go back to when this leg of his press tour is over. Black Enterprise had been losing money for a while and with the launching of his own branded products the financial aspect of the company had to turn around putting Black Enterprise back in the black; no pun intended. I don't know how much trouble the company is in, if any; the loss could be as insignificant as being uncomfortable for their bottom lines and non- effective in the grand scheme of things, to being cataclysmic and a potential company destroyer; for a company built by Paul Black and has been intended by him to be a legacy to his family and his work; the demise of it would be tragic. Whatever had caused him to stress and take those late nights, hush-hush phone calls when he thought I was asleep should end. At any rate, he hasn't been on any of those calls since we arrived in London, or so I thought.

After a quick exercise session with Hennison to relieve both of us from the pressure of the company-sponsored event, it is GAME TIME! The venue dripped from floor to ceiling with an opulent, over indulgent facade; something had been brewing underneath it all. The air in the room had been so palpable it's as if is all or nothing; I didn't like this feeling at all. Is this how the rich and elite conducted themselves when stress is present? I know when you're broke, stress usually manifests itself with a trip to the liquor store, the buffet, or to church; the vice depends on the person.

Taking my seat next to Hennison, and not Clair, I watched the show as if I had been an audience member waiting to be impressed. Black Enterprise sponsored the event, which featured a dozen well named and up-and-coming designers. I had been especially happy to see they had chosen Attali Santiago as a featured designer. I had never seen so many gorgeous, husky male models grace the runways of mainstream fashion; only in event halls where local fashion shows took place. Attali would be the only one in working memory that has been invited to take part in a show of this magnitude. Even Julius Banks had never been to a stage with as much prestige as this one; when Julius started out, men's fashion had still been in the dark ages and very one-dimensional. His styles and designing took men's fashion to a new level, but by the time mainstream came around to taking husky male models seriously, he had been above showcasing his creations the way others know it to be now. Though, that doesn't keep him from keeping an eye out for prospective collaborations and/or competition. I'm sure if Attali is worth his salt, he will be recruited by Nevie or Julius himself to join his team of influencers.

The lights dimmed, the show started, and for a second I felt like one of the most important people in the room. The most beautiful garments floated down the runway, one after the other. As the last designer showed their newest line, Hennison slide from by my side and quietly made his way to the backstage entrance. When the last model left the stage leaving the adoring audience still in awe of her killer signature walk, the center spotlight shone and out walked our generous benefactor of the wearable arts. With a dazzling smile, expensive suit, and the confidence of ten thousand executives, Hennison took center stage and every hand in the building erupted into a thunderous applause.

As he began his well-rehearsed speech, the room quieted. "Thank you all for joining us this evening in showcasing some of the best and talented artists and designers of our time. Since its beginning we at Black Enterprise have prided ourselves on our hard work, ability to evolve, and our determination to be more than just a media publication; but to be the foremost force in the fashion industry. When my father started this company all those years ago, he could have never imagined that we would be here today celebrating his legacy with all of you. In its beginning The Black Company, as it was known as then, was a small publishing magazine that trolled the club scenes for the newest innovations in wearable art; my father at heart was an artist. Though he couldn't make art with his hands, he made it with words. With bold ideas, a retro style, and using his version of a weapon of mass creation, he started several of the thriving magazines that are still being published today."

I listened and watched him intently as he paused. His body language had shifted, what started off as a celebratory speech had taken a weird turn; it nearly sounded like he was giving a verbal 'pink slip'. I felt my mind drift, but then I realized where I had been and attempted to concentrate on Hennison.

"In remembrance of my father, each of you will have the honor of taking home with you tonight Black Enterprise newest additions to our family (insert dramatic pause here). I hope you've all been enjoying your drinks tonight, for you've all been drinking TIMELESS BLACK cognac one of our newest endeavors that has been tantalizing you with every sip…" the room erupted in applause at the mention of free drink samples to take home to party with later. "But that's not all." He began again. "You'll all also be the first to have the soon to be released provocative, alluring fragrant aromas of JET BLACK men's cologne and grooming products, and LITTLE BLACK DRESS eau de perfume for women."

The cheers and whistles grew louder at every mention of a free product that isn't exactly free and will be given out in swag bags; the attendees pay for them in the ticket prices for the event. The only people who aren't paying for the freebees are the celebrities present hoping they would advertise that product to all their adoring fans on social media, on tours, or any personal appearance where there will be visual or individual interaction. In an event of this magnitude, the company sponsoring it will expect to take a monetary loss, but it's a minimal loss in the grand scheme of things. Once the plan is carried out properly, a company can make the money they invested back tenfold by making the right business contacts, endorsements, paid ad space in their publications, retail sales, sponsorship exchanges with other entities for more consumers, the possibilities are endless.

The room quieted again, for Hennison had not been finished delivering the entirety of his speech. "Yes. This news is all very, very exciting and I think I can speak for everyone one in the company when I say we are all very proud to be sharing our future ambitions and successes with all of you. However, with much to be gained from pursuing new endeavors, it will come with noble sacrifice to our company. As Black Enterprise transitions in a new direction, It's with the deepest regret that some of our nearest and dearest entities of our company will not be joining us. Some of our oldest running publications will be dissolved to make room for an exciting new future. And while I thank those publications for years of hard work, unbridled sacrifice, loyalty, and service, we must all give a fond farewell and wish everyone on those publications success in future endeavors. I thank you all for your contributions to the company, and hope we can work together again in the future. Please enjoy the evening; the after party will start soon. I once again thank you all for celebrating Fashion Innovation with us." And with the continued confidence of ten thousand executives, he strode off the stage, leaving us all in awe of what just happened.

Immediately the chatter in the room became deafening. Everyone wondered what magazines were getting the axe, and which ones were safe. As I sat in my seat, still in shock, I understood what had been going on around me. I had been so caught up in working and getting back at Jayshawn, that I hadn't realized the company I have been keeping. It's clear now why Clair had been such a nervous wreck, Indulgence must be one of the magazines considered for dissolvent. Once I took a step back and in fact put thought into the different publications under the Black Enterprise umbrella, there's no need to have three different fashion magazines when they could all be combined into one entity.

The question becomes… Who will be Editor and Chief of this new consolidated magazine? Also, which staff would make the cut onto the new team and which ones will apply for unemployment? At any rate, I now understand why Gavin McClarin could shut Clair down as easily as he did on the plane. Did Clair already have prior knowledge of her magazine being on the chopping block? If so, that explains her erratic behavior the past few days. Come to think of it, it could explain Cassidy's behavior.

I didn't speak much to Hennison on the way back to the hotel. He had been conducting this shady ass takeover with McClarin leading the charge with his wallet in tow. Why was McClarin so interested in the publishing business? He had made his fortune in advertising, as well as a slew of other endeavors; why is Black Enterprise on his radar? These questions and so many more had been reverberating through my mind. I had been so distracted by my thoughts I hadn't realized we arrived at the hotel. In the suite, I couldn't bring myself to look at Hennison. This isn't the man I spent all this time getting to know; this is a different side of him... the side that's a shark.

As he undressed, I packed; we had an early departure in the morning and I didn't want to wait until the last minute to get myself together. In good conscience, I couldn't look at him. I'm upset with him not just because he stabbed his own people in the back, but because I don't know what this setback could do to me. I know it sounded selfish, but I've just started this job and I had been looking forward to moving out on my own; especially since Dee's couch is getting uncomfortable. To get a good night's sleep, I've been crashing at Hennison's house; well, I slept at least some of the time. The point is, I needed this job to work out so I could do what I needed to do; there's no way I will have another Malik situation.

Our lovemaking had been very purposeful. He knew my mind had been in an upset; though nearing the end of my period, my body yearned to be touched by him; so he took his time. I want him, every inch in fact; but the evening's events had both aspects of me in a tug of war. I hate to think it, but it felt as if he had been reassuring me I would be ok. I know that way of thinking is foolish, and no doubt how I ended up at Dominique's apartment in the first place; I want to believe it.

On the plane no one uttered a word, not even a deep sarcastic sigh had been attempted. Whilst the rest of the team headed home, we had to make a detour to the Montréal Music and Arts Festival to make an appearance; and low key, check out McClarin's investment in the event. Hennison is a smart guy, so I'm confident he did his homework on Gavin before allowing him to infiltrate his already established and profitable business; I just wonder how lucrative Gavin's business stands to be. Our stay wouldn't be long, we would tour the grounds for a few hours, probably have lunch with a few of the other well-to-do investors and important organizers and be on the next flight back home. Whereas, Gavin and his assistant Phoenix would be there for the long haul.

Despite the fact that we toured the grounds and everyone seemed to be on their best behavior, I felt an icy chill creep up my spine and had the sensation that eyes had been watching me. Out of the corner of my eye I saw the outline of a figured that looked vaguely familiar, but I didn't want to give myself away by being obvious that I had noticed. Whoever the person is, I wanted to catch them off guard. I walked close to Hennison, so close I had been in perfect timing with his strides. I shifted my weight slightly as to appear to be fatigued after a lengthy flight and not be too noticeable to anyone else in the group. With a quick turn, I got a glimpse of our semi stalker; it stunned me to see it turned out to be Malik, figures he would bribe his way into an event like this to promote his no talent having ass clients'. He didn't seem to notice me at all, he had looked past me; someone else in the group had captured his attention. In my mind I hadn't doubted it was a woman, I just wonder who the next victim would be in his web of lies; following his gaze, my eyes rested on Phoenix. I had been so stunned; I couldn't stop myself from letting out an "OH SHIT!"

The guide stopped what he had been saying and like the rest of the group, they all turned in my direction. I excused myself, but in doing so I alerted Malik to my presence and also to whom I saw him gawk. Trying to out walk my embarrassment, I ducked into the closest refreshment tent and ordered whatever infusion cocktail seemed to contain the most alcohol. Easing behind me, he couldn't resist making himself the center of any available woman's attention.

"Hello Chloe." He whispered softly.

This time it was me that had been caught off guard. Anytime he's ever spoken to me after the breakup had always been callous, sarcastic, or just plain foul; what changed? "Malik," I stated flatly.

"How have you been…" he began to say before I cut him off.

"Look, Malik, cut the niceties. What are you doing here?" I asked accusingly.

"Working, baby, what else would I be doing here? The real question is why are you in the group of high rollers? You come into some money I don't know about?" he said with humor in his voice.

"Malik, what do you want from me?" I asked, exhausted by his presence.

"Chloe, I want nothing from you. Just to say sorry for how things were between us. That's all."

"Oh, that's all." I rebuked mockingly. "What do you really want to know? I saw who you were looking at, are you trying to add another bird to your flock of pigeons?"

With a slight chuckle he countered, "As a matter of fact I am interested in the other girl with your group. What do you know about her?"

I knew it; I knew he was eyeballing Phoenix, that she was next on his merry-go-round of hoes. Just as I was about to unleash my fury upon him, Hennison found us. He had been the gentlemen I wished Malik would've been when we dated. He excused the both of us to rejoin the tour. Malik would have to get the answers he'd been searching for on his own. I loved the look of disbelief in Malik's eyes as Hennison lifted my chin to kiss me and we left him at the bar still wondering who Phoenix had been; we had a plane to catch.

Cassidy

Of all the Fashion Week Events I've attended in my professional life, straight size and plus size; this one by far has been the most turbulent. Clair knew about Hennison's ideas for the magazine the entire time and didn't give me so much as a warning to what she intended to do to derail his plans. What's worse is she didn't include me; she went outside of our business/personal relationship and sought the help of an ageing playboy. Gavin is an impressive man, and to his credit has taken mediocre business and brought them back from the brink of bankruptcy; but Clair should have told me what she's planning so I could be prepared. Not a second after Hennison left the stage did everyone run up to me asking me questions about their positions at Indulgence, and if Clair had a plan. Truth is, I'm not sure my position is secure, how can I assure them that their positions are protected?

Clair had been visibly uneasy the entire trip; I should have known something had been brewing under all her concealer. First that scene on the plane with Phoenix, next she requested a separated hotel room when we usually shared a suite, and the hush-hush conversation I walked in on between her and Gavin, and finally the call I intercepted from her lawyer in New York. I had been so preoccupied with trying to perform my job, worrying about leaving my son with a nanny for a lengthy periods time, and my insecurity regarding Kelly and I and the lack of relationship, that I had no room for any other baggage; perhaps Clair could sense that I hadn't been able to handle anything else or maybe she just as I had been is too busy trying to secure her own slot in the company to think twice about the people who helped to get her into the position she holds. I held and still hold many of Clair's secrets, and I love her like a sister, but I sincerely hope she knows what she's doing. I can't help her if she doesn't trust me enough to tell me what she's planning that requires Gavin's.

I want comfort in the worst way; I looked for Kelly so we would leave together; we only had one night left in this beautiful city. Why not make it a lasting memory? The venue had been buzzing with chatter. Everyone had been speculating of what would happen once we returned home. Spotting Kelly near a backstage exit, I walked briskly in her direction. I could see she was speaking to someone, but I couldn't see who it is until I got closer. Standing in the doorway with a cigarette in her hand is Isabella. From a distance it looked like the two of them were having a heated discussion with Kelly appearing as if she's being scolded; if I hadn't known any better, I would've thought I had been watching Clair during one of our meetings. I got closer, and the two hadn't spotted me on my approach. Through the noise in the background, I could hear Isabella saying...

"I can't allow Hennison to dissolve Rouge! Indulgence is taking up valuable space in the company and let's face it, Clair's audience of overweight house moms cannot compare with the elegance of Rouge and our viewership. He has to be still considering keeping them if he didn't invite me to fly here with them. What hold does Clair have over him? Why is he allowing the charade to continue? Perhaps it's that chubby girl I have seen him consorting with that works there. She's not even important on the job; she's just as disposable as Clair, so that couldn't be it." She questioned.

"Isabella, what do you want me to do? There isn't much time before someone comes back here and sees us; I have to get back!" Kelly whispered with urgency.

"Push the assistant," Isabella ordered. "She has to know more than she's letting on. Clair wouldn't know her right from her left foot without Cassidy. What have you been doing all this time? I sent you to Indulgence for recon! Gather the information so I can bury them once and for all! You know how disappointed I get when someone doesn't do what I ask Kelly. Do whatever you have to do! Fuck whoever needs to be fucked in order to get me what's needed. I promise you if you help me get Clair out, the Creative Director Position will be yours." She explained sternly.

I turned away, maneuvering myself through the crowd of people hastily before Kelly could see me. I don't know if I'm angry for being used or heartbroken because I thought we could really have something between us. I couldn't stomach being around these phony ass people any longer. Without so much as a glance in any direction, I headed to the door; I'm fucking done! Clair is hiding information from me, I could be redundant in the coming months; how will I take care of my son? And the icing on the cake, Kelly is a fucking liar; what else could go wrong tonight?

I didn't have anywhere else to go besides the hotel. I had too much adrenaline in my system to sleep, and everyone is still partying and gossiping at the venue, so I had the hotel bar all to myself; let the pity party commence! How could I have been so stupid as to think I interested Kelly to start a relationship with me? The way she flirted with me was so aggressively blatant, I should have known she had an agenda. I haven't had good sex since Shane and I broke up, so maybe Kelly caught me at a vulnerable moment and I didn't know I had, and she pounced on it; I gave her a way in. However, by the sound of Isabella and Kelly's exchange, they had learned nothing that could help Isabella sway Hennison's mind into getting rid of Indulgence permanently. Sipping my drink, as one thought drifted into another, I didn't notice that someone slipped into the seat next to me.

"Has it been that rough?" the voice asked.

Looking in the direction it came from, I replied, "You have no clue."

"Want to talk about it?" she questioned.

"No. I can't deal with it right now. Thanks. No offence." I blurted quickly.

"None taken, by the way my name is Akeelah." She offered.

"Hi Akeelah, I'm Cassidy." I returned with indifference.

"I know who you are; I've seen you at some shows. I design with Justine Wong." Akeelah explained.

"So, what are you here to probe me for information? Let me make this easy for you, I don't know what happening with Black Enterprise, I don't know what Clair is planning! Is there anything I forgot to answer?" I immediately went on the attack.

"Wow, I can see that I disturbed you. I didn't mean to bother you or anything, I just wanted to meet you and I saw my opportunity; that's all. I'll leave you alone." She countered as she retreated.

"Akeelah wait! I'm sorry it's been a very weird night. I shouldn't have yelled at you or assumed anything. It's just that I got some bad news not too long ago and I'm trying to deal with it. That's no excuse, but I... It wasn't meant towards you." I offered.

"I'm sorry I caught you at a bad time. I just wanted to talk with you and tomorrow everyone is flying out and I'm headed back to Cali..." she explained.

"No, this is all me, not you. Please sit back down; the next round is on me." I offered with an awkward smile.

She cautiously sat at the stool next to me and quickly ordered another drink, possibly to soften the next blow if the need arose again. I laughed gently as to make her aware that I put the bitch back in the cage. We sat silent for a while; I didn't know how to begin a conversation with her. Our first interlude had been a mini squabble I had caused that; what sort of impression did I give her? Sensing that I didn't want to talk, but I also didn't want to be alone, she told me how she and her sister went from Glendale California to the runways of London. Her sister Akira (whom already is on the return trip home) and she had started a small designs studio out of their parents' garage. They had local success with the aid of fashion shows out of recreation halls, and mall venues; with a steady income from online sales. However, they only achieved mainstream success when they partnered with Justine Wong for Wong Style Designs. Justine signed the duo as head designers and the sisters negotiated to retain a large portion of their design portfolio within their contract as to not have Justine use them, toss them aside and take all the credit for their work.

Akeelah seems like the free spirit of the duo. She's the go with the flow and letting her imagination drift into the weirdest recesses of the mind type. Once she became comfortable talking, there's no stopping her. Her conversation surged with ease from one subject to another without pause. She's wildly expressive when she speaks, as if she has to use every part of her body to weave her stories and describe each moment with passion; her energy is relentless. I must have gotten caught up in her story, when I realized that I had been following every shoulder roll, every flick of her wrist, and position her fingers rested in as she continued.

"Look at me talking your ear off! I'm so sorry when I start talking and I get caught up in the moment; watch out!" she laughed.

"No, I enjoyed watching you talk; since you didn't let me get a word in. It was exhilarating." I replied with a slight chuckle.

"Well, I aim to please in all things I do. It's been a long day, and a longer night. So, ugh…" she started to say as I interrupted.

"Yeah, it's late, I don't want to hold you up. You probably have a lot of packing to do, so it's ok if you have to go." I offered.

"Um, Yeah, I am a little tired. Would you like to take this to my room? I have it to myself since Akira is gone; we won't disturb anyone." She suggested.

Taken aback by her suggestive offer, I didn't know what to do. The last woman who flirted with me did so under the pretense of getting information on how to bring down my friend and boss. Is this girl serious? She can't be proposing what I think she is; maybe she's lonely since her sister's gone. Not wanting to be alone myself, I agreed to go with her to her room. Walking to her room, I could barely feel my legs; it's incredible that you don't realize how much alcohol has affected you until you stand. Unlocking the door, she led the way into the darkened room by interlocking our hands. Again, I thought she did this because she'd noticed that I'm not too steady on my own. Switching on the lamp on a nearby credenza caught me off guard and shone brightly in my eyes. Dimming the light quickly, she turned to cradle my face in her palms and wiped away the tears caused by the light. Her hands are uncharacteristically soft for a designer; usually their hands are rough, but not hers. As her thumbs brushed my cheeks, my eyes fluttered rapidly, producing more tears. Sweeping from my eyes to my cheeks again, and finally resting beneath my chin, she gently drew me to her lips. That question has been answered! I haven't been misinterpreting her intentions at all.

As far as lesbianism goes, I don't like labels. I don't consider myself Butch or Ultra Femme; I rest comfortably in between (no pun intended.). As far as what type of woman I prefer, I'm open. In the past I've dated Femmes, but some are frequently high maintenance and assertive; there's only one boss in my relationship... me. I'm a fantastic partner, but I need someone who can balance out my personality; not make it worse. Shane was the only women I dated that had been an Alpha, believe me the right one can love you, leave you, and have you thanking them for the ride. I've sampled a few tourists, but those chicks are one nighter's; a woman exploring being with another woman for the first, and possibly only time. Akeelah... she's different, she'd be my first free spirit lover; at least that's how I will remember her.

For her to be more petite than I, I hadn't expected her to be so aggressive. She dominated our interlude as she took her time with me. I know this is our first time together, but she handled me as if this had been my first time with a woman; being gently and reassuring; I just followed her lead. Where she touched me, I touched her in rotating, fluid motions. Occasionally her long twists would come between us, it didn't hinder us one bit; it smells like Shea Butter, and her skin feels irresistible as it brushes against me.

Her skin is so smooth that it felt like the most delicate silk in my hands. While she straddled me I roamed her body, first with my eyes, then with my hand. The more adventurous my fingers became, the deeper her moans. She has breasts sculpted by Gods the way they perfectly fit her small frame, her nipples had gotten so erect that the slightest brush of my tongue nearly sent her into orgasm; neither Kelly nor Shane had ever been this slick.

Our danced lasted late into the early morning hours. I woke up with a radiating a sense of pleasure when I realized I had to leave. Glancing over my shoulder to check if she's still sleeping, I tried to gently slide out of bed and into my clothes.

As I slid on my shoes I heard a voice say, "So, you're not going to ask me for my number before you leave?" She asked accusingly.

"Oh, I didn't want to wake you." I tried to offer as an excuse. "I was thinking about leaving you mine." I continued to lie.

"Yeah, sure you were. I get it, you're the hit it and quit it type. Hey, if that's what you want, it's cool with me. But, I'm looking forward to seeing you again." She expressed while she began to re-twist her hair that had loosened most likely from our tryst.

"Would you?" I asked as I sat on the bed next to her.

"Yes, I would." She breathed slowly and intentionally as she leaned in to kiss me.

Grabbing my phone from my hands, she took a selfie and began to rapidly write something into my phone and handing it back to me. She entered her phone number, address, and email into my contacts and saved the selfie; no doubt to remind me of our night together whenever she called, or whenever I became lonely for her. Planting a deep kiss on me before I left, I made sure I gave her my information to save as well; it had been a questionable start, but I'm glad it started. I don't know if I'd ever see Akeelah again, but I would always have this memory of her and I would hold it close whenever life became too much to handle.

Stepping off of the plane, my first thought is seeing my son, scooping him up in my arms, and kissing him until I lost my breath. Leaving my bags at the door to my apartment, I crept in slowly as to not alert the household to my presence. The nanny, probably sensing that someone had arrived in the space, entered the living room from the kitchen. Startling her by my sudden appearance, she regained her composure and pointed me toward Cairo's room. Finding him on the far side of his bedroom near the window, he had been on the floor playing with all the toys he owned; in my absence, the bedroom floor had become a semi-permanent place for his playthings to live.

"Hey Ya, Kiddo!" I yelled as I crashed through his wall of play to give him a squeeze.

"MOMMY," He shrieked as he returned the squeeze I had given him. "Did you have fun at work?"

"Oh, yeah, I had loads of fun!" I replied falsely, "The best part of my trip is coming home to see you! Did you behave for Nanny Margaret?"

"Yeah mom, I even ate the round cabbages she made in a soup." He informed with a disgusted look on his face.

Laughing at his description, "You mean Brussels Sprouts? Yeah, I wouldn't eat that in a soup either. But Nanny Margaret is a Vegan and you are lacking in eat your veggies, so a little soup won't kill you; and you have to see Dr. Abioye soon."

"Ok mommy." He agreed.

Leaving him to play, I retreated to my bedroom to recount recent events. That cunning bitch Kelly, how could she infiltrate Indulgence! Had she been trying to recruit me to turn on Clair, or did she just want to pump me for Intel to take to that human walking stick

Isabella? I know one thing for sure; I'm weary of the ménage of sex, lies, and secrets disguised as stylishness that seem to follow everyone who works for Black Enterprise... no, this industry. Maybe I should accept the offer Nevelynn proposed?

Falling into the loving embrace of my bed, I let the doubts and the worries I've been holding onto since London leave the confines of my mind. I don't know the future of Indulgence, Clair, nor the possibility of seeing Akeelah again. I know that I have to look out for my son and I, and I have to preserve whatever is left of my sanity even if it means leaving Indulgence, which is at this point may very well be a sinking ship; at any rate, I don't know how long Nevelynn's offer will last.

I have a few days to unwind, so I spent that time with my son. I can't put words to how I'm feeling, but I know that I need to spend as much time with him as possible; maybe it's because the next few weeks will be a nonstop parade of fools (self-included) that will attempt to secure their position by outperforming someone else; that offer is looking better and better.

Cairo and I finishing up a game of hide and seek with him finding an excellent hiding place that has me running from one end of my apartment to the other. My phone buzzes, glancing at the screen briefly as I looked under my bed for Cairo. A Blasian (Black/Asian) beauty appeared revealing the caller. I had been so stunned to hear from her I temporarily forgot to slide my finger across the screen to answer the call.

"Hi!" I said abruptly.

"Well, hello there gorgeous. What are you up to?" she cooed.

"Oh, not much, just looking for a very handsome man under my bed." I cryptically replied.

"You're looking for a what?" she shouted.

Laughing uncontrollably at her outburst "My son; I'm playing hide and seek with my son, and I have to admit he's winning."

"Oh," She expressed in relief. "I didn't know you had a son. Um, try the bottom kitchen cabinets, my niece likes to hide there when we play." She suggested.

I hadn't even thought of that. Slowly creeping from one cabinet to the other, I hear soft laughing. Quickly opening a random door I found Cairo laughing and covered in cookie crumbs, I guess he got hungry waiting for me to find him, so instead he found the cookies Nanny Margaret had been hiding. Sending him to clean up, I returned to call.

"That was a good tip." I admired.

Akeelah responds with "You know if you and I had been playing hide and seek it would be with a twist, and could you guess where you would find me?"

"I bet I could guess." I flirted.

"So, when can I see you? I can't stop thinking about you." She questioned.

"I don't know there's a lot going on here and I have my son..." I began to say.

"It's ok, whenever you get some time to get away, and I love kids, bring him with you; he won't be lonely I have a niece remember?" She offered.

"I might take you up on that offer. But for now, how about we get to know each other first before we plan trips?" I surmised.

We spent all that day, and most of the evening, on the phone. Our conversation flowed like we had been friends for years, Kelly and I had never had talks that lasted this long. Ending our exchange close to midnight, I hung up the phone and grinned like a love-struck teenager.

I smiled an authentic smile as I arrived at work the next day. I didn't even care that people saw me without the company of my alter ego, I'm just so happy to connect with someone that I want to revel in the feeling for as long as I can. Most of the staff is still enjoying a day of rest, I wish I could join them but we have a magazine to save and an Icon Edition to put out, so we don't have the luxury of wasting time.

I have a half hour before I have to meet with Isabella's assistant Erica, and Hennison's assistant Margo more affectionately known as Ms. Margo or Hennison's "Gate keeper," and assistants from other publications. In addition to planning Spellbound: Indulgence's Anniversary Extravaganza, we also have to coordinate our annual office retreat. The retreat is needed now more than ever, especially since Hennison dropping that bomb at London's Fashion Week erupted in mass hysteria. The upcoming weeks will be a flurry of appearances, meetings, deadlines, and pink slips; the crazy train has officially left the station and unfortunately I'm tied to the tracks.

Tons of rumors have been circulating not only on other various forms of media outlets, but around the organization as well. Ms. Margo would only discuss the retreat with Erica and I, when pushed about Hennison's plans she shut us down like an old schoolmarm; swiftly and with strict enforcement of not needling in a business that isn't ours. Though, I can't ignore the presence of new faces and some old ones disappearing around the building.

Jada McKenna-Hanila has been taking quite a few meetings with Hennison and the other Editors and Chiefs of Black Enterprise Periodicals the last few days; not even Clair would discuss with me what goes on in those meetings, I'm sure Hennison enforced an NDA or Non-Disclosure Agreement to be signed to prevent all information from leaving his office. I'm not sure the role Jada is playing in all of this, I had been told by Ms Margo to schedule private meetings with Clair and Jada on specified days. Another face that isn't native to the

Black Building though widely recognized is "Spin Doctor" himself, Sidney Graham Crisis Manager and Owner of P.I.P.E.S. Prepare Identify Problems Eliminate and Secure. This guy has successfully bulldozed every scandal from pregnant mistresses of high-ranking officials, to Ponzi scheme tycoons; he's the real deal. Why would Hennison bring him in for something as low browed as eliminating departments? That's a chilling, and questionable move on Hennison's part. What could he be trying to cover up?

My mind is spitting rapid-fire questions as to what's going on right under my nose that I can't seem to see with my eyes, I ponder as I walk into Sloan. Both apologizing to each other, I watch as she makes her way to the elevator as I had been exiting onto the dining floor. I stood for a second and watched the dial on it when it stopped on Hennison's floor. My breathing picked up quickly as my heart pounded so hard I felt the blood rush into my veins, and my hands to twitch uncontrollably; I don't want to show signs of anxiety in the middle of the cafeteria where I'm on exhibition for all to see, but I'm having an internal panic attack from not knowing what the hell is going on!

By the end of the day, I'm drained from every part of my body to where even my toenails cry out for relief. Realizing that I'm breaking down from the immense pressure of my known life to be uprooted and changed without so much as a warning, I send a text to Chloe and give the reins of the Icon Edition Issue of the magazine to her. In the middle of relieving myself of the responsibility, I also inform her she would have to attend the meeting with Janeicia the Marketing Director and Hazel the Art Director.

I would normally ask her to team up with Kelly, but to be honest I know Chloe has been doing more than most of the work when assignments are passed out; and she does a damn good job of them on her own. I let Kelly get away with not pulling her weight because I wanted to explore us and I couldn't do that if she's being weighed down by a heavy workload, so I turned a blind eye. I was selfish and undoubtedly compliant in whatever scheme Kelly had been brewing; though willfully unaware of the extent.

I haven't talked to Kelly since; she tried calling and texting, but I've been ignoring her calls. Today Jillian from Human Resources informed me that Kellendra Bowden has resigned from her duties at Indulgence Magazine and has joined the ranks of Rouge Magazine. The ship has officially sunk, and now I had to pull out the life raft for my son and I.

First thing in the morning I'm calling and accepting Nevelynn's offer. I have to secure my son; I don't know or care what Clair's plans are at this point. She would usually confide in me, but not now; NDA or no NDA, our roots run deep. She should be able to trust me with her secrets, as she has always done in the past; at the very least I never and would not even think to use those secrets against her as Sloan has done repeatedly throughout the years. I've also made other provisions for Cairo after he was born to ensure my baby has the best life possible; I know his dad would at least want that.

I have so many fears I never thought I would have before Cairo came into my life. I had been a curvy girl with little world experience until I entered the fashion world and met Clair and Sloan. They schooled me in the ways of the world, Clair more so than Sloan had been my mentor and protector. My youth had been a magnet for the lowest of scum to try to take advantage of my naivety; Clair wasn't having it! I love her and will always love and support her; but I have a young black son to rise all alone, with all the worries that come with him growing up in a world where some people don't understand why his life matters. If I had a choice, I would do it all over again; I'm a proud mother. I hate the circumstances for which he had been given to me; and also despise being unsure of what has arisen as of late. Through it all, he's my priority.

I sent separate text messages to Clair and Chloe notifying them that I'm taking a few days off of work because I have a virus. Following up with Nevelynn and ensuring that all my terms and conditions have been met, I negotiated a start date that allowed me sometime to transition.

On the day of the Spellbound Masquerade and Anniversary ball, I dressed with intention and purpose. I wanted my last event with Indulgence to be memorable. The other coordinators and I outdid ourselves. If this is to be the last Anniversary Indulgence would have it would be one for the history books. No expense is spared, and attendance is mandatory. Clair insisted we present a united front in case Hennison, the king of drama, drops another unexpected announcement. Clair is jittery than her normal caffeine overload; she's worried.

I reached out to Akeelah to be my date, but she and her sister and been in the middle of a creative firestorm. So, once again, I have to fly solo. I think I've outdone myself, admiring my handiwork; I strolled to the bar and ordered one of the signature drinks of the evening when an exquisitely dressed man stood at my side and ordered the same drink. It could be the drink I'm consuming on an empty stomach, or the near possibility that Indulgence will be dismantled and replaced, or the longing I felt to relieve pinned up frustration; but he smelled as good as he looked. I couldn't help wanting to revisit my old flame. I wondered if he had continued to be as good at navigating my curves as I remembered.

The Master Card Madam herself has yet to make her reappearance since London Fashion Week concluded; and I'm grateful for it. Spending time away from her has given me a chance to re-evaluate our relationship. I held on to the idea of Tarin and I being together again like a dope fiend leans. I convinced myself that if we had another chance, we could make it work… I could make it work. Being in love, or so I thought, with a woman like her is dangerous. A more susceptible man would let her behave however she wanted and feed her ego. Maybe once upon a time I had been that man. The initial breakup has made me a smarter man with my heart, but with her returning to reclaim her old position, it has been easy for me to slip back into old habits when dealing with her. Tarin being gone gave me a temporary reprieve, and by a stroke of fate (or self-sabotage) I allowed myself one night of behaving like Hennison and Malik.

I watched her freshly sewn in tresses sway around her body as she bounced on top of me and wondered how it had been able to still maintain its body wave style. She was a good lover and always has been; if I hadn't had fallen so hard for Tarin, she would have been my perfect match. I hadn't intended for the night to end the way it has, with Yanara's orgasm so intense that her body convulsed as if she had been experiencing an epileptic shock; I haven't lost my touch.

We have known each other for years; she had been one of the first people to school me in the industry grind. Yanara Ford and I ran with the same crowd of hungry kids who wanted to party and make dough. You know how it is, people would go to clubs or bars with a group of friends and see the same faces no matter what end of the city or abandoned building an event was being held. She wanted to be a part of the party scene, make music, date ball players, and get money; she practically had a sign across her chest that read 'insert fame here'.

She interned for a record company with dreams of one day becoming their A&R person, so she regularly went out clubbing when the rest of us worked to pay for our instant noodles. She presented herself as the 'good-time girl' just so the men that were trying to cut her throat wouldn't be threatened by her ambition, but I saw through her façade and every now and again would get a glimpse of the wolf that would peak out behind her eyes. As we relaxed from our interlude, I remembered that I had met Malik through her. He was her connection to a potential artist she could bring to her boss; it's crazy how meeting her created a lane for that asshole to make his way into my business, but that meeting also led me to Chloe… it's just all kinds of fucked up.

The night started with us discussing a listening party for her newly acquired R&B group Legacy. The group had been with another manager who had no intention of developing their sound or dropping a single. Being the wolf she is, she saw her opportunity and took it. Between her and Julian Cole entertainment lawyer of REPRESENT Attorneys at Law, they negotiated a deal that let the group out of their contract for nearly nothing; seems like whoever they were signed with before didn't put up a fight.

I watched while she pulled up her panties, snapped the hooks of her bra. She tossed her tousled hair back and forth to make it presentable and fully dressed. She and Julian formed Boss Babe Productions and Legacy will be their first girl group, their listening party had to be over the top and fortunately for Yanara we have some history so I'd pull a few extra strings for her. I felt a twinge of guilt being with her when I'm still in a relationship with Tarin, but it quickly left my mind when I remembered how easy it was for her to fuck Hennison in Miami; maybe this sense of euphoria is what she felt.

Straightening up my office after she left, I let out a deep breath, and slouched down in my chair. All I've been doing is grinding, I'm feeling the burnt out that everyone talks about when their careers took off; but it's happening at the wrong time. When I booked my clients, I had no idea that I would feel this way. For the first time I considered canceling a few events, but then I recognized I had an assistant I could rely on to handle the tasks associated with making sure everything comes together.

Quickly I began texting Fallon to inform him I would take a few days off to recharge between events and I'm leaving the Boss Babe Listening Party in his hands. Immediately he called me with a slight panic in his voice, which is rightfully so. I had basically dumped an entire event on him more or less last minute. I had to make this work, so I reminded him he is capable of doing this alone, and that I trusted him to make the best decisions for whatever catastrophe would occur in my absence. It's a small event and I had ironed most of the details out. All he had to do is make sure it came together and worked cohesively. After reassuring both Fallon and Yanara that the event would be one worthy of both my company and client, I reached out to the fellas to see who would be down for a quick trip out of town for a week or so.

Griff replied immediately! Taking a break between women and pyramid schemes, he had enough money to book his flight. Next on the list is Dane, Zuri, Saddiq, and Kelvin. By the time the text thread ended, we had all begun booking the flights and hotel room; it's about to be lit! I needed a weekend with my boys. Have these women in my life have been draining me to where I'm willing to lose money? Hell, No! I don't even know how that notion even crossed my mind in the first place. Before I pull a disappearing act, I have to see "The Guru" of expert advice, my father Emmanuel.

Only a mere few hours before departure to South Beach, I strode into my family's restaurant to seek some last minutes advice. I knew he would be here; he's always here, still carrying out the same pattern I remember from my youth. My mother and father had always had an extreme work ethic. If power couples had been a term the old heads used back when they got married it would be them. They came with a plan that gets side tracked like everyone else's once children become part of the equation, but they stayed focused on their goal; even if it took them years to accomplish it. My parents have always put family first and ground their bodies down to the bone to make sure everyone prospered. One by one they helped to bring family members to the United States for more opportunity; and to their credit, each one of them helped to elevate the family as much as they could. As a family we've all had our fair share of adversity, first with being black, the second not being from this country; but we're a powerful people and do what needs to be done to get where we want to go.

Making my way through a sea of customers, my aunties taking orders, cousins serving the food, my mom running the kitchen, and my sister delegating tasks to her cooks, I'm wiped out from playing ghetto hopscotch, and nearly forgot why I had bothered to show up at all during the lunch rush. Away from all the chaos, my dad had found a little nook all his own. He wore his age well, and has always been the most reasonable man I've ever known; if anyone could give me any advice, it would be him.

"Hey boy, Why are you standing other there blocking the door? Come wash your hand and start cutting." He demanded before I could catch my breath.

Obeying him, I washed up quickly and grabbed an apron. Leaning over to kiss him lightly on the cheek, I greeted him "Hi dad."

I began using the cutting rhythm he had taught me when I was a teenager. It had been as natural as breathing, so much so that the simple rhythm comforted me. I knew he had been waiting for me to say something; it isn't often I stop by unexpectedly, and even more unusual that I hadn't been at work; he knew something had been on my mind.

"So, are you going to tell me why you here?" he asked with his deep Caribbean English as he went about his task.

With bated breath I slinked out, "I confused dad. I feel like I don't know what I'm doing anymore." I confessed.

"Is it your business, son? Do you need some money?" he probed worriedly.

"No dad. It isn't money…" I trailed off. "Have you ever been torn between two women?" I blurted.

I had never seen his eyes get so wide. Immediately putting down the knife, he briskly walked to the edge of the room, and looked around to see if my mother had been anywhere in earshot. Returning to his former stance, I could tell he had been.

"Jayshawn, tell me what's happening son." He spoke as calmly as he could without alerting anyone else to our conversation.

"Well, I met this woman. Not really met her, we've known each other for a long time and I had only seen her as a friend; that is until I didn't. We had a short-lived but very intimate relationship. Long story short, I let her… No, I pushed her away because Tarin as you know had come back into my life. When she did, my first thought was maybe we can make it work this time. But, I didn't stop to consider where that left Chloe and I. I didn't consider her feelings at all or if she had developed feeling outside or our casual relationship. I mean, I thought about pursuing things further but didn't really make a move. After I ended the intimate part of our relationship, I thought we would pick up our friendship where if had left off, but she stopped seeing me and taking my calls; ghosted me. She Worked for Hennison's company and he knew that we had… Something, but I didn't even pause to think she would develop a relationship with him, who had also been the reason for Tarin and I breaking up. I should've known he would make a play for her once she found out I had been interested…" I slipped into a rage just as my father interrupted.

"So, you think that guy purposely set out to sleep with Tarin? No, son. She allowed him to do it. If a woman isn't interested in a man that way, she'll let him know. And as far as the other girl goes, you voluntarily pushed her out of your life, and then expected her to not find a life of her own? Has living the fast life made you selfish? You

155

and the young lady were friends, you say, then you threw her out to the wolf the moment you had a different opportunity. I didn't teach you that son, that's not how you treat someone you call a friend. Now, because Tarin isn't what you thought she would be, you regret how you treated your friend."

"It's a lot more complicated than that dad…" I attempted to clean up, but he interrupted again.

"But nothing, are you so blind as to think another man wouldn't see in her the same beauty that you've seen? How do you know he wasn't pursuing her the entire time, and she chose you? That man had no way of knowing if you knew her or not. Sometimes son, your choice has the power to create something beautiful or cause chaos within yourself and others."

"When I was a young man, I was in love with this girl…" He paused briefly to look up again for my mother. "She was stunning, and all the boys at school wanted her to be their girlfriend. We would all dance and strut around her trying to get her attention. Every day I would walk home from school with my best friend and speak of how I would get the girl to notice me. My friend would laugh at my ignorant schemes and advise me on what I should say to her. This went on for months, me scheming and my friend advising me. One day I got enough nerve to ask her to dance at a village gathering. We danced together, eat delicious food and enjoyed each other's company. We slipped away from the crowd and talked a little." He pauses and gave me a wicked smile, then continued the story. "We kissed, and moments later I saw my friend sneaking away with a boy we also went to school with; and they too began kissing. I didn't know what to think, I didn't even know she had been interested in the boys at school; we were so close I thought she would tell me if she had been. Anger rose from my gut, and before I knew it, I sprinted to where they were and punched the boy in his chin for touching her! She yelled for me to stop hitting him and the girl I was with tried to pull me off of him, but I had been too strong for her; the fury had taken hold of me. When I came back to myself and stopped swinging, I remembered the advice my friend gave me on all those walks home… she would say, if you want her, show her. And I showed her, I grabbed my friend and kissed her with the intensity of a hungry man devouring the most delicious food he had ever tasted. We became even more inseparable, and years later we married and came here." He ended his cautionary tale.

"You see son, they very thing we need has always been by our side the entire time; we were just too blind to see it. I saw what I needed and made her my wife and mother of my hard-headed children. The question now becomes, will you continue to be blind to what or should I say whom you really need?"

Just as I was about to answer, I looked up to see my mother standing in the doorway looking at me strangely. "Jayshawn, boy, what're you doing back here alone? Are you ok?" she asked with concern.

"Yeah, ma, I'm good. I had a few things on my mind and thought I would come here and try to sort them out. You know dad would always have a story for every problem." I remembered out loud.

"Yes, that old man would tell stories." Her voice trailed off, "I miss him. Sometimes I think I hear him back her chopping vegetables like he used to when you kids were young and telling you stories of how we met. Maybe my age is catching up with me." She tried to laugh away.

"No mom, I think I still hear him too. His birthday is the week, are you going back home to visit him?" I asked, already knowing the answer.

"Jayshawn of course, if I didn't the old fool's ghost might haunt me! I love that man, you know the place he's buried is where we had our first kiss…" she said.

"Yes mom, I know…"

Leaving the restaurant, I felt my body relax. All the tension I had been carrying for months went away for the moment. I knew visiting this place would bring me comfort and remembering my father's advice would help. He'd been gone for nearly seven years. After opening our family's restaurant, he began to get sick. He walked into the hospital one night and never walked out; the Pneumonia had taken root and had been too far gone to stop with medicine. But that's not how I choose to remember him, I remember him in his quiet space beyond the kitchen, chopping his vegetables for the stew of the day, and being proud of what he and my mother had accomplished together.

Checking in a few more times with Fallon as the plane landed, I pulled myself away from wanting to call the office again to make sure he had the number to my hotel room in case Yanara had a meltdown and the event became disastrous. I had to take my mind off of work. How could I continue in my greatness if I didn't make time for myself to recover from its stresses?

The room was decent enough; I hadn't planned on spending too much time in it, anyway. Most of the guys should be here already, with the exception of Kelvin. I know my brother had to do some fast talking to get out of the house, Lauren had dude on a serious lock down; who could blame her?

I sent a text for the guys to meet me at the hotel bar for a round of shots before heading out to find out what South Beach offers. The night started great, quick drinks with my friends, grab a little street food on the way to the first destination so that the liquor wouldn't wreck our stomachs; but after that the night had become a blur. Every club we went into we had bottle service, we drank excessively and partied with limitless beautiful women; I can't remember that last time I had this much fun with my bros.

Some of the girls we ran into had a hard time getting into the clubs because the bouncers had been given instructions to only let in a particular Eurocentric skin tone with a Melanin flavored body size, but my boys and I were not about to let that go down! So we scooped them up and told the guy they were with us. We all partied together for the rest of the night. I don't know why colorism is still an issue; all women are beautiful to me, but I can't stand by and watch my Queens be disrespected because of their appearance, because upper management wanting to impress a particular clientele or maintain an impossible image.

As an Event Image Consultant, (Damn, I should put that in my phone before I'm too drunk to remember.) I know the value in people and having the right people to be present at an event. Every encounter with someone has the potential be the one that will lead you to another, then another that may end up opening doors that were once closed. All businesses need word-of-mouth advertising, which is someone or a company that can vow for your company's ability to perform and or move a brand to the next level; however, not to that extreme. Yes, we want people with connections to various Enterprise; that's how we keep all our business thriving. By the same token, we cannot possess a disdain for the people who help us pay the bills when the big clients don't want to take risks on an individual or business who they don't consider to have the right connections as well. It's all about opportunity, sometimes we create it out of nothing; but most of the time it's given to us. We have to pay it forward to keep progressing.

Damn! It's so easy for me to slip back into work mode unintentionally. By the time I woke up all I heard is the sound of Zuri snoring, and the smell of Griffin's feet! I got up (the room spinning) found my room key and left. I took a shower to wash the smell of alcohol coming out of my pores, then crashed again, going back to get another forty winks to sleep off the rest of our good time. The next time I awoke, it was around one in the afternoon. By this time I had been slowly starving myself. I nearly nodded back off to sleep when I heard a loud banging at my door followed by Saddiq yelling for me to get up.

We could only make it across the street from our hotel to a small outdoor eatery that served breakfast all day. Recapping the night, the boys went in on Griff! Homie had been acting thirsty all night, keeping in close proximity to this one girl that had been rolling with us. I think she was into him by the way she was smiling and laughing in his direction, but one never knows; she might've been trying to be nice.

"Griff... Griff... Griff man, old girl last night! Did you propose to her or not? Your boys just to know?" Saddiq questioned as he laughed.

"Man, get out of here! I was just conversing with shorty. She had a little body, I'll give her that; but it was a little too much of it. You know what I'm saying? She's not my type." Griffin attempted to explain his infatuation.

"Oh, man, don't be like that!" Kelvin chuckled. "If you're feeling her there's nothing wrong with that."

"I am not feeling her; she was just nice, that's all." Griff made another attempt to clean up his interest. "I like my women sweet and petite, old girl is cute but not my style of female."

All the while the banter is going on; I chuckled along with the jabs and commentary. For the moment, I forgot all about the drama that awaited me in New York. It wasn't until I chimed with my own playful repartee that my friends turned the tables.

"Man, it's ok if you want to see her again. It doesn't matter how thick she is, if you have chemistry it can't be denied." I advised.

"Look at this fool trying to give someone advice." Zuri took notice. "This guy drops a fine ass thick girl like Chloe to be with a washed up, wannabe trophy wife like Tarin! How're you trying to give him any advice when you don't know who you want to be with from day to day? And you let old boy scoop both women! Seriously dude, do you in doubt of how your lil man performs or something?" he continued to clown me.

"It's way more complicated than choosing one girl verses another..." I wanted to defend my actions. "And as far as Hennison goes, the only way he can sweep a woman off of her feet, is to lay her on her back. Dude has no game whatsoever, just funding. Oh, and

Tarin, she's canceled! I'm putting an end to that as soon as I get back home."

"Look dude, all we're saying is that we've seen you with Tarin and with you with Chloe and there's a tremendous difference in the person you are when you're with each of them." Kelvin elaborated.

"Tarin is a leach man." Griff stated.

"And you would know all about leaches, wouldn't you, Griff?" I said condescendingly. "I thought I left all this shit back in New York. Can we just not talk about any women while we're here? Let's just have a good time and relax." I said in an attempt to take the pressure off of the subject.

"Oh, so you want us to leave it alone?" Zuri questioned.

"Yeah, Zuri, I want y'all to leave the subject of my love life alone." I enforced.

"Oh, so leave it alone?" Griff questioned again.

"Yeah fool! Let it go!" I concluded.

"Ok cool, but what if I told you one of your ladies is here? What would you do?" Saddiq inquired.

"What the fuck are you talking about, man?" I blurted with in frustration.

"Look." Kelvin asserted as I followed his gaze towards the other side of the street, towards our hotel. Who he could be referring to, I wondered as I attempted to steady my gaze to find the subject of his teasing. Is that Chloe?

Dominique

Of all the thoughtless things I've ever done, who would've guessed this would be at the top of my list?

I left the wedding content that I'd settled whatever yearning I had for Chase. I had fully convinced myself that I could do it... I could move on and explore building a friendship with Elgin. Sure, Elgin and I hadn't entertained the idea of dating; and it doesn't take a Master's Degree in the opposite of sex to figure out he's interested in me, I'm just not aware of where he is in his pursuit.

The person's pursuit that I've been susceptible to is Chase. A few weeks after the wedding, he'd began texting me. I had no idea how to react to it at first; I more or less tested the waters by keeping our conversations above board so to speak. Whenever I tried to text a normal conversation, he would steer it to contain some sexual innuendo. I played along for a while, hoping he would eventually get bored; he didn't.

Admittedly, it felt good to have contact with him, even if it wasn't exactly the contact I wanted. I didn't realize what had begun until I had been pussy deep into the situation. It started like any non-relationship, first with texts, then with phone calls. When the calls got boring, he would ask if I could meet him at the most inopportune times. Which under normal circumstances in the courting process would be ok, but the times he would want to meet would be, oh, you've guessed it! Booty call hours or a text to meet up for a few minutes of lunch time loving, or some BS like that.

I indulged his wiles, and would meet up with him in random locations in the city; and for a while it was fun. It was almost like role playing; it created excitement. The feeling of getting caught by a passerby or a museum employee had been thrilling, I engaged in it because in my mind I made myself believe it had been a part of the making up process, and this is what we both needed to bring the fun and spontaneity into our courtship. The only problem is that it really hadn't been a courtship. He had been using my feelings for him as a way to get two things out of me: 1. To get back at me and treat me like the whore he perceived me as, and 2. To have on call sex, and the satisfaction of relying… knowing that I would make myself available to him. What he didn't count on was my patience running out and wising up to what I had allowed to happen.

When I wasn't having spontaneous sex with Chase, and working with Hershel, I spent my spare time with Elgin. Chloe is so incognito these days, I can't tell if she's still living with me or is using my apartment as storage. The more time I spent with Elgin, the more I realized he's more than a handsome face; he has a great ass too! But seriously, he's very considerate and caring to things you wouldn't expect from a high-powered executive. He has to maintain his shark-like persona at work, but when I'm with him he's like a teddy bear. Again, I don't know for sure if this is game on his part; though something in the way he caters to me lets me know it's not.

We do the things friends would do when we're not working; like for instance, he loves to eat; so we go to nearly every street vendor between where we would meet up and where our eventual destination would be and buy food along the way. We'd take it back to his in home art studio and have a picnic on the floor as we decided if we will visit the cart again or if we would pass on it on the next food excursion.

Most of our conversations would be interrupted by him suddenly leaping up from the floor to sketch something quickly. He would never let me see what it was he'd been drawing, I'd just continue to sit, eat, and watch him do it as he would chew large globs of food as his food stuck fingers latched onto the paper; meanwhile, the painting that sat by the window remained covered. If he worked on it at all, it was never when I was with him.

Elgin is quickly becoming the person I want to spend my weekends with when I'm not being held hostage by Hershel, badgered my mother, or wondering where the hell my best friend had been. It's so easy for me to forget about feeling bad about myself when we're together; he even has me considering an alternative career path because of his influence. If I knew where we stood in our friendship I would want for him to be my boyfriend, but hurdling into that arena without us having a conversation about it would be foolish.

In all the time we spent together we've never done more than kiss and groped each other here and there; nothing major, and he's certainly hasn't slid my panties to the side and caress the honey inside this pot; maybe he just isn't interested in me in that way. I'm the daughter of Marcellus Lawrence at the end of the day; it's possible that because of that unavoidable reality, he doesn't want to get too cozy with me. Also, it could be he doesn't want to get too serious being that if the powers that be send him to another city to acquire another business to breakdown and sell he'd have to go no questions asked; he doesn't need romantic entanglements holding him back. Though every once in a while the rebel artist in him peaks out and he mentions wanting to start an art gallery one day; he told me he'd name it Urban Chaos.

As good of a time I have with Elgin, Chase continues to linger in the background waiting to summon me at the most inopportune moments. Again, I didn't notice it at first; it happened slowly. He gradually demanded more and more of my time, and it became more like I had been a plaything only for his amusement.

The first time it happened I had been on an outing with Elgin at an art gallery when I received a text demanding I meet him at his apartment. This was a major leap that I hadn't been expecting from our casual hookups. As much as I wanted to go to him the moment he asked, I couldn't do that to Elgin. We had been spending more and more time together outside of the office, and I'd genuinely liked him; whatever Chase had up his sleeve would have to stay there, I'm not his damn toy!

I'm not sure if I misjudged Elgin, or if he put his best foot forward when I had been with him, either way he grew on me; and the once annoying things he used to do became the things I started to love. For example, Elgin is an undercover artist; he loved to visit galleries and dissecting an artist's work. He would speak of the lines a brush stroke made, the blending of colors and the intricacies of insinuation and deep thought an artist would provoke. I listened at the intensity and passion in his voice, and the sound of it as words I've never heard before flowed pass his lips memorizing me; I loved to watch him as he spoke so passionately about ideas I'd never knew existed.

We'd talk about career paths and why I hadn't been motivated to be more than Hershel's assistant. Elgin didn't understand that I am motivated to make a change; I just don't know what it would be. With all my education, I don't want to follow in my father's footsteps. I want to create my own lane and build my brand; I'm afraid to do so. It's easy for someone like him to casually ask me that he's so good at everything that crosses his path. I on the other hand have no actual working skills to back me up; the last thing I want to do is embarrass my family. Still, it made me wonder what I could be if I got over my fear of failure.

I really need my friend. I want to talk to Chloe about what's been happening, but she's so wrapped up in the glamorous life I feel like I don't know who she is anymore. She stayed home briefly before taking off again to a work-related retreat I didn't have any time to explain the chaos that has ensued. However, she managed to tell me she'd be moving out when she gets back and wants me to help her look for a place close to me. I'm relieved that she still wants to remain nearby. My first thought had been that she would move closer if not into Hennison's home; I'm happy to see that she's learned her lesson from the last time she lived with a man.

I love that she's found a job she's passionate about and a man who adores her, but I feel abandoned. As far as I know, we still live together, though she hasn't been at the apartment in weeks. When she came back from London, her demeanor felt off. She became secretive and withdrew. We used to talk about our bosses and laugh about the asinine tasks they'd have us perform; now I have to schedule time for her to pick up the mail. I know her work is important to her, and for a long time she didn't have a job that fulfilled her or an amazing partner to share it with; now that she has both, it doesn't negate the responsibility of being a good friend. I miss our regular outings together; despite the comings and goings of the men in our lives, she's always been my constant and I hers. It hurts that we've grown apart.

Nothing in life is a guarantee, but when the ice and snow melt, and the winter clothing gets pushed to the back of the closet one thing is certain... The invitations for the Manhattanites Business & Social Networking Event will be the first of many invites that will magically appear in your inbox if you're worthy enough to have been chosen to attend. This is one of the most anticipated events of the new season; it gives business people, companies, and new entrepreneurs a chance to pitch ideas, brag on their fiscal year, or schmooze with the who's who of the top corporate 1%. This very exclusive, elaborate affair is invitation only and requires a generous donation to attend. Most clamor to be the first to reserve a ticket, for if you delay too long you give someone else a chance to have an association with the utmost elusive people who will be in attendance; hesitation is not an option when attendance is based on a first come first served basis.

The firm would only pay for three people to be in attendance, and as a courtesy the event hosts allowed those who participate to bring a companion at no extra cost; how generous of them. The people who are representing the company are high-ranking officials. No low brow associates would be permitted to even see the invitation, as per the host it helps to prevent stowaways; Hershel would not be flashing that cheap "I'm your man" smile dripping with thirst at this party.

Of course my dad and his top partners will be in attendance, spouses aren't usually invited to attend. The company representatives usually say it's too boring for them with all the business chat, really I think they don't alert them as to not have to explain why they rub elbows so closely with the attractive women in the corporate 1%. No longer are women the minority, they are the most sought after, viciously attractive, no nonsense majority of the business world. Which give the men (single or otherwise) a chance to get into their good graces.

The partners of the people invited are usually the most productive business partners in the firm, that way no addition money will be spent and the appropriate people who have the power to propel the company will be in attendance; just because the company has the money to spend doesn't mean it's spent frivolously… in other words they're cheap. I only made the cut because Elgin had asked me to go with him, of which I happily obliged.

Usually for an event of this magnitude, I couldn't wait to get home and tell my girl what's happening. This time I can't. Not only is she not there, she's still at her corporate retreat and as part of the rules she can't use her phone! That's bullshit; I know that senior management will all have access to a phone. What if there is an emergency, how will they be contacted? Most of them are married to their work, so I know they won't be able to sit in isolation, for God knows how long, without communication to the outside world or Wi-Fi; impossible!

If all the world is a stage, then all the principal characters with the acceptation of some riffraff will be a peak performance tonight. We drove for an hour outside of the city to an undisclosed location. Maneuvering up a slopped driveway, the car approached a large, extravagant mansion. As if beautifully coordinated by the drivers, each arrival and departure took 1-2 minutes as to not have the other guests wait too long to exit their vehicles. If you were wondering about the drivers, let me put the speculation to rest; the drivers are the only people who know the location of the event and are instructed to arrive at your location at a time chosen by the host, then drive you to the event (no stops permitted, as per a tracking system that alerts the host if a driver ventures off course), and take you back to the original location in which they've retrieved you; all a part of the price of admission. I'm sure compromises are made if an emergency occurs, or traffic becomes an issue, but only the driver knows that such securities exist.

The partition remained raised as we drove. The windows are darkened, and the ride is so smooth it was like we aren't moving at all. We haven't spoken a word to each other since leaving his loft. In the corner of my eye I saw him ogling at my breasts as they ever so slightly peaked from the rose gold, off the shoulder, bodycon jumpsuit I wore. This event can be a career starter or a career killer, there's no way I'm not going to show up and show out. I knew most of the women attending the event would be dressed in the classic business sexy way; either with a sleek dress or pantsuit. The only element that would make them stand out would be an incredibly beat face the Gods would envy. Most of them would come straight from work or would've taken the day off to pamper themselves, but would still want to be taken seriously by the men in the room; I had to stand out. Yes, I'm attending this event as a companion and I have no extensive experience that all the people attending will have; but I know the importance of positioning and strategizing.

It's likely that at some point Elgin would leave me to my own devices and I would have to hold my own and not appear a ditzy date of an important power player. I had to not only shut it down when it came to the fashion, but in the intellect category as well. I had to be memorable; one never knows when, where, or if an opportunity will present itself. I've been giving a lot of thought to branching out on my own, and I would need to squeeze these people of all the information expensive alcohol would make them utter as the night wore on.

Exiting the car, I saw Elgin's eyes light up as he helped me. The lights near the entrance danced perfectly on my body, highlighting my smooth chocolate complexion against the glistening hue of my outfit; YES, I came to slay! And slay I have.

Like most social gatherings, the usual ambiance had been expected and achieved, but it felt different. Nothing seemed out of place right away. By how the organizers coordinated the event, I got the feeling that more had been lurking under the surface. I tried to shake the feeling of uncertainty and chalked it up to nerves as we floated from one group to another. The usual suspects made an appearance, along with a few new faces. Being the attentive and doting date, I listened to the mindless chatter of the business people as they spoke; and also as they watched and sized up their competition.

Annalisa Trevino COO of Mindscape App Creation is first to signal the group that Titus Rainier and partner Gavin McClarin have entered the party. I have no idea who any of these people are, only that as soon as the words left her mouth I noticed that most of the partygoers had also detected their appearance. Immediately the whispers began. The pair omitted an air of immense affluence, and all the company reps want a piece of the action; I could tell by the glint of anticipation with a side on envy that bubbled up from the shift in their body language and the salivation dripping from their lips.

I overheard Quincy Keegan of Behind The Chronicles online news and top columnist/reporter Sabrina Hadid murmur to each other that the duo had recently gained a publishing and media company, which enticed me to listen on in hopes of my eavesdropping not being detected.

"They're buying up everything." Keegan spoke softly. "What's their agenda, they have to know that by doing this they will monopolize…" He expressed as Sabrina interrupted.

"That's exactly what they're doing!" Sabrina concluded. "If they buy small pieces of the most profitable Enterprise not only do they create a conglomerate that forces other business to outsource their services exclusively to their business, but they also place themselves in a power position to crush any or all opposition that may threaten the machine." She spoke proudly.

"Go talk to McClarin," Keegan suggested. "He loves beautiful women; strike up a conversation with him, do all the usual. Tell him you admire his work, he's an inspiration, how handsome he is… etc.

lay it on thick, then try to pull him in for an interview." He added sternly. "Get the exclusive, I want BTC to be first to drop the story! The traffic to the site will be astronomical. We could very well break the Internet once the story goes viral!"

"What makes you think he'll fall for a little flattery, Quincy? A man like that, just look at the woman; who isn't his wife that's draped on his arm (referring to a familiar-looking woman he's with). He has to have a harem of women at his disposal; my flattery won't make it past his ego to even suggest an interview." Sabrina retorted.

"Because he likes powerful women," Keegan explained. "He collects them like trophies, first his wife Megan Bellacena who owned Savage Mind Advertising. He met her when she was at the top of her game; her company was one of the first he acquired. He's dated a slew of models; even some women in his room have been rumored to have warmed his bed. Hell, even as we speak rumors have been circulating that he has another high-powered woman in his pocket that's he's pillow talking in order to take over her business. He and Titus want to get rid of any competition. Titus works the numbers and Gavin works the ladies," Concluded Keegan.

I got to stepping away from that conversation as briskly as I could before they noticed I had been taking mental notes. Aimlessly strolling from one area to the next, periodically joining one conversation or another, I can understand why spouses didn't attend; it is lackluster at best. In the beginning of the evening the event was very formal, but when the top shelf refreshments made an appearance corresponding with all the invitees' final arrivals, the party turned up in a major way.

In the span of only thirty to forty-five minutes, it went from a IT business convention to Mardi gras in the middle of Las Vegas with no transition period. Suddenly, the uptight 1% got loose! I mean there's alcohol all over the place, men and women dancing horribly to decent music, and an obscene about of money being tossed on tables with handshakes accepting whatever deals were offered; this upscale networking event had quickly turned into an Eyes Wide Shut situation.

Stumbling through the sea of dancing bodies, my eyes landed on my father chatting it up with Titus Rainier; a minor part of me wondered if my dad is preparing to make a deal with the devil. The beginning of the night had been a total façade. Deciding that this isn't my scene, I frantically searched for Elgin. On my search, I'm surprised to see that there are people are for the most part continue to network and socialize; but as soon as I turn the corner, fuckery greets me. Noticing a small group of women entering and exiting a corner sitting area, I strode in that direction hoping to find Elgin; and find him I did.

In the small area they line the walls with a symmetrical sectional sofa and tables, a few high boy tables, and a small bar/bartender; the host made sure there's a party in every room, complete with optional of nose candy. On first glance, I didn't see him. Then someone caught my eye as I turned to leave; Gavin McClarin's head quickly popped up. Across from him sat Sabrina Hadid, on one side of him is Elgin and on the other is the woman. After taking his hit of booger sugar passed to him, he shook his head as his nose absorbed the shock of the drug. When he opened his eyes and stabilized for a second, he realized I had seen him. I realized I had seen enough!

Pushing my way through the sea of hoes, I dashed to the exit. In the first few seconds of my rage Elgin attempted to follow me, but stumbles because the potent drug worked so fast he'd lost some balance. Once outside, I scrambled into the first car I saw and shouted at the driver the name of my escort. After a momentary pause, the car roared to life and began its decent down the long driveway.

I am livid! Is that what goes on when dear old dad is handling business, or is this just something that happens occasionally? Does my mother know and is that the reason she never attends these parties? And Elgin! I wouldn't have taken him for a cokehead; usually my type is emotionally unavailable men, not drug addicts! The driver made quick work of dropping me off at Elgin's. Projecting from the car, I stormed off in whatever direction my feet took me in to hail a cab.

My phone rang relentlessly. The first few hundred times it had been Elgin, the next few had been my father, the last call that I had actually answered is from Chase; he sure had great timing. After securing a late night interlude, I dialed Chloe, hoping she would answer. As I held the phone to my ear and listened to the ring over and over; I felt my head spin and my breathing become labored and heavy, imploring her subconsciously to answer the damn phone! The last long ring is an indicator that the call is being directed to voicemail; my heart sank, and a chill washed over me.

Directing the cab driver to Chase's, I toiled between calling my mother to let her know about my fathers "business", calling Chloe again, or just having angry sex with Chase; I chose the latter. The walk down the hall to Chase's door seemed longer than usual. Did I want to have sex with this guy or was he a means of getting out my frustration? I hesitated before knocking on his door; I felt an icy surge of embarrassment when considering what I'm doing. If Elgin hadn't had taken me to that glorified "lock door" party masquerading and an upscale social gathering, would it be him I'd conclude the evening?

I went in fast, furious, and with intent to take out my mixed emotion on Chase; and for the first few minutes, I saw that he'd been enjoying it. He didn't care or ask why I had been dresses to impress, why I'd been angry and pounced on him with little warning, all her knew is that he wouldn't have to do much coxing to get me out of my panties, and his dick moving vigorously inside my vagina. After all is said and done, the sex did nothing for me; I still felt as I did when I arrived. I made an attempt at a casual conversation as I redressed; he was unmoved. When I applied a little more pressure on him to clarify the status of our flings, he remained unmoved.

"You could at least call me a cab and walk me to the door!" I spat at him sarcastically.

"You know where the door is," he retorted. "I didn't call you a cab here, so why would I call you one to leave."

"So this is how it's going to be?" I thought. Absentmindedly, I mumbled my thoughts aloud. Before I could catch my words from leaving my mouth, he answered.

"How did you think it will be? Goodnight." He uttered dismissively.

No more words needed to be exchanged between us. No more calls, secret rendezvous, or wasted hopes. He'd thought I'd be on a string forever; I knew it's over. This had been it, the thing I needed to let go. Closure is for characters in a movie, or a magnificent book hidden among some of the best works of self-published fiction. This isn't closure; this is self-punishment for what I've done to him. I knew he would react this way. What man wouldn't as an act of revenge? I foolishly thought having these trysts with him, fully aware that our situationship wouldn't go beyond the physical, is what's needed to right the wrong I did; so I entertained him, not prepared for the cost. I think I have sated my guilt, and the debt on my soul paid.

"Goodbye Chase." I mumbled to myself as the door to his apartment click with finality. My last glimpse of him had been him drinking water in the kitchen when the door closed.

A week had gone by, and no one in upper management had mentioned the party. Everyone went about tasks normally. Nothing and no one had changed except me. I saw their actual faces behind the facade of expensive clothing, million dollar deals, habitual lies, and pseudo-intellectual language; and I realize it's time to move on.

We avoided each other, Elgin and I. I didn't know what to say, and I assume he didn't know how to explain, so we just didn't speak; I miss him though. We would glance at each other from time to time, but nothing more. I felt the sting of loss whenever our eyes locked. In those moments, I instantly went back to how we were; in my mind I would see flashes of the fun times. When I realized we aren't in that space anymore I recoiled inside myself; I think I've lost another friend.

After another week of office eye hockey, the awkwardness had worn off; as much as it could, anyway. Chloe had been home from her retreat and had become more solemn and withdrawn. We picked up from where we left off. But she refused to tell me about what had been going on with her, and frankly she'd still been in the dark about the work of art my life had become. I wanted to tell her everything, but if I do, how much of it will she actually hear over the madness she's hiding behind her eyes?

Operation apartment hunt is proceeding as scheduled, with little to no information about what exactly she's looking for and what's in her budget. We went building to building, street to street, hood to gentrified area and nothing had been what she wants. I'm literally exhausted. Not just by the endless searching, but also with the stress of trying to deal with my own shit, and I can't take another step before knowing what the fuck is going on!

We drifted into the amazing building to see a studio apartment that had been listed on an open house website for a newly renovated building. The building has a fresh paint and sanded wood smell from the rehab, and if I didn't already have a place, this would be on my radar. Following the balloon marked signs to the units, we found the show studio set up with mock furniture to give the prospective renter ideas of how to set up the living space. The unit is a decent size; I estimate it at about six to seven hundred square feet with an exposed brick and painted walls, one window in the main room, and another window in an alcove. In addition, it has a small kitchenette, and an even smaller bathroom, and a closet that wouldn't even hold my shoes; the apartment is tiny, but it has so much character and the staging increased the enticement. We looked around the room and peaked into the bathroom; because we both couldn't fit in there together.

"This is it!" I proclaimed with undoubted certainty. "This would be perfect you, what do you think?"

With a weary look and turned up lips, she squeaked out, "It's ok. I don't know if this is what I'm looking for." Chloe stumbles.

"What do you mean? This place is nice, renovated, a decent size, and if I knew what your budget is, I would say it met that requirement too! What's not to like?" I questioned.

She looks around the apartment from floor to ceiling before answering, "I'm just not feeling it." She concluded flatly.

"Not feeling it, not feeling it? Then what the fuck are you feeling? Because if you asked me, you've been on autopilot for a while now and I'm not sure you're feeling anything! You got me going from pillar to post without so much of a hint to what you're looking for… FUCK! Am I supposed to read your mind?

"Dee, what the fuck is your problem? Why are you spazzing out, is it because I'm not sure about the apartment? Or it is because you're upset I'm moving out? Either way, you don't have to look with me anymore!" she spat at me while waving me off and attempting to walk out.

Blocking her path, "you want to know what my problem is. YOU'RE MY FUCKING PROBLEM! You used to be my friend; we used to be there for each other. Now all you do is run after your job, or a man, and don't care about us anymore. You can't even decide where you want to live, maybe you should send a memo to your Indulgence friends so they can help you decide since you don't need my opinion or even have one of your own." I retaliated.

"Funny, talk about running behind a man. You've been doing that since I met you. And seriously you are just now figuring out that adulthood is more than men, sex, and money bitch so don't get too high and mighty on me!" Chloe declared.

"You know what, you're right. I've been with plenty of men, and that gives me experience that you don't have. So, take some advice; don't settle for the first guy who tells you you look pretty, move in with him, and then let him fuck your sister!" I finished.

When I said that, she hauled off and slapped the shit out of me! I gave her a mean backhand slap in return. We tussled a bit until we both became too tired to keep going. I had a red mark on my face, and she's sporting a bloody lip and smeared makeup; we looked ridiculous.

"Why would you say that?" she asked between sniffles. "Why would you bring up Malik and China? You of all people know how far I've come after that. For you to throw that in my face because you're feeling some kind of way is fucked up." Chloe stated. "How could you?"

"I... I didn't mean to. I was just so mad at you for not being around for me, like I had always been for you, that I wanted to hurt you. I wanted you to feel that pain and understand that I hurt too, and sometimes I need you to be there for me. I've picked up your broken pieces so many times and this time I need you to return the favor; but you left me high and dry." I explained. "I shouldn't have brought it up, I'm sorry."

She gazes at me through glassy eyes, "I've got things going on too, that I can't talk to you about; especially things that concern Indulgence. I'm sorry you felt abandoned, I'm living my wildest dreams, and I didn't stop to consider the people who helped me get there. Don't think I couldn't see that something is bothering you, it's just that it feels good to have all eyes on me, I figured you could handle whatever it is on your own." She expresses.

Before I could add to our heart to heart, voices and footsteps rapidly approach. We stand up and straighten out our disheveled clothes and walk out of the unit briskly before anyone could suspect a disagreement took place. Once outside, I broke. I told her what have been going on while she's been absent. Flashes of shock and awe appear in waves across her face as I fill her in on everything from attending the White Wedding to the Manhattanites party her eyes bulged at the mention of the people named in attendance, and even more so when I mentioned the woman Gavin McClarin was with; she later told me the woman is Jayshawn's girlfriend, Tarin. I even shared with her that since my last encounter with Chase that I hadn't had my period; I'd been late a few weeks before the party even happened, but hadn't noticed until the day after.

My body ached and felt relived at the same time from the hurt I'm feeling by explaining everything and laying it out as if it had been someone else's story; maybe I wished it had. She asked if I went to the doctor or took a home pregnancy test to confirm, when I explained I hadn't she insisted we go to the closest pharmacy to get one. On the way she told me about some of what had transpired in London, and only pieces of what occurred on the retreat. Because of the NDA that everyone had to sign; which explains why her phone had to be confiscated. She couldn't reveal much. But she told me that the news had been like a gut punch to everyone and that because of the severity of what had come out that the information would eventually make it to the blog pipeline and all the shit will hit the fan in due time.

Arriving home, tired from the clusterfuck the day had become, I lugged my body to the bathroom. Peeing on the stick and waiting for the results, my mind drifted to all the events that led me to this situation and the wrong paths I took convincing myself they were the right ones. As I waited, I looked at the ceiling and prayed to God if I got out of this that I would change my behavior. I want to change and I've seen that it's possible; I just need to believe in my ability to do it.

The waiting is the hardest part; this cheap ass test is taking too long. While I wait, I looked up on the FIND search engine to look up the name of the company who staged the building we had come from seeing. I'm curious to see who had such excellent taste for a compact space. In my search, I found that brothers Castor and Pollex Tyndareus of Rare Creations Staging furnished the spaces used for the open house. As I probed further, the alarm sounded on my phone, snapping me back to reality and the problem at hand.

Entering the living room to a waiting Chloe holding a towel with ice in it to her lip, I handed her the stick. She looked at it confused and I sobbed and thrust my head into my hands and stomp my feet angrily on the concrete floor, as I omitted sounds she's never heard come out of me before. Not knowing what to do, I dropped the stick and immediately pulled me in for a hug. I continued to wail uncontrollably; she whispered that we would face it together and that she would never abandon our friendship again. She also included that if I wanted her to stay in the apartment with me, she would.

I couldn't take it anymore, and I let out an unyielding laugh. She looked even more confused; maybe she thought I entered into a psychotic episode, or that my clock is ticking to have children, so in my conflicting feelings I laughed; none of that is it. I'm laughing because God had answered my prayer and gave me one more chance at redemption. She figured out my ruse, pushed me and chuckled as she turned away. Expressing that I had not been with child, we laughed at the thought of the two of us who could barely take care of ourselves attempt to take care of a baby.

Knowing that sometimes home pregnancy tests give a false positive/negative, I made a doctor appointment to confirm the results. The idea of having and raising a baby alone is scary, and I'm glad that now isn't my time to do it; if it ever happens for me, I want it to be real. Genuine love, devotion, and a real relationship that will be one for the romance books.

Chloe decided on the renovated studio with my urging and moved in slowly. As I have before, I helped her bring box after box in to the space. This time it's hers, not mine, not some guy she's dealing with, but her own space. I'm proud of my friend; she's coming into her own; as am I. Of course she has more clothing than furniture. After collapsing on her new bed still in plastic and on bedding still in the plastic carry cases they're purchased in, we air high five each other for a job well done. Now all we need is wine, a hot shower, and a vacation.

My lips missed the feel of kissing her skin. Placing small kisses on her face as she sleeps, I realized that I've never yearned for someone as much as I have with her. Something about the way she carries herself keeps me intrigued.

I didn't think I would see her again after Montréal, but after watching her I couldn't stay away. At first it was purely for the conquest, but when I looked at her... really looked, I knew she had the potential to be more. Ok, I'm still booed up with China and we still have professional dealings, but I can't ignore how I'm feeling. No woman could ever tie me down, or hold my attention long enough for me to see her as more than a quick fuck. It's harsh to say, but let's be real, the only thing that has ever interested me is getting paid; until her.

It took some maneuvering, after the interview I had some downtime before the festivities would begin; sound checks and press junkets would be in the following days, which gave me more time to work on my minor project. Still believing that she's with her rich daddy, I waited until she's alone at the hotel bar before I approached her. I snuck up behind her as quietly as I could and whispered, *"Hello, beautiful."* She turned quickly to see whom the voice belonged to, realizing it had been me her eyes bulged out of her head, and then darted around the room quickly. At the time I did not understand what or whom she had been looking for, but I quickly found out.

"What are you doing here?" Phoenix hurled.

"I'm here for you, doll. Did you think you could get rid of me that easily?" I questioned.

"Yes. No… What?" she stuttered. "You can't be here! You have to leave now!"

"Whoa, I haven't seen you in weeks after you throw me out of your apartment unexpectedly and this is the greeting I get? Did I do something to offend you? If I did, I apologize." I offered, putting my hand to my chest, appearing as sincerely as I could.

"No, it's not that. It's just…" she trailed off. "You just can't be here."

"Ok, then tell me where should I be? Tell me and I'll be there." I responded. "I'm not going to leave your side until you meet me, and if you stand me up, I'll just keep popping up unexpectedly until you'll agree to go out with me."

With a look or horror in her eyes, she agreed to meet with me the next day at noon. Making sure she understood that I wouldn't leave until she promised to meet me, Phoenix agreed relentlessly before I rose to leave. No sooner than I left to exit the bar, the old guy I saw her with waltzed in and immediately took the seat next to her. I watched her talk to him, as her eyes urged me to leave without another word; I left but I'll defiantly remember this, this piece of information might come in handy on a later date.

I couldn't shake the feeling that I knew that cat from somewhere; I never forget a face. Back in my hotel room, I did some digging on the investors for the event. Previously I had only been concerned with the acts and the money, now I have more to inquire about. I searched the event web page until I landed on the information I needed. The guy Phoenix is with is none other than Gavin McClarin. As soon as I typed his name in the search engine, endless information sprang up. This guy has his hands in a little of everything from music and fashion, to information tech and land development; if this is her father, I've certainly hit the mother lode with this one.

We met up as planned; she had been in incognito mode, walking up to the table where I'd been waiting. I threw her some appetizer charm to warm her up to me, catching on quickly as she conjured up some charm of her own; this girl is challenging me, I like it. The other women I've dealt with never presented a challenge; they just fell in line like they had been doing so for years. Phoenix matched me toe to toe, blow for blow. She's sensual and elusive at once and the combination had me floored; yeah, I like this girl.

We spent most of the afternoon together. We strolled along the festival grounds and she opened up a little, and I decided this is a good time to inquire about McClarin; maybe she will give me something I can use, but she dodged me like a hood girl in a fight about to get her ponytail pulled out. Every time I made an attempt at extracting information, she changed the subject; I would have to leave it alone for a while until she became more comfortable with me.

When she probed about why I had come to Montréal, I obliged by telling her the actual reason I had shown up; she looked impressed, as if she had no idea a man like me could be so ambitious. As we walked, I observed that she had been present with me in the moment, but when she became quiet, I noticed her mind would drift elsewhere. Taking note of the silence that had grown between us, I suggested we make plans for dinner before the chaos of the event is in full swing. Noticing the time, she broke into a panic and scrambled to go back to the hotel.

"What a minute Doll, we haven't made dinner plans yet. We've got time." I assured her.

"Dinner… I'm sorry we can't have dinner, maybe when we get back home…but not now." She said sternly.

"Why not, we don't have to go out in public; we can have dinner in my room." I offered with a double agenda.

"I can't. I have to work tonight." She explained.

"Blow it off. How often do you get to come to Montréal? And for us to link up again, come on baby, its fate." I tried to convince.

"Fate." She say's sarcastically. "You have no idea what fate has in store. I have to go. It was nice seeing you again, but I really have to go."

Ok, I can take a hint. I walked her back to the hotel. When we got close enough to see the rotating doors, she asked to walk the rest of the way on her own. Now, what sort of gentleman would I be if I didn't see her safely to the door of the same hotel where we both are staying? Insisting I continue to walk with her. She became increasingly nervous on approach. I don't know what had baby so jittery, but no sooner than I thought it the answer rolled down a darkened window to the town car that waited.

"Phoenix." Gavin uttered smoothly.

"Mr. McClarin." Phoenix responded.

"Where've you been? We have a business that needs your attention." He demanded.

"Just talking." She gave without further explanation.

"Well, if you're done talking, we have business. Please get in, we're running late." He commanded without waiting for a response as he rolled up the window.

This asshole didn't even acknowledge the fact that I had been there or that Phoenix has other things going on besides work. She whispered that she would talk to me later and slowly opened the door to the town car and slipped in. When the door shut, the car immediately pulled off. The only thing I could gather from this encounter is: at least I know he isn't her father; but there is something else going on between them.

I know the signs. Hell, I've even done it myself with many female artists that I manage. But I didn't expect to be the outsider looking in on the exact same situation. I didn't see her again for the rest of the night, and the next few days that passed. After our meet up, I didn't have time to chase any female, anyway; TNT had to prepare for his performance. TNT is performing alongside established and season artists who are used to a crowd of this magnitude like Trigger Warning, Flawless, Voodoo, and The Lyrical Assassin. Most of these artists had the backing of major record companies or are branded under an established artist new label; we're strictly underground for the time being; we have to be able to keep up with the front runners to survive. Hell, even the women had the game sewn up tighter than a virgin on prom night.

While I busied myself with my artists, my mind would drift to Phoenix from time to time; I haven't seen her since she disappeared into that car. I caught a glimpse of Gavin McClarin during a sound check, but no Phoenix in sight; maybe he sent her back to New York; he must be afraid of a little competition. In the hours before the show, they gave us an agenda and producers' assistant personally assigned to us to keep us on schedule for the press junket and performances. I could tell Tee had been reveling in all the attention he had been receiving since we arrived. The women flocked, and the men made offers to do deals with cash incentives; WE MADE IT BABY! I told him if he stuck with me that the money and fame would come pouring in, I'm glad to see that I could hold up my end of the bargain.

TNT had been getting restless in the months leading up to the festival, and I got the distinct feeling that he had been approached a few times by other managers. Even that stupid bitch Makayla had been in his ear about jumping ship for a record company that will promise him the world and then make him sign a shitty contract that equaled to indentured servitude. At least his contract with me would allow him to keep his publishing rights, with me as a co-writer of a few tracks and EP of his albums. When I found out she had set up a dinner between TNT and a one of the suits, I crushed that shit and sent Malaya's ass back to the secretarial pool she came from; nobody will ever fuck up my money flow and not pay the consequences. Now, she had no contact with me, my artists, or any industry connections to make any more moves. Her only way back into the entertainment fold is to give some mean sloppy toppy to another upcoming artist or exec, because with me she's canceled permanently.

The artists I had performing ROCKED THE SHOW! I couldn't be more proud if they had been my own children. Exiting the stage I saw the look of accomplishment on each of their faces and it felt good to know that I made this all happen for them. After the celebratory drinks, after parties, and after-after parties in the hotel suites of high profile people, I left with the satisfaction of knowing that this is all just the beginning. By the time I got to my room I'm still feeling wired from the entire experience, so when China called for updates I had only been too happy to brag on my work. Undressing as I re-accounted the stories of the people I met, what we discussed, and the plans we made, I heard a slight knock at the door. Muting China to answer, a bellhop presented me with a bottle and a note. Mumbling "Thanks man," and closing the door promptly without passing the guy a tip, I placed the bottle down on a chair next to the door to read the note; it read:

"Open the door."

Obliging the note, I turned swiftly to do as it said; perhaps one of the people I met tonight sent me a little something-something to my room to sweeten whatever offer they were about to make. Oh, I was propositioned all right; but it had been Phoenix who is doing it. Making up a quick excuse to get off of the phone with China without alerting Phoenix, I watched her as she sauntered into my room. She grabbed the bottle from the chair and pulled out two glasses from the mini bar. I remembered the bottle; it had been the same cognac we shared in her apartment. Holding up a glass to me, I accepted it and chugged it down hastily; it also had some bite to it. After she too slurped down the drink, the real after party began.

She let down her hair from the loose ponytail it had been in and removed her heels. I had already begun the undressing process when she showed up, so I'm more than halfway ready to finish whatever she's willing to start. I began sipping another drink, as I watched her remove her blouse and slip out of her skirt. She has the four F's every man of means wants in a woman: Fine, Fuckable, Fierce, and most importantly FINANCED! The removal or her clothing is as effortless, smooth, and full of as much bite as our first interlude; I wait for her next move; I don't want any misunderstandings between us that could result in her leaving as quickly as she came.

She walked up to me, taking the glass from my hand and setting it on the credenza. She stroked my face with the tip of her fingers; the coldness felt soothing on my hot face. I cradled her in my arms at her waist as she continued to explore. We spoke no words, what's left for us to say. We have mad chemistry; it was apparent from the start; she just needed opportunity to act on it. With the continued silence growing, and the sexual desire mounting, she finally gave in to what she had come to my room for. Normally, with my other women, I would make the first move. But after Phoenix kicked me out of her apartment abruptly, this is my chance to build the anticipation between us and make her come to me... after some strategic coaxing from days prior.

She kissed me slow, deep, and with intention devouring my mouth like this is the first time in a long time she's had this much mounted passion. Her skin is smooth and soft as her lips glided across mine; she tasted of Timeless Black Cognac mixed with brown sugar, her body smelled of expensive perfume I couldn't place, and her hair smelled of Shea Butter and Almond oil; this woman is a true queen.

I followed her lead as best I could without being mechanical. When she touched softly, I did it too. When she became more passionate, I did too. I wanted her to feel me match her tempo note by note until she sang with immense pleasure; I'm not the old man trying to intimidate her out of her panties, I'm the young ruler who doesn't require panties at all; it ladies' choice.

Using a bed in every sexual encounter is for rookies, the real artistry is in the manipulation of your body to adjust to unique environments, positions, and stimuli; with a slight display of my stamina, I showed her just how stimulating I can be. Her feet never touched the ground once during our interlude. I needed her to understand that no matter how hard it became to support her and my weight at the same time that I would never drop her. I don't know why I wanted her to be so aware, but I did.

By the time the night had ended we eventually made to the bed, I knew that whatever I had with China is over and I got a new thang to take her place. Re-running the escapades of the last few hours in my head, I glanced down at her with a smile. Home girl is sprawled out on her side of the bed looking exhausted, but I can go another round before it's time to check out of the hotel. It's time to wake her ass up so she can finish daddy off before my flight.

After checking in with my artists and giving some time off, I caught the next flight home; but not before I stopped at the airport bar to grab a quick drink and make "the call" to China. She was understandably upset. Who would want to lose a meal ticket like me? She sobbed and asked questions I have no intention of answering, and then she asked the one I waited for. She asked what would happen to her career, I didn't have the heart to tell the girl she has no career and that the most she can expect from me is a severance check. That would be too cruel; instead I gave her the same ultimatum I gave Chloe when I broke up with her. She has a month to leave, don't touch my shit, and oh yeah, she would get something that Chloe didn't get a pink slip; I'm dropping her from my client roster.

China suited her purpose for a time, and now that purpose has come to an end. I'm about to become a mainstream producer/manager I no longer have use for mediocre artists.

The next few weeks are a blur of meetings, concerts, interviews, luxury shopping and dining, and of course spending as much time as I could with my new bae. Phoenix is everything I want is a woman, she's intelligent, resourceful, and cunning; everything I desire in a girlfriend. She'll be able to help me run the business and satisfy me in the bedroom; the kind of woman I could bring home to moms, I only have one thing standing in my way; his name is Gavin McClarin.

McClarin is a ruthless son of a bitch, he devours everything and everyone is in his path. Something had been going on between them prior to us hooking up, I could tell by how agitated she became whenever he called. He tried to monopolize her free time. On her off days he would call all hours of the day and night, during the work week he would make her stay late to work on projects, he'd also show up unannounced to her apartment and demand that she meet with him; leaving me for hours to wait. As a businessman, one would think he has more going on than trying to keep tabs on his assistant. It seemed as if he couldn't close a deal without her. Word on the curb is that he's also planning a coup de grâce on yet another high profile business owner.

I think the old man is jealous and can't handle a younger man stepping on his arthritic toes. I don't care who she entertained before we got together; sometimes you have to be nicer to the boss than normal, especially if that boss is as egotistical as McClarin; just as it's known who comes first, and who's here now. If his interference keeps up, we're going to have to have a one on one grown man conversation. With men like McClarin, he's used to getting what he wants; I'm here to let him know that Phoenix is my woman, if he wants one younger than his wife then he need to find a quality escort service because Phoenix is taken. I don't care what he does just as long as he keeps his weak ass knees away from Phoenix's direction.

I felt nothing like this with no woman. I find myself wanting to leave business dealings early or canceling them all together just so I can spend more time with her. More often than not, I find myself going girly shit that I would never have done with Chloe, China, or any other female I dicked down. Occasionally she wouldn't answer a phone call or text, but I understand that work has to come first and what we have is brand new. I don't want to fuck anything up, so for the time being I'll play by her rules.

As I insisted on booking my heavy hitters for more studio time, we also entertained the offers from a few record labels; some major, others either startup or underground; it felt great to be in high demand. When I had late night sessions, Phoenix stopped by and gave me some inspiration to keep going until the mix was just right, and when I was running on empty, I would fill up again with a few strokes of her deliciously juicy pussy; it was a good time until it wasn't.

I still messed around now and then with some of my old faithful women like Sienna, but if ever Phoenix required my presence they no longer existed; what can I say, she's the lady in my life. I began to finally relax. The business is flourishing; I'm now entertaining offers from multiple sources for once; instead of my artists and I sneaking into events just to get in speaking distance of the power players.

The weeks passed, and it seemed like everything I worked, lied, and cheated for had begun to finally pay off. TNT, Fox, and a few of my other artist and I had taken a few meetings with Gretchen Terrell and Oren Shah at The Cypher Continues label. The offers they presented at this point didn't favor our agenda; they must have thought I had been some kind of rookie in the game. They basically offered us slave contracts written to coil words into circles to confuse the signer; I'm not having that, especially if it means cutting me out of my due.

Hiring the best Entertainment Lawyer a favor can bargain, Julian Cole of REPRESENT Attorneys at Law is ready and waiting for negotiations to start by the time we arrive. Finally, taking a much-deserved seat at the table, LET THE GAMES BEGIN! They wanted my artists; they're just not willing to compromise albums vs. compensation. We left the meeting not accomplishing much; we settled on a viable figure for each artist, but length of time and royalties are a different matter entirely.

I arrived at Phoenix's apartment just as she's looking for her keys to leave. She had the slight look of panic when she saw me; it was like she hadn't expected me to be there; granted I had got there earlier than I told her I would be, but last minute I decided not to go to my apartment to shower when I could just use hers.

"Babe, I thought, you be here late. How was the meeting?" she probed anxiously.

"It was aight. They tried to jerk us as usual. I'm just glad Julian was there to help us fight it out; we rescheduled for two days; where are you going to in a rush?" I probed.

"Oh, I have to run out for a minute; I'll be right back." She responded quickly as she hurled out the door.

I had no time to respond before the door slammed, leaving nothing but a violent echo. I took a shower, raided her kitchen, and watched tv. I finally got bored enough to doze off. I don't know what time she got back, all I know is when I woke up she had been asleep with her head in my lap. I gently eased out of my seat while cradling her head as to not disturb the deep sleep she's in. I don't know what's going on with her, but whatever it is it's taking a toll on her.

I left early before she could wake up; I have a lot of preparations to make. Not only do I have to prepare to go back to battle with Gretchen and Oren, I have to hit up some old friends to find out who's on the guest list for Spellbound Masquerade Ball. Once I got to my office, I scrolled through my contacts until I found Chris's number. I needed the guest lineup, which else but a caterer would have access to not just the head count but the picky palettes of the elite and influential; this time I didn't need him to sneak me in. They had gifted me with an invitation.

Phoenix had been acting weird since that night she barreled out of her apartment... well, weirder than normal. She stopped wanting to spend as much time, and when I called she made an excuse for why she couldn't talk; if I didn't know any better I could swear she is attempting to ghost ya boy... no, she wouldn't do that, would she?

Negotiations went better than expected; we agreed on a mutually beneficial contract about time! I was afraid if we stalled too many times and didn't come to an agreement that the Label would re-send their offer to sign my artists. After some much deserved congratulating and handshaking, all parties agreed to meet the day after the Spellbound event to sign the final contracts.

I cleared my calendar for the day of the event; I wanted to pamper myself O.G. Style. I knew the event will have people I haven't seen since my 'come up' days, and I want to flex on them a bit. They all counted me out as a bum ass dude, and all out schemer that will never amount to anything; tonight, I would show them all just who they've been dealing with. The money is pouring in, especially since tomorrow I will finalize the deal with the Record Company, my artists have been on sold out tours and festivals, I look even more handsome than ever, complete with a new 'stunner' on my arm; I can't lose! I wonder what washed up Jayshawn will have to say now. Everything had finally come together.

Waiting for Phoenix to finish dressing is like painfully watching your accountant tally up all your receipts for the year and you owe on your taxes; my anxiety due to the waiting had kicked into high gear. The wait was worth it; she emerged from her bedroom wear an emerald green gown, with matching gold and jeweled accented shoes, accompanied with a feathered mask; my bae is stunning!

We arrived on time; the party is in full swing with guests still arriving because they're being held up on the Red Carpet taking pictures. I felt my chest poke out broader as I strolled in, invitations in hand. A few months ago, I would have snuck into an event like this just to elevator pitch a Financial District reject about sponsoring a new artist, and sleeping with their secretaries so I can be eased onto their meeting schedules; not anymore! I'm the real deal, legitimate business man now! And these Hedge Fund stooges will beg my secretary for a meeting.

The usual suspects are in attendance, but I'm not interested in them; I want to holla at a few of my artists that had arrived and make sure they remember to be at the meeting promptly. Phoenix excuses herself to talk to someone, and I continue on the path towards Julian and TNT. On approach TNT is visibly upset, words exchanged between the two left frustration in the form of bulging veins in TNT's neck; I hope doesn't fuck up this deal!

"Hello gentlemen. Is everything good?" I addressed both men.

"Yeah, we good. Right 'T'?" Julian insisted.

"Yeah." Responded TNT in a grumble. "We good." He looked from Julian to me and then walked off without another word.

"Julian, man what happened." I probed.

"Nothing, man. He's just got little cold feet. What's good with you? Are you enjoying the festivities?" he switched subjects.

"It's cool." I tried not to seem too impressed. "It's the same old, same old, you know?"

"Yeah, I know. Well, listen man. I have to catch up with a few people here. Excuse me, won't you?" He said as he walked away without an answer.

It's not like TNT to get an attitude out of nowhere. Something happened between the two men. After the ink is dry, we won't have to worry about it anymore. It will be bye, bye Julian; I might keep him on retainer in case anything comes up, but I will limit his interactions to me only, he'll have no contact with my artist.

I became swept up in a whirlwind of conversations and floated from one group to another for a long time before I noticed that I hadn't seen Phoenix for a while. Looking for her, I ran into Hennison Black. We looked at each other, blatantly sizing each other up, before he took his Champagne glasses and left. I heard he had been dicking Chloe down. I'll give it to the girl, I taught her something. She went from messing with Jayshawn to Hennison Black; at least she got her come up game correct. But at the same time she's losing, because I know good and well that no white dude can hit it better than a black man can; but then again it's Jayshawn he probably isn't any better so I guess Hennison would be a for real come up in comparison. Neither one of them are better than me! I know that shit for sure!

Searching the crowd, I still couldn't find her. I noticed servers and followed the direction they came from; maybe one of them had seen her. As I slow jogged to catch up to one of the guys, I saw Phoenix walking towards me. My eyes were bouncing from wall to wall, exit to entrance, and everything in between to understand why she had been back there.

"Hey babe, I was looking for you all night, where have you been? What's back there?" I asked her.

She looked up at me with genuine surprised and responded, "Nothing babe, the restrooms are down the hall that's all. Let's go back to the party." She insisted, as she strangled my arm and briskly walked me back towards the party.

The rest of the night had been amazing; I will mark this date on my calendar as the anniversary of truly achieving my success. I reveled in the notoriety, and recognition I received from the other partygoers. People, whom I never knew, knew who I was and wanted to be a part of my ventures. It had happened! I finally had them eating out the palm of my hands. Damn! Success feels glorious! The only downer on the evening had been Phoenix. She seemed to have been distracted, and withdrawn for the remainder of the evening. Every so often, I would glance through the crowd and catch McClarin staring in our direction. The silly old man had finally realized he'd lost! Thank God, I'd get no cool points for beating up the elderly.

Ending the night on a high note, all I want to do is make love to my girl. When we got to her apartment, she seemed even more distracted. I tried everything I could think of to cheer her up, but none of it worked. As a last resort, I decided to tell her of a surprise I'd planned. I wanted to wait until after the meeting to tell her, but I think she could use some good news.

"Babe, I noticed you've been distracted all night..." I began to say.

"Um, yeah, I've got a lot on my mind. Malik, we have to talk. My apartment..." she said when I cut her off.

"Yes, the apartment. Well, I noticed it's cramped in here, and that there's no room in the closet for all of our clothes. Look at the living room; we have no walking space anymore. I wanted to wait until after dinner tomorrow to tell you, but… I put a down payment on a three bedroom, two-and-a-half bath condo today! I know its sudden, but I want us to live together permanently. I want to do whatever I have to do to make you happy, and I bet Ms. Sofia will be happy for us to move out; maybe she can start back sleeping at night. I heard her complain to the super about all the noise we make. So, what do you think, baby? You want to do this?" I asked.

"Malik." She said flatly.

"I know, I sprang this on you last minute. Just sleep on it, and tomorrow night we can discuss it at the celebration dinner. Sound good?" I tested.

Agreeing with a nod, she undressed and crawled into bed without another word. Needless to say, I didn't get any that night. The next day I woke up with a purpose. Everything seemed to look better. The sun shone brighter, my clothes were crisper, the food tasted magnificent, and the opportunities are limitless; today will be a marvellous day!

Arriving a little ahead of schedule, I wanted to show the label that my artist and I would come in early, stay late, work harder, and bring in the most return on their investment than any other artists signed to them. Everyone else must have had the same idea, because when I walked into the conference room everyone who needed to be there had already arrived. Checking my phone quickly, I took note that I didn't get a call, email, or text that they had pushed the meeting up; Kamaya's ass will be fired for this!

"Hey, everyone apologies if I'm late. No one told me the meeting has been pushed up early. Where are we?" I asked.

"Um Malik, we weren't expecting you yet." Julian stuttered.

"What do you mean, man? We have a final meeting today? Granted, I'm earlier than originally planned... What's' going on? All my artists are here and Gretchen and Oren are here, I see contracts on the table. So, you tell me man; why weren't you expecting me?" I said declared.

"Have a seat, Malik. We have things to discuss." Oren stated.

"No, I think I'll stand Oren. Now tell me what's going on." I demanded as I looked at the sunken in faces and slumped shoulders of the people whose careers I've either started or nurtured.

"Malik, we all are happy to be making this deal with all these wonderful artists. But there are some adjustments that have to be made before we can proceed to the next step." Gretchen explained.

With a hurry up and explain look on my face, she stopped to gage if I'd been following her. "Well, what are the adjustments and I will talk with MY ARTISTS to find out if they are plausible." I insisted.

"That's just it Malik, you are the adjustment that has to be made." Julian interrupted.

"What the hell do you mean, man?" I asked.

"We want to sign these remarkable artists, just not with you as there manager. We all acknowledge the work you've done with them, but it's time for you to move on. We want to offer you a generous finder's fee, buy you out of your management contracts, and maybe work with you as a freelance talent agent. You have a great ear, and an eye for talent; we'd love for you to bring us credible artists from the underground scene." Oren offered.

I stood in stunned at what I heard. These ungrateful sons of bitches are trying to take my clients away from me; not without a fight! I tried to regain some composure, took a few deep breaths and asked my clients to leave with me. But when I turned to walk out the door, none of them stood up.

"What the hell are y'all doing? Let's go!" I demanded. One by one I called their names, and each of them looks off in shame. I couldn't believe what is happening.

"Malik" Julian muttered. "No one is leaving with you. They've all signed their contracts, all except Foxy. Malik, take what they are offering, sign the contract, and leave with some dignity."

"Dignity, Julian, you are supposed to make sure we came out on top, not stab me in the back the first chance you got! How you going to do this, man! I hired you to protect my interests." I countered.

"No man. You hired me to protect their interests. Don't get mad at me! They all were approached with the same offer; you or them, they chose them. It's not my fault 'your artists' betrayed you.' Julian replied. "Listen, sign the contracts, take the money, and try to maintain some relationship with the label. They might bring you on in a different role in the future."

"Terrod really man!" I implored. "Is this how it's going to be? So, now I know why you were mad last night. How long have you known this was going down?"

"Look Malik, this is how its got to be. I'm sorry, man." He offered.

I didn't believe what I'm seeing and hearing. These ungrateful bastards are abandoning me! ME! The man who took them off the street and put them on the stage, paid for studio time, put food in their bellies, clothes on their backs, and pussy on their dicks! And they deem it wise to leave me! Ok, if that's how they want it, that's exactly what they get! I'll crush every single one of them; ruin their name in the streets so badly they will beg me to come back!

"I'll sign your little contact, but where's my money?" I spat. No sooner said that Julian slid a check and a contract to where I stood. Signing the contract, and snatching my check, I called for Foxy to follow me; again she didn't follow.

"What's going on now? I thought everyone had been signed except Foxy?" I threw out for someone to answer.

Sheepishly looking at Julian for help, he stepped in to explain to me that Foxy signed with Boss Babe Productions, the same label that signed Legacy; formally known as Hell's Angels and also owned by Julian. Also, her young protégé Bella Donna is also signed to Boss Babe with Foxy, taking a writer/producer credit with sign-on bonus. I've been fucked in every orifice without the cutesy of petroleum jelly.

I took the money and left. Every single one of those sorry motherfuckers will regret this, as much energy as I put into making their careers, I will break them just as easily.

Seeking some comfort from my girl, I stopped by Phoenix's apartment. I tried to use my key to open the lobby door and it wouldn't turn. Looking down at my keys, I checked if I had used the wrong one. Noticing I didn't, I tried again, but the lock wouldn't budge. Growing frustrated, I buzzed her apartment. Usually, she would buzz me in; this time she didn't. I buzzed over and over until finally she got on the intercom.

"Baby, my key isn't working let me up!" I yelled into the intercom.

"I can't Malik, I'm sorry but we can't do this anymore; I don't want to be with you." She said coldly.

"Phoenix, stop playing and let me in! The day I've had baby... I don't feel like playing." I said sternly as I continued to yell through the sounds of the bustling city.

"It's not a game, Malik." She insisted. "I told you I can't be in a relationship, and you just didn't listen. I can't be with you, it's over."

"Phoenix, maybe I'm came off a little aggressive. But baby I had a terrible day and I just want to be with you right now, can you please let me up?" I pleaded.

I heard murmuring in the background that sounded too deep to be another woman. Someone is up there with her; urging her to continue the assault on my heart. She returned to give me one last warning to leave or she would call the police. I can't believe she's doing this to me now! And today of all days! Not only have I lost a large portion of my roster, but I already sold my condo to put the money down on a bigger one for us to move into. How the hell can I afford that shit now? The money from The Cypher Continues won't last forever. What else could go wrong?

Cassidy

I woke the next day to my head aching, my phone ringing, and my body satisfied. I accepted Elgin's offer, but didn't expect that I would seal the deal with wonderful sex; though I would do it again.

Elgin and I had dated for a while when we attended the same college. Before I pursued a career in modeling, and on and off for a brief time afterwards. We continued to see each from time to time when our busy schedules would collide, but it was never anything more than a one night hook up, then we disappeared to our respective corners of the world. While Elgin graduated in person, I did so via email. We would run into each other from time to time, but we never hashed out any bad blood between us if any existed. So, when I was approached by Nevie to have a meeting with him, I was speechless.

When we were together, we had always fantasized about opening a business when we graduated, but I thought he'd abandoned the idea when he entered real estate and private equity. It was good to hear from him, and it felt like we had picked up where we left off. The timing couldn't be more perfect since Indulgence is on the verge of publishing its last issue, and people from both Indulgence and Rouge are unsure what will happen with their jobs; I have the feeling last night will be the last anniversary Indulgence will have.

We have always been good together, Elgin and I, but life has taken us in different directions; last night was a display of that. We are two old friends that needed comforting, by no stretch of the imagination did I think we would become anything more than what we are; business partners. After the retreat is over, I'll break the news to Clair that I'm moving on. My decision shouldn't upset her since she's been doing things behind my back for some time.

As I attempted to steady my swirling head, Elgin walked into his bedroom with a mug in one hand and painkillers in the other. Peeping at Akeelah's missed call; I noticed the time and began putting myself together while explaining that I had to get home. He urged me to stay, but the only thing on my mind is getting to my son. I sipped my coffee and dressed as I offered excuses that didn't seem to be relevant enough for him to accept. Finally, I let the cat out of the bag and told him I had to get home to my son. Stunned for a second by my sudden confession, he fired question after question at me; apparently when he had Nevie research my professional background, she left out the private one.

"Wow, a son. How old is he? Are you still with his father?" He fired at me.

"Cairo is five, and no we're not together." I answered quickly.

"So, when were you going to tell me you have a son? We're going to be partners and eventually I would find out." He accused.

"I'm not hiding my son from you! It doesn't matter if I have a child or not, obviously when you were background checking the fact that I have a child never hindered my working abilities. I've traveled, ran a magazine, managed people, finances, and things I won't mention out loud. Why would you think that running an art gallery would be difficult for me?" I threw at him. "You haven't changed. You're still the self-centered asshole I remember, not everything is about you! Just because I'm a mom, doesn't make me less capable or running circles around your ass."

"Ok. I'm sorry. It's just that I didn't expect for you to drop that bomb on me after we just had sex. I thought we could pick up where we left off, but you having a kid changes things." He admitted.

"Elgin, last night is a onetime only deal. I've been dealing with some things lately and I needed something I can feel as an outlet for the tension. You are no different, I can tell you are trying to get over someone, by getting on top of someone else, so you can stop right there; I know you remember, I'm not just a woman you picked up in a bar. Anyway, I haven't slept with a man for a long time, I actually just broke up with my girlfriend (and working on another one), so don't flatter yourself; you don't have that much swag. Let's just keep everything between us professional and we'll get along just fine, ok." I concluded.

"Ok, just partners then. But you said Cairo is five? If I recall correctly, we messed around a few times maybe five or so years ago." He said.

"Do you have a point, Elgin?" I said with annoyance.

"Who's Cairo's father?" he asked sternly.

I grabbed what's left of my clothing and walked out of his bedroom without another word. I knew that once I left Indulgence that people would ask a lot of questions about Cairo; like people have never seen a single mother handling her business. I don't enjoy telling people my business, especially since they're not helping me raise him or provide for him financially; they can FUCK OFF!

I hadn't expected to make an unscheduled stop in Elgin's bed last night or I would be home and tucked safely in my bed before Cairo can wake up. Thankfully, when I walked in the door, I didn't hear the sounds of a kid tussling through the apartment. I have enough time to get out of my evening clothes and get into the shower without him being the wiser. While in the shower, I thought about Elgin. I can see how he would question the parentage of Cairo. Back in the days, I was a wild girl, and sex was like a casual handshake for all parties involved. And as far as us hooking up, we did so whenever and wherever we ran into each other; so I understand. But, if I had thought for a second that we would have a child together, I would tell him without hesitation. Sadly, it just isn't possible.

Realizing the water had gotten cold, I reluctantly snapped out of my daze. Entering my bedroom, I found a wide awake Cairo jumping on my bed. He looked so cute with milk stained pajamas, and his wild, brown, curly hair swaying as he jumped. I just stood and watched until he realized I was there.

"Hi mom, I brought you some juice and toast!" He said excitedly while he continued to bounce. As the toaster is the only appliance he's allowed to touch in the kitchen, I would hate to see the mess he would have made if I let him anywhere near the microwave without supervision.

Watching him have so much fun, I tightened my robe and joined in with him. These times we have together to be silly are the ones I treasure the most! With things making a sudden change, I want to keep stuff like this close to my heart. I may need them to get me through the rough times that are sure to come.

Chloe

I want to say that working at Indulgence has been a dream, and all the novel experiences have given me multiple avenues to expand my career, but it's been one disaster after another. Instead of using my occupation as a stepping stone to a great opportunity, I became complacent. I love working there; it is the dream of most chubby women and girls who has seen Indulgence Magazine on a supermarket shelf and pictured themselves on the cover(or at the very least a regular columnist). But with recent rumors becoming more and more of a reality, I'm beginning to picture a clock counting down to zero every time I enter the building; I have to give myself a chance to win with or without Indulgence.

Being a semi single woman, and living in the city, I have to find creative ways to generate multiple streams of income. In the few quiet moments that I have, my mind drifts and it tries to determine which of the skills (if any) I've gained over the years while working odd jobs; as I do so, I try to mentally stitch together ideas to create those avenues. Some girls make videos on various social media platforms, target a niche, and use their views to monetization their page/channel; which can lead to other opportunities such as becoming an influencer and/or product endorsements. But this like in all things take time, I have to build an audience and constantly stroke their particular taste and their egos to eventually build myself up to become a blip on the radar of a major player (or startup) that will pay me for my opinion, or market their merchandise. The next idea I have is to partner with someone who is already established to piggyback off of what they've already created, and lastly if push comes to shove I can create downloadable content like teaching a Master Class (since they're all the rage now), and show people how to mix a drink and call it *Chloe's Master Fusion Class: Mix like a professional Mixologist*. If none of those ideas pan out, I can sell Salon tresses hair extensions or Smooth Belly Teas (if the need for a quick coin arises, money is money, and it all spends).

Instead, I've been hoping Black Enterprise along with Indulgence Magazine will see my potential and give me the space to be more of an asset. The anxiety I've built up from thinking so much about my future has me waking up in the middle of the night after only a few hours of sleep, I toss and turn for the duration of the night in a vain attempt to rest. It rarely works, and when I finally manage to quiet my mind long enough to doze off, it's just in time for my alarm to ring reminding me that the side hustle will have to wait, because the nine to five has to be where I focus my energy on to live. I remember on one night of mindless scrolling on social media, I once saw a post that said something along the lines of '*Work gives you an income to overlook your dreams.*'

Finally arriving home from an arduous trip, the first thing I wanted to do is wash off the debris from the bomb Hennison dropped, and the feeling of my skin crawling from seeing Malik in Montreal. My mental state of breakdown had morphed into a physical one and I wore the look of an exhausted woman, like Kelly wore out a chair from sitting on her ass the entire event and watching me perform like a trained show pony.

Sensing my weariness, Hennison asked Mr. Bassett to take me home first. Unlocking the door to Dee's apartment, Mr. Bassett sat the bags down near the door and handed me a brown envelope. When I questioned him about what had been inside, he gave me a *'you know what it is'* look as he smoothly left and closed the door behind him. I tucked it inside my purse and stripped myself of the travel fatigue I had been wearing. After draining the shower of all the hot water it had, I grabbed my pillow and blanket and immediately fell asleep on the couch without a second thought.

Luckily I had a few days to rest up before returning to Indulgence as a clown in the circus, in time for us to give the performance of a lifetime at the upcoming anniversary party, and the corporate retreat that will be soon to follow. By the time I woke up Dominique is already gone, with nothing to do for the first time in nearly a year, I took a few moments to have a thought that's my own, and not one that had been assigned to me by Cassidy.

As I sat on the couch, still in my pajamas, with a throw blanket wrapped around my shoulders; I sat still and in silence for so long that the coffee in my 'Real Diva's Move in Silence' mug had gone cold. Have you ever been lost in a thought so deep that time seemed to stop? It did for me, and I found myself in the same place I had been before when I sat in a coffee shop and stared out of the window and contemplated... Where do I go from here?

I saved some money, not enough to support Dee's shoe habit for a month, but enough to gain my own space. I depended on her too long and even though I don't know what will happen with my job; I have to stand on my own; and I also have to figure out how to make an extra income. Like a spark from a distant memory, I remembered the ideas I had for monetizing my blog (that I haven't written for a few months) but still it was something. Leaping quickly from the couch, I grabbed my laptop, opened up my program, and stared at a blank page. And I stared... and stared, and stared some more, willing an idea to come to me. And when it would finally present itself, my fingers will take off in a frenzy of eloquent, insightful turns of a phrase that different media outlets will clamor for me to be a columnist. But none of that happened; I just continued to stare at a blank page.

So many things had happened to me that I should be able to put out a decent piece of work! The problem I'm finding, when attempting to have an original thought, is that all the things that happened had already been reported on; in other words it's old news, and I've missed my opportunity to discuss it with the small group of readers I managed to get, and they've grown into an even smaller pool after my lengthy absence.

Growing frustrated at my inability to write, I remembered the envelope Mr. Bassett handed me. Rummaging through my purse to find it, I opened it to discover a sizeable amount of money. I don't know if this is a compliment or an insult. Was Hennison paying me for services rendered while we were in London, or is this a pre-severance payment for when he shuts down Indulgence? Either way, I'm in no position to turn it down by getting on a moral high horse. If I'm going to lose my job, at least I'll have a small nest egg to live on until I'm able to get back on my feet. Honestly, what would you do if a man you are seeing regularly gives you a wad of money out of nowhere, and with no explanation?

While I marinated for a few days on what to do about the money Hennison had given me, time passes by quicker than a dope fiend can lean; it was time to return to Indulgence. One would freeze from frostbite by how everyone behaved in the days following London. Clair had been in continuous closed-door meetings, which are so secretive that even Cassidy isn't welcomed to attend. Cassidy seems to be operating in a fog of uncertainty, Kelly has disappeared entirely, and everyone else is strategizing on which Black Enterprise competitor they should submit a resume.

I tried to busy myself with as much work as I could handle, which isn't hard due to the fact that Cassidy practically gave me full autonomy over the ICON Edition of Indulgence, since she's also been in closed-door meetings planning the corporate retreat; which is great for me because I can list manager experience on my resume if the need arises. Maybe full autonomy is too broad, I'm not authorized to give final approvals on anything; I just assist the photographers, keep the individuals being featured happy, make sure the project stays on budget, and if I run into any problems with staffers involved, I'd threaten them with the wrath of Clair and that very thought of her turning them into sawdust is enough to make them get back in line.

If this is to be Indulgence's last issue, it's sure to be the highest selling one to date. The Icon Edition will include plus size female professionals from some of the various industries. Other publications feature, endorse, and support women in business; but not one of them focuses on the various sub-groups of women who never become a positive focus. If a plus size woman is featured in a mainstream fashion magazine, it's only to compare her to a smaller counterpart or to typecast her as a stereotype that happens to be a profitable trend for the moment. But the worst one of all is the one that fetishizes a fuller woman by featuring an emerging, popular plus size star (whether she's a movie heroine's funny sidekick, or a musical artist) on the cover to sell magazines, then add insult to injury by having advertisement after advertisement of diet fads, or designers that would never make clothing for women larger than a size 10(and a size 10 is pushing it, some designers consider it to be plus size) when the artist being featured is clearly and size eighteen and up.

The ripples from Hennison's announcement sent Human Resources into an uproar, so much so I overheard one assistant talk about Hennison hiring a Corporate Actuary to evaluate the effectiveness of all Black Enterprise staff. With the revolving door of unfamiliar faces that entered and exited the building daily, it's hard to find the one that has been hired to fire.

The tension in the air had gotten so thick whenever I entered a room, that I stopped eating in the cafeteria, and began eating in my cubical. I tried to be as inconspicuous as possible, but the relationship between Hennison and I is well known, and I've heard whispers as I pass by, accusing me of knowing all about Hennison's plan, and not warning them to their pending unemployment; they must have forgotten I'm going to be jobless along with them! With only a few days to the Spellbound Masquerade Anniversary Ball, I hope the animosity calms down enough for everyone to pull it off with dignity. Just because this could possibly be the last party Indulgence has, doesn't mean it should miserable; and with the retreat around the corner, we should all be putting our best face forward so that when we won't leave with a pink slip in hand and a sizable severance package in hand.

Corporate retreat... What's the point of going forward with it? If most of the Black Enterprise media catalog will be broken down, bought and sold, or dismantled altogether to disappear into obscurity; it certainly isn't a moral boost. In my opinion, it's a ploy to get the most profitable staff in one place, all at once to evaluate our effectiveness and contribution to the company without alerting us directly. But now isn't the time to worry about that.

I dressed for the anniversary ball in Hennison's apartment on "Billionaire's Row." Have you ever had a sudden memory aimlessly flash in your mind as you're doing something? I did as I dressed. Not so long ago, when I prepared for a similar event, I had my best friend with me. We drank a mixture of top self and bottom shelf alcohol, smoked a little and passed it back and forth, turned the music up loud, and danced around as we did each other's hair and makeup; having a good time... just us. Now, I'm dressing alone, in stone silence, and eager to get the night over with; the fun is gone.

It's been replaced with strategy and obligation. I now understand the women I met years ago; the sorority of housewives and kept women, with the best designer clothing money can buy, wealthy partners were for the most part aloof or unavailable (from work or having affairs of their own), accompanied by children (if they had any) that they hardly knew, paired with the loneliness of an unrequited love to keep them warm at night. It also explains why they entertain themselves with scandal and gossip. And busy themselves with planning parties and having affairs when their children were away at boarding schools, or being watched over by a nanny.

With Hennison in the next room, there's just no excitement; he approached us (our relationship) as a job, and the perspective from an outsider looking in would be that we are a settled, married couple, that only stays together because we have business tied into one another; which isn't the case, but I seemed to have outlived my usefulness; we don't even make love (if that's what you call sex at arbitrary moments) anymore. I began this causal relationship with the intention of it not becoming serious, and I tried to approach it as a good time, and when it was over I could walk away unscathed. Somewhere along the way I drifted back into my old habit of wanting more than the other person is willing to give. Does every woman unwittingly fall into the same patterns in new relationships, even when you try your best to avoid them?

We are barely a couple, and if we hit this "roommate patch" vibe now, I can only imagine what it would be like if we were actually in a committed relationship; maybe the money wasn't a gift, but compensation for being the hired help with benefits.

I think the enthusiasm has worn off! Hennison complemented me a few times and even gave me a taut kiss on the lips as we departed his apartment; but the ride to the venue is stiffer than the taste of Timeless Black. Out the corner of my eye, I saw him eyeing me a little, but it's different from the other times he's done so. It seemed more as if he's making a mental checklist, rather than omitting feelings of desire. Arriving in record time, we made our way through the sea of photographers and reporters, all vying for Hennision's attention, and hurling questions about which of his infamous publications will receive the ax. He smiled politely, dogged the questions, and promised a spectacular evening of praise for the magazine and its entire staff. But when questioned who I was by a greasy-looking camera guy, he responded that I'm one of the staff members of Indulgence and the magazine chief audience. In an instant my status changed from lover to trophy fat girl, Indulgence's core audience.

The impact from his answer shook me, and I instantly became lightheaded and dizzy. The offhand question paired with Hennision's answer gave me pause long enough for everything around me to feel like it moved in slow motion. The spinning in my head whipped as I tried to regain my composure. At the first opportunity, I gave him the sharpest eye a mad black woman can give in public. If looks could kill, he would've dropped dead on the spot. I tried to save face by continuing to smile, but as soon as the question had been satisfied, I glared at him with the look of a thousand neck rolls, finger pointing, and fuck you implications, that I left him standing in front of the step and repeat with a dumfounded look on his face. The honeymoon is over; now where is the bar!

I had been so angry at Hennison that I nearly missed a step trying to weave through the crowd as swiftly as a mall employee on a thirty-minute lunch break; thankfully I had kept walking without further incident. Reaching the bar area, I sipped drink after drink, trying to formulate a plan to leave as soon as I could. I wish Dee is here to offer a few encouraging words, or at least offer to re-arrange a few of Hennison's front teeth. But she's not here, and I have to defend myself. Truthfully, I didn't have an official title as his girlfriend; though he could recognize me as his date.

I found Ingrid in the middle of the dance floor, doing a version of the two-step that looked like more like a half step with a guy from accounting. Spotting me, she whispered something in his ear quickly and dance/bounced in my direction, Whiskey glass in hand. She slurred her words a bit, but that's to be expected if you drink Timeless Black straight, Hennison made sure he stayed on brand, especially with all the free publicity the company had been getting.

She nearly knocked me over when she hugged me; I had to catch her and her drink before they could hit my dress and the floor.

"See that guy I was dancing with? His name is Ellis and his in the accounting department." Ingrid indicated.

"Yeah, I know Ellis, he's Vincent's first assistant." I informed her, as I gave him a lazy wave. "So, you've found the next love of your life, I mean besides me?"

"Of course you're my number one darling, but he's so fit, just look at him; I could lick the sweat from his abs." She said with as much emphasis as the alcohol that raced through her. "I love my men tall, dark, handsome, and nerdy." She laughed.

"Really, I didn't take you for a sapiosexual." I countered.

"Oh yeah, I love the brainy lot, but I have to tell you what he told me. The retreat is a setup! Isabella has had someone stashed at Indulgence for months trying to get dirt; she knew this entire deal is going down before everyone; except Clair. Clair also had a mole at Rouge, and when she found out that Hennison was beginning to lean more to the Rouge side, Gavin showed up. So, not only are the other magazine staffers out, we might just be too. Hennison and his cronies aren't trying to boost morale by continuing this charade, so now one leaks anything to the press. They are going to eliminate us as soon as the retreat is over. They'll offer us a rubbish severance and leave us in the dust. And that Gavin, he's brilliant that one; he's bought up so much of Black Enterprise stock that Hennison could have possibly lost controlling shares; Ellis doesn't know for sure, he's a bit daft after a few drinks so. I'm sure I can get more out of him. I'll be right back." She said as she re-joined Ellis back on the dance floor.

I stood stunned by what I had learned, so many questions turned in my mind; and it made since why Kelly had been incognito, but who had been feeding Clair information from Rouge? This also explains Hennison's anxiety before London, and why he had become calm in the days before the last show. Worst yet, what part did I unknowingly play in all this? Between the information and the alcohol, my head slowly spun until it turned into a raging tornado.

Seeking a moment to catch my breath, I ducked into the ladies' room. I heard people in the stall giggling and moaning as the scuffing of their shoes scrapped the tile floor. I smiled to myself thinking, '*Well, at least someone's having fun tonight; I hope they enjoy it while it lasts.*' No sooner than the thought entered and exited my mind that the stall opened and Gavin and Phoenix stubble out. At first they didn't notice I had been standing there watching as they continued to kiss and grope each other, but as soon as they detached Phoenix looked up to see me and realized they had blown their cover.

Walking pass me as hurriedly as she could, Phoenix exited without another glance in my direction. Gavin lingered for a few moments before flashing me a cocky smile as he smoothed down his beard, rubbed his hands together, and finally checking his appearance in the mirror, then left as abruptly as Phoenix had.

Rejoining the party, I watched as Gavin walking toward his wife, and Phoenix had already joined her date; Malik! God, that asshole can to weasel himself into any situation! I should've known he would make a play for her, I thought she was out of his league; but judging by how she had practically mouth fucked Gavin and now doing the same with Malik; what little respect I had for her is gone, she just as opportunistic as Malik's dirty ass; they deserve each other.

Between my drunk, work best friend, the amateur porn demonstration in a bathroom stall that's so cliché it's painful, and Hennison's stuck on stupid ass (or maybe it's me that's stuck on stupid?), I cannot hold in my anger and contempt any longer. By the time Clair had been introduced to the crowd and began her opening statements; I had already been walking steadily to the exit; I'm over this shit!

I caught a glimpse of Hennison as I walked toward the exit. He gave me a confused look as if to inquire where I had been going, but I had seen and heard enough for the evening. Catching the first cab I saw I quickly went inside, as the driver navigated his way through the busy streets I contemplated the events that led me once again to be in a cab alone leaving a party, but this time I wasn't chasing a man; I had been leaving one behind. Why do I feel like I've done this all before? Possibly because I have; I'm repeating the same circumstances as before when I thought I'd been in a relationship with Malik. The difference now are the players. Am I really pursuing the road less taken, or am I just meeting new people on the same road that I've been choosing time and time again? These are some of the thoughts I have to sort out. The only solace that I have is at least Hennison doesn't know China.

I wish I was the type of person where I could turn off emotions, and/or thoughts, even cut off people that didn't suit my best interest; I'm simply not. I carry everything, and the load is getting heavier by the day. The only solution I can think of is to keep going, the problem with that idea is it's not a permanent fix, and eventually I will burn out. In an effort to reclaim my life, I've seemed to have gone further off course.

Trying to prove to myself I didn't need to be in a relationship, and I could be self-reliant, I stumbled into two of them; first with Jayshawn, and again with Hennison. Neither worked out, and both left me with a sense of disappointment and hurt. I moved in with my friend, and while that was ok as a temporary situation; I feel that I've overstayed my welcome and I need to find my own place and lastly regarding my career; I've gotten comfortable and lost my hustler spirit. On this leg of my journey, I have to figure out how to get back to me; and not the idea of me those suites everyone else.

Packing for the retreat is easier than it had been to pack for London; the only thing both trips had in common are preparing for long hours and short temperaments; this trip would be at an isolated destination with only my co-workers for company. Like previous on-site events that didn't involve the masses to participate such as photo shoots, the occasion required only a few pairs of jeans, sneakers, and decent shirts; but of course this is a retreat with people who not only live for fashion, but govern it as well. If I'm going to be casual, it has to be the fashion industry's version of casual chic. Between the freebies from work, a few borrowed pieces from Indulgence's fashion closet courtesy of Ingrid, and the tidbits I find here and there that will suit an assistant's budget, I think I have enough outfits to get a pass from the FBI (fashion Bureau of Investigation).

The site selected as our prison for the weekend is a camp that is vacant until summer begins, when it'll be filled with the wonderful sounds of moans and groans of adolescents and teenagers; while simultaneously filled with the sounds of thankful parents looking forward to being stress free for a few months. The site being a far cry from the ski lodge where we traveled to previously, this time there are no models to burn their hair extensions, and no Greer to keep a watchful eye; they would be replaced with experts in group therapy and exercises that will give us skills to adapt to the new work environment (for those who don't leave the end of this emotional challenge with a pink slip!).

Instead of traveling with Clair, Hennision, and Cassidy, I traveled alone. When I alerted Cassidy to my travel arrangement, she was fine with it; one less person for her to worry about, but Hennison he had no clue of my plans; I ghosted him like an online dater swiping left. The first few days had been easy enough, Hennion is in such outrageous demand I bet he didn't even notice. But after a few days of his dick aching, he noticed he'd been lacking; that's when the calls started.

It didn't end there, texting, random visits to the Indulgence floor under the guise of Margo meeting with Clair, and of course he would send his number one guy Mr. Bassett to track me down. I evaded them at every turn, first at work I recruited Ingrid and Vivian (who is still the front desk receptionist until further notice) to give me the heads up whenever Margo was on the move and headed to my floor, I became the invisible assistant. Mr. Bassett was harder to avoid, I traveled on alternate routes home. Sometimes I took a taxi, or called the Pick Up Car Service, and other times I would take a train then walk the distance to Dominique's; I shouldn't have underestimated him. Figuring out my pattern, he waited for me in front of Dee's apartment with a 'gottcha' look spread against his weary face.

"Darling, how long did you think you could keep this up?" she laughed slightly.

"As long as I could," I answered, defeated.

"What's going on young lady? Did you and him have a spat?" he inquired.

Gesturing him inside the apartment, he took a seat on the couch/bed and waited for my reply. I explained why I had been avoiding all Hennison's attempts at communication, and what he'd done at the anniversary ball. As I explained I could tell he was exhausted; so I wasn't the only one tired of Hennison's games. Mr. Bassett has witnessed the coming and goings of many people in the Black family, and the company itself, so he understood why I'd withdrawn. As he stood up to leave, he gave me one last word of advice.

"I've been with this family for years. Before I drove for Hennison, I drove for his father. And that man also had someone he couldn't let go of. I don't know if it was love, lust, or infatuation, but whatever it was he couldn't let go. It's like for them they have to possess someone to ensure that it stays under their control, and when that control is lost, obsession grows, and sometimes secrets spoken from the warmth of pillow talk can bring down a mighty dynasty and the debris that follow can be lethal to anyone who's standing in its path. Do you understand what I'm telling you, Darling?" He finished.

Nodding my head in agreement, he left the apartment; but not without telling me that when prompted to give Hennison information, he would insist he'd lost me on the subway in a crowd of people. I don't know if the lie would fool him, but at least it will buy me some time to figure out what I want to do.

Arriving at the New Haven camp grounds, the hair on the back of my neck stood on end when I saw how seriously they took the idea of camping. The company must have been attempting to save money as to not spend too much on people who would be on their way out. The organizers had registration tables set up, complete with staffers going through luggage taking our devices. They seized everything from cell phones, to curling irons; anything that could leak information to the public or cause an electrical fire has been deemed not allowed; good call, it'll be fun to watch the prima donnas go an entire weekend without communication to the outside world.

Of course no retreat hosted by Black Enterprise would be complete without an NDA agreement signed, dated, and handed off to the Human Resource personnel on staff. As I checked in, relinquished my phone, and signed the NDA, Hennison appeared from the recreation cabin with a woman trailing behind him I didn't recognize. Could this be the Actuary everyone has been whispering about? With not so much as a sideways glance in my direction, he ordered everyone inside as he delegated assignments and expectations for the weekend. After giving a schedule of events, he introduced the instructors that would lead our group's meetings. At the last minute, he introduced a fresh face to the fold; none other than the Corporate Actuary herself, Rosalynn Torres-McKenna.

Also, at the retreat, Gavin made his presence known by giving brief statements, and handed out mild humor as if it belonged in dry humored, out dated tv show; his comfort within the company had noticeably grown. After we had been dismissed and relegated to our sleeping quarters, I noticed he hadn't had his right-hand woman Phoenix with him. By the way they were dry humping in a bathroom stall at the Indulgence masquerade anniversary ball, I expected her to be at his beck and call; what would be more fun than having raunchy weekend sex with his mistress and save money by firing people at the same time? He brought a companion, but it wasn't Phoenix or his wife; it had been the least likely person I would have thought of... Tarin!

This weekend has not been set up for us to be comfortable, but to be on point at every turn; no special considerations were being made for anyone, regardless of position at the company. The cabin assignments must have been chosen by tossing names in a hat, because the most unlikely people are bunking together. Just because the camp is co-ed doesn't mean the directors will allow cohabitation (at least not for the peons); all the campers are separated by their sex and assigned four to a cabin. No standard size beds for us, from this point going we are all sleeping on twin size bunk beds. As we settled into cabins, one of my bunkmates from the Scullery & Garden Magazine (another Black Enterprise venture) had been whispering to another colleague about Gavin and his callous and recklessness of flaunting yet another woman when he's married. Overhearing the conversation, all the women in the room sighed and nodded their heads in agreement at the statement. No one knew why his wife had allowed him to behave this way, or if she knew about the rumors of his many affairs. Maybe she loved him, or maybe she married him with a prenuptial agreement and had to stay in the marriage for a certain amount of years to get a substantial payout? Whatever the reason, he's certainly making a fool of her.

As she continued to gossip, she said that Gavin and Tarin (no one knew who she had been except for me), met while she had been working on a beauty campaign for a cosmetic line Gavin's wife had been starting up. Since he bought and sold her last business endeavor, the cosmetic line would mark her comeback as a businesswoman; little did she know that her husband had been looking for a beauty of his own, but for the life of me I couldn't understand why he chose Tarin? Rumor has it that she had been looking for a comeback, and Gavin had the pockets deep enough for her to mooch off of. Sloan must have taken pity, and sent her on the job as a last ditch effort to revive her career; but it's already too late, Tarin is nearly aged out, so Gavin really is her last chance; I guess Jayshawn just isn't able to bring in the money she requires to be a kept woman; that relationship is over… again.

We endured endless hours of corporate structure, awareness, conflict resolutions, etc. Everyone had to attend their meetings, and everyone had to participate including Clair and Isabella; who also ended up being bunkmates. Their fiery exchanges made Smoky the grounds keeper nervous, and he brought back extra fire extinguishers from his supply run. We all ate together in the mess hall, and there's a clear divide between whose team Clair and team Isabella; no need to wonder where Kelly had gone, the puppet had returned to her master; no doubt full of information that can give Rouge more of an edge over Indulgence. It's like watching a scene from the Angry Chicks movie. What made these women hate each other so much? It can't only be solely about business? As we shuffled from one session to another Rosalynn observed.

After the first few sessions, I would see Rosalynn talk to Hennison, and then I observed her handing off paperwork to Gavin;

and in between, people slowly vanished. By the end of the weekend, more than half of Black Enterprise publications had been dissolved, and the staff eliminated. The tension between the staff that's left is thick enough to slice; the tension between Hennison and I as well. He made no attempt to speak to me and looked through me whenever we were in the same place as if I was just another employee and as if he hadn't sent Mr. Bassett to track me down a few days prior; he runs hot and cold fast. Maybe the money was a *'Thank you for your services'* tip, which is more than I ever got from Malik or Jayshawn.

Finally arriving on the last day, all they summon the staff that had not been given the boot into the sitting area of the recreation hall for a final meeting. Arriving just as everyone had begun to settle in for a long-winded speech, Hennison stood in front of the stone fireplace as Gavin sat legs crossed next to him. There is a clear division in the room. Everyone sat and awaited the next move. Clair and Isabella glared at each other with contempt in their eyes from opposite sides of the room; the only staffers left are from Indulgence and Rouge, the other magazines that haven't been eliminated are in the clear to either continue printing or have been demoted to online publishing only; their fates in this industry have come down to who's the most profitable without causing the most expense.

This is it, the last time both publishers will be able to make their cases for continuing on the current path. I sat on a worn couch; that smelled of corn chips and underarm sweat; clinching my fists and ready for anything; I wish some would talk already! Hennison began by thanking both teams for their hard work and dedication; both editors hung on every word he spoke, hoping to hear a phrase that would give one a leg up over the other; I continued to watch Hennison to see if there was a crack in his armor. Just as he was about to make a final decision on which magazine would reign supreme, Gavin interjected.

"Hennison, do you mind if I say a few words?" Gavin interrupted, gesturing to continue. "I know that I as well as the Black family cannot thank both Indulgence and Rouge for the amazing work, and dedication to the dream of Paul Black. As a newcomer into Black

Enterprise, I understand the feeling of a family dynamic within each division. However, this industry isn't what is used to be and we have to change with the times. Both publications have made sacrifices and adapted to the changes we, as a company face; but those changes simply aren't enough. Hennison and I, as well as the Board, have to come to a decision that would benefit the company and move us forward. As you all know, we have eliminated some of our publications, and others downsized. Both magazines have a great staff and have been very competitive and productive over the years, but only one will emerge as our number one, go to magazine for fashion and lifestyle."

We all sat with bated breath, Clair was literally on the edge of her seat, and Isabella was cool as a cucumber, as if she had known what the outcome would be. I only half paid attention to Gavin, I mostly watched Hennison. When I caught his eyes, I gave my attention back to Gavin, but he continued to watch me; the ice had begun to melt.

At that moment Tarin walked in and stood next to Gavin as if she belonged there. Gavin continued his speech and announced that both magazines will merge and there will be an Editor and Assistant Editor of the newly formed Legend; as Sloan slid into the room undetected, he announced the new Editor and Chief Sloan Genesis Hill and Assistant Editor Kellendra Bowden. The announcement sent Clair fuming!

"Excuse me, did I hear you correctly? Sloan is Editor and Chief? Gavin, we had a deal!" She confessed.

"It wasn't set in stone, and I reserve the right to change my mind whenever I please." he stated cockily.

"You've been an intricate part of the successes of our endeavors, but it's time for new blood to lead the magazine into more profitable territories." Hennison attempted to explain.

"Profitable, I built this God damn company! I was here when there was nothing but an old camera and a typewriter, Paul wouldn't have built this without me! And Sloan you backstabbing bitch, how could you? I expected this from Euro trash (referring to Isabella), but you!" Clair rambled off. And you what do you get out of this? She motioned towards Isabella.

Isabella must have had a heads up of what they had planned, because she didn't flinch as they had announced the new leadership; only Clair and the rest of the former Indulgence staff had been blindsided.

"Simple, I get to run the European Division." She said smoothly. She had negotiated a deal with Gavin over a brief pillow talk session, which he'd also had with Clair occasionally. During that session, he let slip that Kelly had been playing both sides to secure a position, so Isabella negotiated her own arrangement; which subsequently left a portion of her staff out of work.

Sensing that she had no more cards left to play, Clair had to use the only leverage she had left. "So, do you all think this is the last you all will see of me? I've planned for this day, even though I hoped it would never come. I built everything your family has Hennison, I've built your so-called family name with noble sacrifice to my own. You do not understand what I've done for Paul, and the secrets I've kept. You all owe me your careers, especially you, Sloan! You were a dancer at the Stiletto Club, spreading it wide and laying it low for a few dollars! I elevated you, and this is how you repay me!"

"How the mighty have fallen." Sloan spewed at Clair. "And you never let me forget it, you and Paul always kept me on a leash, to afraid that I might give you completion. And poor Cassidy, you brainwashed her into doing your dirty work. You've stepped on many people to be nothing more than Paul Black's hired whore, and Indulgence was something for you to do when you got too old to walk the runway. Sorry not sorry Clair this time you lose."

The rest of us stood in awe of the exchange, I tried to read Hennison's expressions, but he hadn't been at all surprised at Sloan's confessions. The rumors have all been true about his father and Clair. Could this be a motivation to take down Indulgence? I looked to him for an answer; he ignored my glances. At the mention of her name, Cassidy stood and announced her decision to leave Indulgence; so there's no need for Rosalynn to give her a pink slip. In between the unveiling of secrets, Clair still had her power move she'd been saving.

"Ok, Hennison. Since Gavin is running the show, I think it's time everyone knows why you brought him in. Truth is Hennison wants to start his own legacy, and to do that he has to destroy his fathers, by scrounging up capital from every nook, cranny, and shyster willing to make money on his stupidity. We all know that Hennison has no head for this business, and he will never measure up to the greatness of his father. He's just a trust fund kid with no real talent of his own. And one more thing, you can't get rid of me that easily, there are a few shares in this company that haven't been accounted for, so that means you don't have all the voting power you need, I have control of those shares they belong to my son!" Clair revealed.

You could hear a pin drop after Clair's confession. As far as anyone had known she had no children, and if she did, how would she have control? We looked to each other for answers. No one dared to say out loud what they'd all knew all along. The only person who had known the truth is Cassidy; I watched her as tears fell down her cheeks.

"Yes, my son was gifted with shares from his father. And as a push present, I had also been gifted with a few of my own." Clair declared. "Yes Hennison, Your father and I have a son together and he is also heir to the Black family throne. So, if you want me out; you have to buy us out, and we don't come cheap."

"What son?" Gavin asked in disbelief as he looked to Hennison.

Cassidy stood, back straight and ready to unleash a weight she had been carrying for far too long. "My son Cairo isn't really my son. His birth parents are Clair Winters and Paul Black." She turned to Clair and continued, "Clair, I will fight you in court if you try to take him from me, and I'm still his legal guardian!"

We all were stunned at the revelation. As Cassidy left, leaving murmurs of confusion in her wake; some of our coworkers soon followed, waiting for the chance to gossip and unpack what happened. The peanut gallery threw around wild scenarios to when Clair could have given birth and gave the baby to Cassidy to raise. By gathering pieces of information overheard, there were a few months unaccounted for when Clair had supposedly "worked from home". The official excuse was that she had been traveling and worked remotely, that might have been around the time her pregnancy began to show and subsequent birth. To maintain a foothold in the industry, she had to keep the baby a secret and must've given the baby to the only person she could trust to love and raise him while keeping his parentage a secret, Cassidy. How else would she be able to explain a mixed-raced baby?

Like everyone else, I cut my losses and packed up to leave that night. On my way to my cabin, I saw Kelly try to talk to Cassidy as she brushed her off, and slipped into an awaiting taxi. Kelly isn't the only one on damage control; I had been summoned to appear at Hennison's cabin, declining the invite; I waited for a ride of my own when I spotted Tarin attempting to be charming as she and Gavin groped each other on their way to an awaiting car to what I can assume is another event by how they're dressed. Locking eyes briefly, she winked at me and smiled wickedly as they slipped into the darkness; well played bitch!

By the time I had returned to the city, I'm worn out from the chaos of the last few days. I returned home with a larger sense of yearning to be on my own. After a few days of moping, Dee and I apartment hunted; that didn't go well. After touring a few places with no real direction, we wondering into a building to see what's available; that's when all hell broke loose.

We got into a shouting match that turned into an actual fist fight after she mentioned my backstabbing ass sister; the lowest blow she gave me without physically touching me. By this point I've had enough crazy, lies, sex, and love triangles to last me a lifetime. I was ready to let go of everything right then and there; our friendship, my job, Hennison, Jayshawn, EVERYTHING! We tussled a bit, long enough for her to get a hit off. But, believe me that was the only one, I have enough built up aggression to fuel the police force for a week. It had been a while since I've been in an actual fist fight; a few minutes into it, we both became winded.

Trying to regain composure, she revealed the actual source of her anger, and the part I had to play in it; it seems I can't recover from one catastrophe without another one starting directly after. She had finally told me what had been going on under my nose, and the emotional turmoil she'd been suffering through alone. By no means is that an excuse to bring up my trifling ass sister and sucker punching me; but I understood where it was coming from…but don't mistake it, she left that fight with just as many bruises as I had, and with a few less hair follicles; Jersey don't raise no punks!

After a brief celebration following Dee's false pregnancy scare after our fight, I rented the apartment we tussled in and began the final steps to gaining my independence. The move is daunting, and I'm scarcely able to fit all my belongings in the tight space, but it's all mine and that's enough. Settling in, I tried to stuff my clothes in the smallest closet ever created when a sturdy knock at my door announced an unexpected visitor. Turning the doorknob without verifying who had been on the other side, I opened it to find the disapproving glare from eyes that are a mirror image of my own.

She had tracked me down, no doubt paying a visit to Dee first to get the details of my whereabouts since I've gone rouge; Meredith is very calculating and resourceful, that's why she knew not to show up empty-handed. Before I could utter a single word of excuse, she gave me a bag from my favorite bakery; moms... they always know just what to do.

"Did you think you would hide from me forever? And by the way, your father is expecting a call." She pointed out.

Letting out a tremendous sigh, "No mom, I didn't want to talk about what happened. I know you guys know by now. I was upset and embarrassed... I didn't want to talk to you and dad about it and feel worse." I confessed.

"You're damn right I know what's going on! Your sister spilled the tea when your father overheard her on the phone with that cretin, saying things you shouldn't to your sister's boyfriend. Honey, I get it. This thing that happened between you and her is unfathomable and for some unforgivable, I wouldn't know how to behave if it had been one of my sisters and me; still, you should have come to us instead of disappearing. If you ask me, that boy wasn't good for you or her! He's a con artist and an opportunist, he used you both; don't get me wrong I don't condone your sister's actions; she's dead wrong for putting her ambitions ahead of blood. However, you both are my children and I raised you better than that." Meredith explained. "Now, go get me something to drink; act like I didn't teach you any manners on how to treat a guest." She commanded.

I chuckled slightly as I retrieved bottled water from the kitchenette. "I was embarrassed; Malik used me for whatever he could get from me and kicked me out! I had nowhere to go!" I blurted.

"You always have somewhere to go! You could always come home, and we could have worked this out as a family." She spat at me.

"I know I could have come home, but then what? I had no money, no job, nothing to show for myself. I didn't want to go home to you guys a failure. China always has to come home because whatever scheme she had going on went wrong, or she needs money, or a way to avoid responsibility. I didn't want to be a burden on you and dad, you

have enough to worry about; I didn't want to drag y'all into this mess."
I confessed.

"No, ma'am you are not about to say that to me; you are not a
burden! I love you just as much as your sister, and if one or both of our
children needs us, hesitation isn't an option; BRING YOUR ASS
HOME! I don't care if we have to drive, fly, or hitchhike to get you
there; do you understand me? As far as China goes, she has always
required looking after. It's a relief that I didn't have to watch you as
closely. However, that does not mean you get to disappear on us. Have
you spoken to China?" My mother asked.

"No, I saw her at a party Dee's mother had organized; but we
didn't speak, I nearly slapped her back to infancy though." I said with a
malicious sneer.

Giving me a cross look, then one of understanding my mother
responded "I get it, she crossed a line that few come back from. I'm
not here to plead her case or guilt you into forgiving her, that's not my
style. But I am here to let you know that we are here. I don't care how
absurd the situation, inconvenient, or embarrassing; you hear me? By
the way, you're not the only one he left high and dry." She glanced at
me with a hint of shade in her tone.

My mother sent shock waves through me as she told the tale of
Malik and China Chronicles. Apparently, Malik had kept his word and
got China some work as a performer. Still her performances had been
bombs; a few reviewers tore her to shreds in a performance she'd done
in a club, as the opening act her job was to get the crowd hyped for the
headliner; instead she nearly cost everyone a payout for the event.
Shortly after that, she'd had some dance and vocal training; but that all
stopped when she went home for the holidays. As my mother
explained it, that's when Malik lost interest. Eventually, he broke it off,
leaving her stranded in New Jersey, by the time she got back to the
city; he'd moved on to the next victim (I already knew about Phoenix).
I know I should be upset about how dirty he did her, however she
deserved it. She stabbed me in the back for a pat on the ass and

promises of stardom. For that I'm not sorry; you do dirt; you get dirt, those are the rules and karma is a bitch. Nonetheless, she's my family, the other side of me hurts for her.

I'm at ease when my mom left, as if all the emotional baggage I'd been carrying finally dropped. I don't know if China and I will ever bond as sisters again, but I know in time I'd consider it. Back at the ranch, Indulgence is imploding. With Clair gone the staffers are running amok, and without the structure Cassidy implemented most don't bother to come into work at all; I try to reign everyone in as much as I can, but I have no authority and they know it; at any rate, the company has suspend all publications until the company's lawyers can sort out the madness. All I have in my hip pocket is that some staffers believed I have some power over Hennison's decisions, so they don't ice me out completely; I don't intend to let anyone know our tryst is over.

With futures uncertain, we all clamor to bits of information that's leaked in office, online, and from other media outlets. Thus far, all parties involved have been tight-lipped and trying to solve the problems in house as to not spook the stockholders into getting nervous and selling shares; in the meantime, we wait. I continue to be called into Hennison's office, and I continue to ignore him. Whatever hashing out we need to do, cannot be done anywhere near The Black Building; I refuse to let him turn me into the stereotypical angry black woman at work! It doesn't matter that we quarrel about something in our personal relationship, all the staff will see is an angry black woman being unprofessional at work towards the boss. It won't matter why I'm angry just the fact that I had the audacity to act on it would be enough for them to categorize me, as if my pain is worthless, my feelings even more so, paired with the questioning or my mental and emotional stability while in the workplace; not today Hennison, not today.

I managed to slip out of the office early and unnoticed… who would notice, anyway. Upon my exit I ran into an old friend whom I missed, but didn't intend to see; Mr. Bassett. Informing me that my presence has been requested by you know who. I deciding that I didn't want to hide anymore; I entered the town car and strategized how best to conclude this game. Mr. Bassett must have been watching my facial expressions through the rearview mirror, as I contemplated what I would say. With a deep sigh, he'd asked if he could offer me some advice; since I'd been too embarrassed to seek it from my father, I nodded my head at his offer; he went on to say...

"Darling, whatever he's says to you remember who you are, and where you want to go. Don't let his influence be the standard by which you live your life. I don't doubt he cares for you, God knows I never had to do this much chasin' of a young woman. But I see something different in you than I didn't in the others. You're meant for great things Ms. Chloe, never forget that." He concluded.

Assuring him I wouldn't, we arrived once again at the cinderblock building with the humongous wooden doors. Expecting Hennion to open the doors, I was surprised to see the icy blue eyes of Ms. Margo instead. As her role as his secretary is no longer needed, her role as his gatekeeper continues as she has become his newly appointed House Manager. She led me to the living room where our first sensual encounter. As I waited for him to appear; I couldn't help but remember the times we spent together.

I sat in that room for what seemed like an eternity waiting for him when I realized, this is all a part of his game. He wanted to get me into a place he controlled, and he kept me waiting to assert his power and dominance over me or the situation. I might have been a fool before, but not anymore; if he wants to see me, it will be on my time! Looking around the foyer to make sure the coast is clear, I scurried to the door quickly as to not alert Margo I'd gone.

Making it home in record time, I forgot I have my own apartment because I half expected to see Dee. Having a quick laugh at my absentmindedness, I settled in for the evening. I gave Mr. Bassett's words some thought, and the more I thought about it, the more inspired I became to write. Finally, after months of writer's block, I'd had something to write about; my fingers went to work. It was just how I imagined it! The words poured out, as if they had been waiting for me, instead of me waiting for them. This frenzy went on for hours. In the middle of it I jotted down ideas for other blogs, and while I had been riding the wave, maybe even a book.

No sooner than I hit the publish button, someone had rang on my buzzer; whoever it is had rang it so long I thought it would halt the alarm. Answering the intercom, I expected it to have been Hennion; not surprised at all that he'd tracked me down, but it wasn't him. A smooth, deep voice pulsated from the box. It wasn't Hennison, but Jayshawn who had found me.

Allowing him entry I panicked trying to put on my best '*I'm over it*' face. I stood in the doorway and waited, hoping to gain the upper hand. He is just as handsome as before, maybe even more so. He walked calmly towards me, and asked if he could come inside. Inviting him in, he began to apologize for how we ended our friendship. Trying to explain what he thought I didn't already understand, he went through his reasoning for abandoning what we were building for something more familiar. I understand why he did it, if the roles were reversed and it had been Malik and I there's no telling if I wouldn't have done the same. Sometimes we wish for a second chance to do something right, or get a chance with the object of our affections only to miss it when presented; so, yes I understood his actions.

At his suggesting, we left my apartment to get fresh air. We strolled for a while, until we landed in a neighborhood chicken restaurant. While we waited for our food, he told me about his new assistant, the projects he'd been working on, and a random trip he took to South Beach. A hangover from a night of binge drinking caused him to hallucinated seeing me. He said in that moment he couldn't fight his feelings and he had to see me. Tarin had vanished (surprise, surprise) leaving him with a breakup text, and a huge credit card bill. All the time we'd been friends, he'd never told me the reason for their initial breakup. Homie must have really been in his feelings, because he finally let the truth out.

Unbeknownst to me, the reason why Hennison and Jay had been at each other's necks whenever they occupied the same space is because Hennison had been the cause of the separation. Apparently, Tarin had been sent on a photo shoot for Indulgence; after the session she, Hennison, and another woman decided to have their own party. Jay planned a surprise visit the same night to propose to her, needless to say it didn't end well; that why all their interactions were hostile even years after the incident.

It had all made sense, the verbal jabbing that nearly became real jabbing, the snarky comments, even the rivalry they had with me. I took in all the information, I could without flinching. I didn't want him to be aware of the fact that every word he uttered had been a stab to my heart; I began to question both Hennion's and Jay's feelings for me. Had I been a way for them to get back at each other? The thought was interrupted when Jay scooped me up in one swift movement and submerged himself in my lips. I couldn't help but to kiss him back, I hadn't felt passion like this in a long time and I craved it.

I didn't want to go back to my apartment, so I suggested his; I wanted to see it one last time. His apartment still had the same vanilla scent I remembered. Dropping the food still in the bag it landed on the floor, followed by his keys with a loud thud. I felt his eagerness to have me as he pressed into my body. Jay is equal parts passionate and aggressive, which I didn't mind at all. With Hennison the sex was all play, with Jayshawn it's all desire. We settled into his bed, slowly moving from one embrace to another until all our clothes disappeared. We kept the pace slow in the beginning, it had been a while since the last time we were together and we didn't want to move so quickly that we couldn't fully enjoy each other; it felt like he'd been staking a claim, while I had been making a sweet memory.

As we lay on our sides, my arms are wrapped around his neck as he hoists my leg to his hip allowing his hand roam further; we never broke our embrace for a second. Maneuvering me on my back he took each breast into his mouth, in addition to slowly penetrating my body; I didn't know how much I missed his touch until I was touched. I winced slightly as he entered, it had been a while since I'd had sex, and I grew accustomed to Hennison's size; but Jayshawn had more width than Hennison and he certainly knows how to use it. Jay rotated between long strokes that made me anticipate the next one, and short ones, causing me to arch my back, while lifting my legs higher for deeper sensations; he didn't disappoint.

As the night went on I contemplated what I had in mind, and wondered if I made the right decision. I made sure he was sound asleep before dressing. I left as swiftly as I had arrived. There was no need to wake him up; I'm not going to change my mind. We both entered his bedroom with different intentions, his were to rebuild and solidify a relationship. However, my intentions were to enjoy being with him for the moment and move on. I walked home slowly as the daylight appeared. My mind was torn, so many times in the walk I wanted to turn around. Every time I got to a corner I had to give myself a pep talk to keep going. I got home, and stripped myself of last night's sex. While in the shower, I decided how to handle my job and the Hennison situation in one fell swoop.

I sent a quick text to Dee before going into work to confirm our brunch. Entering The Black Building, I knew what to expect. I didn't need to wait for anyone in Human Resource to tell me my fate at the company; I already knew it. Indulgence is no more and Legend will arise in its place, Sloan converting her Legendary Models Inc. staff into a publishing one. Thanks to Ellis, I'm already aware of the amount of my severance package, and thanks to being able to save some money by staying with Dee I built a small nest egg; it sucks that I'd just moved, but shit happens. I headed straight to HR as per the email instruction to acknowledge and sign for my package. Stopping first to talk to Ingrid and assure her that we will still hangout, I packed up my cubical. Checking my email one last time, there was a message waiting from Mr. Black. Skimming through it quickly, he basically mumbled an apology; I'm not impressed. I sent him the standard *'It was great working with you'* email and ended it with *'I wish you well on the next stage of your life.'* Hopefully, he understood my meaning.

I managed to get all my tasks done by noon, just in time to meet Dee. Stopping at security; I scheduled a carrier to pick up my belongings and delivered for the next day. Standing there I remembered the first day I entered The Black Building, and all the amazing people and events I'd been exposed to; I wouldn't trade my time here for nothing in the world, but now it's time to move on. I may not be a regular columnist, but I have been hired for a few freelance writing gigs until something permanent comes along.

Passing a magazine stand on the way to Dope Soul Café, I shook my head at the headlines concerning Black Enterprise. So far, Clair has lawyered up and began negotiating a palpable settlement of her and Cairo's shares. Cassidy left Indulgence and partnered with Mr. Elgin Reese in an Art Gallery called Urban Chaos; now, I know why Nevie came to London. Cassidy lawyered up too, but not for money; for her son. Skyline Times reports that she sought out a custody lawyer in case Clair decides to be a mother and sue her for full custody, after everything Cassidy sacrificed I don't think Clair would petition for full custody; but partial custody I wouldn't take off the table. Dee and Elgin are courting again, and he had given her a painting he made for her; she left her dads firm and began working for Castor and Pollex until she can open her own Staging and Design Studio. Gavin has his hands full…literally! Not just in business, but at home as well. With his reputation on the line, he cannot afford any bad press since it's rumored that he and his wife Megan are getting divorced. She must be tired of the constant infidelity. Tarin on the other hand couldn't be more elated, the gossip columnists report her visiting bridal boutique's while they battle it out; I wonder if Phoenix is doing the same. Malik has quit the entertainment business entirely for a new hustle. Together with his wife Sienna, they opened up a store front church called Church of the Divine Tongue. I hear they travel across the country preaching the "word" and cleaning up the collection plates along the way.

Then there was Jay, I don't know how that story would end until we crossed paths on my way to the café. He asked so many questions; he knew that answers to before I could say a word. There isn't any ending that can justify our beginning, but here we are with no words left to speak, and no games left to be played. He pulled me in for a consuming hug. It was so strong I felt the rhythm of his heartbeat and nearly forgot we'd been standing on the curb embracing. He'd kissed me with passion as he'd done so many times before, and I knew in that moment that if I didn't break our embrace he wouldn't, so no matter how comforted I felt in his arms, and safe he made me feel I knew that this had to end; and so it did.

We walked away from each other in two different directions. I felt his stare as I walked towards the café to meet Dee, and it took every ounce of restraint I had not to look back at him; if I did, I might never know for sure if I could truly be on my own. So, I continued to walk, wondering if I'd made the right choice. Maybe one day we can rekindle a relationship. Hell, maybe that one day will be tomorrow. But, today isn't that day; today is for me.

ABOUT THE AUTHOR

Dominique has been a writer/author for many years. Her writings have been featured on her blog These Are My Chronicles, as well as a few articles written for online publications. In addition to releasing The Life & Times of a Full Figured Fashionista Parts I and II, she is working on other projects and endeavors. For more information, visit her on social media. Join the other readers on Facebook at TheLifeandTimesBook or on Instagram at DominiqueThaWriter.

Thank You to my Readers!

I want to take the time to acknowledge and show great appreciation to all the readers and supporters of my writing. It's because of all of you I continue to pursue my love of writing and storytelling. There were times in the crafting of The Life & Times Series when I wanted to quit, but it was through my family, friends, and social media family that I continued to create. It is because of the words of encouragement, visits, calls, texts, etc. checking on my progress, and the constant reminders to finish what I started that I stayed inspired. Thank you ALL from the bottom of my heart! I hope you enjoy reading The Life & Times Of A Full Figured Fashionista Part II: I'm no angel. I hope through each character you find a piece of yourself, and like some more memorable characters; I hope you find the strength and willpower to be more than your situation and love yourself more than you ever have.

With Love,

Dominique A.

www.ingramcontent.com/pod-product-compliance
Lightning Source LLC
Chambersburg PA
CBHW070105260626
47160CB00004B/1332